To G.B.G.

Angel of North Africa

A novel

by

James Gottesman

ISBN: 978-0-9911557-6-7

JayEddy Publishing

ACKNOWLEDGMENTS

Thanks go to many. Gloria Brown Gottesman, my longtime co-conspirator, like always, was brutally and painfully honest.

I need to thank the initial readers of the book, all friends, particularly, Chuck Caplan, Marilyn Caplan, Ruth Bunin, Greg Gottesman, Susan Tapper, Gayle and Paul Romain. If I forgot someone – oops.

Thanks to editor, Sydney Weinberg, of London. First time to use Syd and I will use again.

I always thank Diane Mackay Richie, the first person to teach me how to write. She may not remember, but I do.

Although I listened to everything and everyone, I didn't always follow all their suggestions. Alas.

JEG

Angel of North Africa

Forward

When most people today think of World War II, it's Pearl Harbor, D-Day, and the atomic bomb that come to mind. The battle for North Africa between the Allies and the Germans doesn't jog most people's memories.

After Germany declared war on the United States mere days following Pearl Harbor, Roosevelt and the Joint Chiefs of the U.S. armed forces favored a direct assault on Europe. However, the Depression and America's isolationist position after WWI had led to a weak, poorly trained and under-supplied United States Army. Churchill argued vehemently that a direct assault on Europe in 1942 carried too much risk, given the limited forces available. What Churchill actually meant was that the United States was simply not ready to take on the German war machine.

The British Army had been fighting Germany since May 1940, losing badly more often than not. Only the Royal Air Force and Navy had prevented a successful German invasion of England. The German offensives in WWII differed greatly from the trench warfare of WWI. Their concentrated and highly coordinated movements of large numbers of armor, artillery, infantry, and air power known as 'Blitzkrieg' overwhelmed the Poles, the British and the French. Even by the war's end, most scholars believed that the German army, man for man, had the more combat-efficient troops and leadership. Had the U.S. tried to land in France in 1942, many scholars believe the Allies might have lost the war.

A North African campaign offered the Allies the opportunity to secure the Mediterranean Sea for supply shipping. It would give the British and American armies time to learn how to work together. To a degree, North Africa calmed Joseph Stalin's demands for a second front to take pressure off a beleaguered Russia. Most importantly, the North African campaign taught the American armed forces how to fight the Germans. Those initial battles at Kasserine Pass and Sidi Bou Zid offered the Americans their first tests against the Germans and revealed how unprepared the Americans were for war. The American Army performed so badly that the German High Command dismissed them as a threat.

However, the Americans caught on quickly. They changed leadership, with generals like George Patton and Omar Bradley proving able to learn from their predecessors' mistakes, change tactics, and instill confidence and the desire to fight in their men. They learned how to leverage the immense industrial strength of America to their advantage. In short, the Americans learned how to win.

This is the historical context underpinning *The Angel of North Africa*, a work of fiction. While my characters are not real, I do include some fictional renderings of real generals and events in the plot which correspond to actual accounts of the battle for North Africa and its aftermath.

James Gottesman

WWII Glossary of Terms

BOQ - Bachelor's Office Quarters

CO – Commanding Officer

CSurg – Commanding Surgeon

HQ – Headquarters

KIA – Killed in Action

MIA – Missing in Action

GSW – Gunshot wound

SNAFU – Situation Normal, All Fucked Up

SSA –Service de Santé Armées (Medical Department of French Army)

Kraut – Derogatory term for Germans used by Americans in WW2

Bosch - Derogatory term for Germans used by French in WW2

Jerry or Fritz - Derogatory term for Germans used by British in W2

Map – Northwest France

Map – Western North Africa

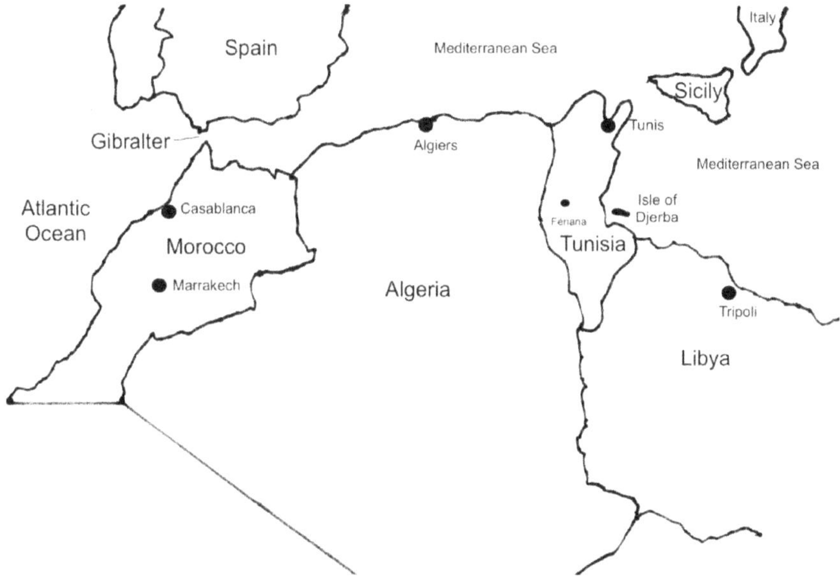

Map – Tunisia

Bizerte
Tunis
Medjez el Bab
Algeria
Tebessa
Kasserine Pass
Kasserine
Thelepte
Sidi Bou Zid
Bou Chebka
Fériana
Faid
Mediterranean
Sea
Gabes
Tunisia
Isle of
Djerba
Text
Libya
Sahara
Desert
160 Km
100 miles

Prologue

Fériana, Tunisia

Midnight on February 20, 1943

For centuries, only the rare bleat of a goat might be heard after midnight in the village at the base of the Atlas Mountains, two-hundred miles southwest of Tunis. This evening, however, and for the past week, sounds of distant shelling along with flashes of artillery filled the air. With Rommel and the German Afrika Corps occupying the region and applying a strict curfew, the village remained bathed in darkness.

On the edge of town, Sophie Sollar slept fitfully in the bedroom of the two-room, stone-and-mud house she shared with her cousin Hélène Al-Hadef. The other room, quite large, served as a medical facility for the women of the village which Sophie and Hélène had been running for three years. Sophie, known in Tunisia as Safiyah Shaloub, was twenty-nine, Hélène thirty-two.

A soft knocking on the door caused Sophie to open her eyes. Sophie and Hélène both sat up quickly when hard door-kicking followed. When alone, the two women spoke French.

"*Qu'est-ce que ça pourrait être*?" asked Hélène.

Sophie's legs had already touched ground. She didn't know who it was either, but she knew who she didn't want it to be.

The pounding continued, then stopped.

Sophie groped for the lantern and matches on her bedside table. After lighting the lantern with shaking hands, she donned a robe and headed into the main room as the door-pounding resumed. Hélène followed. As they walked, both wrapped *niqabs* around their heads, exposing only their eyes. "*Ana qadim*!" yelled Hélène, to assure the stranger they were coming. Sophie detoured to the kitchen and grabbed a large carving knife, which she held behind her back.

"*C'est probablement une femme qui accouche d'un bébé*," said Hélène, who'd served as midwife to all the women in the village.

Sophie thought of the curfew the Bosches had imposed; anyone caught violating it would be shot on sight.

"*Non*," she replied shortly.

Hélène lifted the latch, opening the door a few inches as frigid night air rushed in. She stood aside so Sophie could lift the lantern. Sophie held the carving knife in a death grip behind her back and raised the lantern high above her five-foot-two frame.

Two men were slumped against the threshold, one with pleading eyes, holding up the other man whose eyes were shut, his head sagging onto his companion's shoulder. Blood streaked their faces, and blood on their leather jackets almost hid the winged, white star surrounding a red circle: the insignia of the USAAF, the United States Army Air Force. Sophie exhaled and softened her grip on the carving knife.

"Help us, please," the man with pleading eyes said.

"*Américains*?" Sophie asked.

"Yes. We're hurt."

Sophie handed the lantern to Hélène and opened the door.

Chapter One

Metz, France

May 1928

A week after her sixteenth birthday, Sophie Sollar paused in front of her home in the Bellacroix arrondissement of Metz. She waved goodbye to her two school friends, and skipped inside. Once the door closed, she heard her father's voice asking if it was her.

"Sophie, *Est-ce que tu*?"

"*Oui, Papa.*"

Sophie entered the sitting room to find, her father, Dr. Charles Sollar, a surgeon, reading a medical journal on the sofa.

"Where have you been?" Charles asked.

"I was at Marie's with friends. Her mother has just come back from Paris and we were looking at her fabulous new dresses," Sophie said.

Charles looked carefully at his lovely daughter, whose large brown eyes and head of unruly, black curls always gave the impression of dynamic tension, like Henri Matisse's famous art piece, Dance I. She had her mother's silky olive complexion.

"I thought Marie's mother was with Mama today."

"I suppose."

"So without Marie's mother present, you and your band of mischief makers invaded her closet like the

Huns invading France?" Charles asked.

Sophie put her hands behind her back and looked down as if inspecting the floor for insects.

Charles' eyes narrowed. "And you were only *looking* at the dresses, that's it?"

Sophie continued to search for insects.

"You might as well tell me the whole story so when Marie's mother calls Mama to ask why her closet is a mess, we have a defense prepared."

The anxious line of Sophie's mouth slowly morphed into a smile.

"You're not mad?"

"They weren't your mother's dresses. I'd be more worried about Marie! I bet you looked stunning in the latest fashions."

Sophie squealed, "I did," then bounded over to hug her father, before settling in next to him on the sofa.

Charles took a lock of Sophie's curly hair and twirled it around his index finger. Sophie brushed his hand away.

"Why do you always do that?" Sophie asked.

"Because you're my daughter and the miracle of miracles to me and your mother. No other reason," Charles said. "It makes me happy."

"It doesn't make me happy," Sophie lied.

Sophie actually loved the attention shown to her by her father. Sophie had myriad girlfriends and had spent many nights at dinners, sleepovers, parties and on short trips with her friends and their parents. None of her friends' fathers doted on their daughters like Charles did on Sophie. But Charles didn't spoil Sophie with gifts of jewelry, dresses, shoes and toys. He spoiled her with his time, and she loved it.

"One day you might miss it," Charles said.

"Never."

Charles, now 46, was handsome, fit, fair skinned, with dark blue eyes, and a full head of light brown hair with bits of gray at the temples, belying his Austrian roots. Though on the short side of five-foot-eight inches, he exuded the confidence a surgeon should have. He smiled, leaned over and kissed Sophie's forehead. "I have some very exciting news."

"What?"

"Our family is going to the United States for a year in August."

"What for? I don't want to leave. My friends are here," Sophie cried, sliding away from Charles.

"There are some new surgical techniques that I need to learn. We'll be in a city called Ann Arbor."

"I've never heard of Ann Arbor."

"It's in the Michigan region near the big city of Detroit, which was founded by a famous French explorer, Antoine de La Mothe-Cadillac," Charles said. "Besides, you'll go to school there and learn English."

"I speak French, German and some Arabic already. I don't need another language," Sophie replied, her frown deepening and her arms folded tightly.

"I know it's hard to leave your friends, but it will be a grand adventure to see America. Mother and I are so excited by it all. Anyway, it's decided and your friends will be here when we return," Charles said.

"I think I'll just die," Sophie said, sliding off the sofa onto the floor, spreading her arms onto the sofa's cushions, then throwing her head back.

Charles laughed at Sophie's act of utter

desperation. “Quite the theatrics. You won’t die, and now for protecting you from Marie’s mother, you’ll do me a favor.”

Sophie rolled her eyes. “Do we have to tie surgical knots again?”

“Yes. I haven’t got a son and my only wish in life is for you to join me in my practice.”

“Mama says girls aren’t supposed to be surgeons.”

“And I say, let them stop us. How are you doing in your science classes this term?”

“Top of my class. It seems to annoy the boys no end that I excel over all of them in math and science.”

‘Good.” Charles stood and went to a chest of drawers, removing a spool of black sewing thread. He unraveled an eight-foot piece, snapped it off, then snapped it in half, then half again. Pulling an armchair next to the sofa, they both sat. He slid the four pieces of thread under the arm of the armchair, and gave two ends of one piece to Sophie. He kept the other piece for himself.

“First, we’ll do twenty one-handed knots right-handed and then swap threads and do twenty left-handed. Go!”

Without a hint of effort, Sophie threw knots with her right hand. Charles started a moment later, smiling as they worked together.

A moment later, Mira Shaloub Sollar, Sophie’s mother, entered Charles’ study. Petite with the same curly black hair and olive complexion as her daughter, Mira had given Sophie not only her beauty but her dry wit. In her daughter, Mira recognized her husband’s unbridled ambition, which she tried to hold in check, most often without success.

Neither Charles nor Sophie saw Mira enter; they

were concentrating too hard. Mira crossed her arms and waited to be noticed, but the knot-tyers had placed all their focus on flying fingers.

"Our daughter," Mira announced, "does not need to be a surgeon, or even a doctor. She'd be old and withered before she finishes school."

Charles and Sophie shook their heads at Mira, but continued to tie knots without missing a beat.

"In her own time, my daughter will choose what path she will follow," Mira said.

Finally, Sophie and Charles ran out of thread and stopped.

"I agree, my love," Charles said. "Our daughter can be anything she wants."

Mira smiled and uncrossed her arms.

"As long as it's a doctor," Charles finished. He stood, walked over to Mira and gave her a hug and kiss. The smile on her face had already disappeared.

"Oh, Mama," Sophie said, as she stood. "Papa's being funny. Clearly, I will marry a prince, become deliciously rich, mingle with courtiers, buy my wardrobe from Parisienne designers, and never exert myself at all."

Charles and Mira looked at each other, began to laugh, and walked to Sophie and gave her a communal hug.

Mira, needing the last word, said, "You'll find a Jewish prince in France when dinosaurs lay eggs under the Arc de Triomphe."

The next round of laughs ended when the phone rang in the kitchen. Mira dropped her arms and hurried to answer. Charles and Sophie heard her say hello from the other room.

“Who is it?” Charles called.

“It’s Marie’s mother. She wants to speak to Sophie.”

Chapter Two

December 1933
Strasbourg, France

Despite Mira Sollar's objections, Sophie had entered the six-year medical program at the Université de Strasbourg in 1930, having graduated high school a year early. Only four women in a class of a hundred and ten had gained admission. Sophie had ranked in the top five of her class for the past three years.

Fifty-five third-year medical students, paper and pen in hand, stood at the benches of an enormous laboratory lined with identical monocular microscopes, taking a final examination in pathology. The microscopes, en toto, gave the appearance of thin-necked penguins in a trance-like state, glued to the benches.

Three professors walked around, proctoring the exam. Every five minutes, one of the proctors rang a small bell and the students moved to the next microscope station. The students interpreted what they were seeing on each microscope slide, including the type of tissue, the organ from which it had come, and the disease which might or might not be present.

In the middle of the laboratory, Sophie scribbled furiously in her test notebook then bent over to take another look into the microscope at a slide of a tissue preparation of liver from a patient afflicted with cirrhosis.

The bell rang and the students stood in unison. Sophie smiled confidently, flipped her notebook to the next page, and moved to the next microscope.

A secretary entered the room, whispering to the head proctor, "Please send Sophie Sollar to the office of the dean when the exam has concluded."

Twenty-five minutes later, Sophie entered the office of Professor Claude Beaumont. Bald, angular, and with a full beard, Beaumont stood to greet his star student. A matronly woman dressed in all-white stood next to Beaumont, the school nurse, Madame LeConte.

"Please have a seat, Mademoiselle Sollar," Beaumont said.

Sophie sat, curiosity shining in her face. Beaumont moved in front of her as LeConte took to Sophie's side.

"It's about your mother," Beaumont said.

"She's skiing with my father and their friends at Champe de Feu," Sophie said. "They go every year before the holiday."

"I'm afraid I have some bad news," Beaumont continued. "Your mother, along with four others, has been killed in an avalanche. Your father has been injured, but not seriously."

"I need to go to them!" Sophie cried out, jumping up.

LeConte extended her arms to catch Sophie as she wobbled, then helped her sit back down.

"I need to go," Sophie repeated, beginning to hyperventilate. "Papa will need me. Where is he now?"

"He said that he'll meet you at home," Beaumont said. "Maybe sit for just a moment. My driver will take you to your apartment and wait until you've packed. He'll then drive you to the train station. He's waiting out front in a blue Citroën."

"I was ... to join them... on Saturday," Sophie said haltingly, putting her hands to her mouth.

"We're sorry for your loss," Beaumont said. "Take however much time you need before returning to school."

Sophie, sniffling, stood slowly and faltered a bit, then caught herself. "I'm okay. I need to go. Papa will be lost without my mother. So lost."

Chapter Three

Metz, France
December 1935

Angry clouds hid the sun while whipping winds and freezing temperatures had cleared the dreary streets of children playing.

Sophie exited a taxi in front of her house and quickly wrapped a scarf around her face for protection. The taxi driver dropped her valise on the curb, then hustled back to his taxi and drove off. Sophie, head down, hoisted the valise and walked to the front door of her house.

As she removed her heavy wool coat, she yelled, "Papa, I'm home. It's miserable outside."

Charles came down the stairs quickly.

"I've so missed you," he said. "Living in this house alone, without Mama, is like living in a tomb."

Enveloping Sophie in a bear hug, Charles held her head in both hands, kissing her forehead, twirled one lock of her hair around his index finger in the familiar gesture. Now that she was grown up, Sophie didn't protest.

"Let's go into the kitchen and have a cup of hot coffee and a croissant," Sophie said. "I'm famished and chilled to the bone."

As they sat at the table enjoying a cup and a roll,

Charles looked lost in thought.

“Are you feeling well?” Sophie asked.

“The days are fine. I lose myself in the surgeries and my patient’s problems. The evenings are dark and sadistic,” Charles said.

Sophie didn’t need an explanation for her father’s woes, which hadn’t eased since her mother’s death. She squeezed her father’s hands and let him speak.

“On nights when I come home late,” Charles said, “the cook and housekeeper have gone home. Dinner is left on the table and I’m forced to eat alone. The absence of sound or life in the house crushes my soul. I sit at the table, unable to eat. I miss Mama so much.”

“I miss her too.”

“I know. But I seem to be unable to cope with it,” Charles said.

“Mama wouldn’t want you to act like this,” Sophie said. “You and I have mourned for a year. If you could talk to her now, she’d say life is for the living. If you had died in that awful avalanche, would you want Mama to crawl into a shell for the rest of her life, unable to function?”

“No, of course not, but I don’t know how to crawl out,” Charles said. “I think perhaps that I should move away. Everything here reminds me of Mama.”

“I’ve come home to make you a proposition,” Sophie said. “I can’t live knowing that you’re moping around every day like a dog who can’t find its bone. It’s just too depressing.”

“What then?” Charles asked. “You’ll abandon me and move to America.”

“You know I won’t abandon you.”

“What then?”

"After completing medical school next year, I'll come home and live here with you and join your practice. You'll teach me how to be a surgeon. I've tried applying to surgery programs, but no one in France seems to want a woman to train. Who better than my father to teach me?"

As if a light switch had been flipped, Charles, surprised, sat up erect. "You'd do that?"

"Yes. But I want my father and his smile back," Sophie said.

"Deal. You're home for two weeks now. On Monday we have a colectomy to perform on a woman with diverticulitis, and then two hernias."

"We?"

"Yes. You and I," Charles said, showing a grin from ear to ear.

......

Back at school two months later, Sophie entered the Faculté de Médecine de Strasbourg administrative offices holding the hand of a woman, a head taller, thin as a reed, and dressed in one of Sophie's lab coats. The ill-fitting coat's sleeves ended two inches above the woman's wrists. Sophie said something to the secretary, then she and the tall woman entered the office of the Chairman of the Department of Medicine, Professor Eduard deAtkins.

"How might I help you, Mademoiselle Sollar?" deAtkins asked.

"I'd like to introduce you to my favorite cousin, Hélène Al-Hadef, visiting from Tunisia. She's just gotten her midwife license and is heading off to the Isle of St. Martin to practice. She's visiting for a few days and I hoped she might be able to shadow me."

A random observer would find it difficult to believe

that the two women shared even a single gene.

Hélène, at five-foot nine, towered over Sophie. Hélène had a comforting smile and a presence that conveyed royalty. Hélène had always been tall, Sophie remembered then laughed to herself, “Maybe I’m short.” They had first met when Sophie was seven, visiting the Isle of Djerba, off the Tunisian coast, with her parents. Hélène was called Hilin then, the Tunisian equivalent of French, Hélène. While getting her midwife license in Paris and heading off to French-speaking St. Martin, she also changed her first name to Hélène.

Though Hélène was three years Sophie’s senior, she had included Sophie in every activity. Sophie would never forget those kindnesses.

Besides the height differential, Hélène had stick-straight, brown hair, acne-pocked skin, and tended toward being reserved compared to the outgoing Sophie. That all being true, Sophie and Hélène, whose mothers were sisters, found that blood is thicker than water.

“I don’t see that as a problem,” deAtkins said. “Though you might want to find her a lab coat that fits.”

Hélène looked at her sleeves and shrugged which started Sophie and Hélène to laugh. “That I will,” Sophie said. “Thank you.”

“Nice to meet you, Mademoiselle Al-Hadef. Good luck in your new profession.”

...

Sophie and Hélène sat in a café on Rue Finkwiller enjoying lunch and glasses of Chardonnay.

“As children,” Sophie said, “we swore that we’d be partners in something. I believe the list included restauranteurs, dress designers, African explorers, and dancers. But I can't see myself leaving France for a small island in the middle of nowhere."

"I needed to get out of Muslim Tunisia," Hélène said. "It's too restrictive. Besides, you were gifted with better hands and the stamina to study medicine. I could never do that."

"You think you might meet someone and stay in the Caribbean?"

Hélène shook her head. "I'm not looking."

Sophie hesitated, thinking about her cousin's most unusual response, said with a tone that suggested Sophie should not probe deeper.

"Have you met anyone?" Hélène asked

"I was seeing a dentist here in Strasbourg, only to find he and his family were afflicted with fragile egos. We had much in common and the sex was good but he and his family had trouble with me being a doctor. In the end, his mother quashed it."

"Funny things happen and we may still find a way to become partners," Hélène said.

"Don't see it," Sophie lamented, "but there is no one in the world I would enjoy more as a partner than you."

"You'll promise to write?" Hélène asked.

"And you too," Sophie responded.

The cousins clinked glasses of wine.

After six months, they stopped writing each other.

Chapter Four

Strasbourg, France
May 1936

A month away from graduating medical school, Sophie, in mask, gloves, and gown, stood across from Professor Henri Dubois, Chairman of the Department of Surgery, as he finished removing an inflamed appendix in Operating Suite #12. A scrub nurse stood at Dubois's side as a circulating nurse scurried around the room.

"I hear," Dubois said, "you've not changed your mind about becoming a surgeon."

"Yes," Sophie replied. "Unfortunately, and despite being at the top of our class, I can't find a surgical training program to accept me."

Dubois remained quiet.

"Including here at Strasbourg."

"Women are not cut out to be surgeons," Dubois stated with a professorial air of certainty.

"Nor physicists. But tell that to Marie Curie with her two Nobel Prizes," Sophie said, in a matter-of-fact tone.

The scrub nurse winked at Sophie. Dubois cleared his throat.

"Let's see your technique in closing the incision. I'll take over when it becomes too difficult."

With her lack of official surgical training, Sophie knew that Dubois expected her to be all thumbs. She steeled herself.

"The appendix had not ruptured, so it's a clean case," Sophie said. "I would close with gut and silk."

"Yes," Dubois agreed, his face impassive.

Sophie turned to the scrub nurse. "Two-O gut running on a half taper needle for the peritoneum, then interrupted two-O silk to follow."

The nurse handed Sophie a loaded needle holder and a pair of forceps. Sophie placed the suture into the end of the open peritoneal opening and tied the knot effortlessly. Dubois watched Sophie's technique then cut the short end of the suture. Sophie ran the suture to the end of the peritoneum and tied the knot. Dubois again cut the remnant.

"Hmm. Very nice," Dubois said.

Sophie detected a note of surprise in his voice.

"Have you done this before?"

"No," Sophie lied. In truth, she had assisted her father in his surgeries during summers and school breaks for six years. Over the past year, until his tutelage, Charles allowed Sophie to do a lion's share of the procedures whenever she returned to Metz.

Dubois watched as she closed the abdominal muscle layers with interrupted 2-O silk sutures, and then the skin with mattress sutures of 4-O silk placed four millimeters apart. Dubois, confused, looked at his scrub nurse as Sophie finished.

The nurse, eyes gleaming, said, "I'm afraid, Professor DuBois, this medical student knows exactly what she's doing. Did I say 'she.'"

Dubois agreed. "Impressive. We've residents here in

their third year of surgery training who can't suture or tie half that well. Where did you learn to do that?"

"I've been tying knots and suturing cloth with a needle holder and thread since I was thirteen," Sophie said. "My father wanted a son and he wanted a child who'd become a surgeon and join him in practice. He'll get only half his wish."

Chapter Five

Metz, France
May 1940

A taxi pulled in front of a row of five-story buildings on Rue de la Cheneau, just up the street from the Hôspital d'Instruction des Armées Legouest. Sophie exited the taxi's back door as the driver opened the trunk and placed a small valise at her feet.

The surgical offices she shared with her father were on the second floor.

"Sophie, you're back," said Mme. Louise LaFleur, early 50s, her father's receptionist of twelve years and theirs together for three years. Louise came from her desk to take the valise as Sophie removed her coat and scarf. They pecked each other's cheeks.

Louise had known Sophie as a teenager and called her by her first name. Around patients, Sophie was 'Dr. Sollar.' Absent a mother, Sophie used Louise as a bouncing board for social situations.

"A good time, I hope?" LaFleur asked.

"Paris was wonderful. The professors I visited were not," Sophie said.

Louise tried to smile.

"The part with food, friends from school, dancing, nightclubs ... What's not to like?" Sophie asked, expecting no response.

"Did you meet the nephew of your father's friend,

Mr. Charcot?" Louise asked slyly.

"Yes. His father owns a string of successful automobile dealerships in Paris – Citroën, Renault and Peugeot. He was handsome and quite the charmer."

"And?"

"I saw him only once."

"He didn't think you interesting?" La Fleur asked. "Impossible not to."

"I guess not. He didn't call me again."

"Why?

"We went out with other friends of his, married couples," Sophie said. "One of the wives asked what I usually made for supper. When I said 'reservations', they all laughed until they realized it was the truth."

"Maybe not the wisest response. You have to learn to read the room."

"The charmer seemed upset when I told the table that I had no intention of marrying anyone who expected supper on the table every night when he came home. Still, I wanted to see him again."

"This is not a new issue with you and men," La Fleur chastised. "You enjoy scaring them away."

"No, I don't enjoy it. I want to meet someone, someday. But I'm a surgeon, not a housewife. Patients don't time their illnesses to occur before dinner."

La Fleur shrugged, keeping any further thoughts to herself.

"Where is Papa?" Sophie asked.

"He's at the hospital repairing a hernia. It's the mayor's son. I expect he'll be back any moment."

"The professors looked at Papa's letter of introduction like used toilet paper," Sophie said. "No one believes a woman can be a surgeon, no matter how well I did in medical school, or Papa's recommendation. You know as well as I do that most of the physicians here in Metz have the same mindset and refer only to Papa. They don't know that we share the procedures equally."

"What will you do then? Louise asked

"I'll continue to apprentice with Papa."

"I'm sorry," Louise said, trying a wan smile. "He'd hoped the professors would see what he sees when you work together. I'm sorry to change the subject, but do you know that your father is quite worried about the Bosches? More French and British forces are moving to the border. They must suspect something. He was contacted by his medical unit from the Great War and they want him to visit and look over the new medical facilities in Verdun."

"He's told me he'd serve whether they ask or not. Anything to help fight the Nazis," Sophie responded.

"He wondered if you'd go with him," Louise added, after a pause.

"They won't allow women physicians of any kind in the army. The army is worse than the surgical professors. One miserable professor at the École de Sage-Femme suggested I spend time in America. He thought the Americans might be stupid enough waste their efforts on training a woman."

"Do you remember your English?" Louise asked.

"A good amount. Many medical articles are written in English and I still write to friends in Ann Arbor. Most are already married with children. Papa and I use English when we don't want people to understand what we're saying." Sophie smiled, then laughed to herself, thinking of something funny. "Sometimes we'll mix

English and Arabic. Nobody understands that but us."

At that moment, Charles entered the office. "You're back. Did you enjoy it?"

Sophie leapt to her feet and hugged him.

"I missed you, that's all," Sophie said, as Charles stepped back and twirled a lock of hair over his index finger.

"No luck with the professors, or I assume I would have heard?"

"Not a sliver of interest in training a woman," Sophie lamented.

"And Charcot's nephew?"

"Don't ask. He wanted a housemaid and cook. Not me."

Charles nodded, understanding Sophie's plight. "We must talk of other things. Let's sit in my office."

Sophie sat in front of her father's desk, watching Charles pace nervously around his office.

On Charles' desk sat three different photographs of her mother. Sophie smiled as she picked up a framed photograph of her mother taken in Tunisia before her parents were married. She knew her father loved that specific photograph and kept a copy in his wallet.

"Why are Mama's pictures out?" Sophie asked.

Charles moved behind Sophie and smiled at the photograph. "When you're away, I miss her more. Sometimes, I bring them out and talk to her."

Knowing that Charles often talked to the photographs, Sophie said nothing. She replaced the photograph onto the desk.

"Louise told me you were even more concerned about the Bosches," Sophie said.

“War is coming to France. But our problems are bigger than that.”

“How so?”

“I don’t believe the Bosches can defeat us and the British,” Charles said. “We’re too strong. But if somehow they do, we’ll not be safe in France. We must prepare.”

“Oh, Papa, you worry incessantly. France cannot be defeated. No army in the world can penetrate the Maginot Line or the Ardennes Forest,” Sophie said with a tone of pure confidence.

“Tell that to Denmark and Norway. They fell in a day,” Charles replied. “You were only a baby at the time of the Great War. Had it not been for the Americans and the Spanish Influenza decimating the Bosch troops, we might still be fighting. Outcomes are never certain and one mustn’t be smug, despite what the papers write and what we think or hope.”

“What would you have us do?”

“We need plans if the worst happens,” Charles said. “We cannot be here if the Bosches take control of the Alsace and Lorraine. We are only sixty kilometers from the German border. They could be upon us in less than an hour. We must be prepared to head for Paris at a moment’s notice. Even Paris might not be safe. Being Jewish will be dangerous anywhere under Nazi control. Many refugees tell of special camps for Jews. Once sent to these camps, people are never seen again.”

“My identification card mentions no religion. How would they know you or I are Jewish?” Sophie asked.

“You’re too smart to be so uninformed. They’ll know. They’ll know by names, by neighborhoods, by membership at the synagogue and, for money or threats, the gentiles will tell them.”

"I'm still not worried. The Bosches won't win," Sophie said.

"Your head is in the sand. We should have travel bags packed with necessary IDs at all times. If we're separated for any reason, you must head directly to Aunt Gabrielle in Aix-en-Provence."

"Why not Switzerland? It's close and neutral."

"The Swiss border is closed to us now. They have been warned by the Nazis not to accept Jews."

"I'll not leave Metz without you."

"My unit will be in Verdun," Charles said. "You cannot wait for me. I may head south without returning home."

"You're scaring me. Please calm down. This stress is more dangerous than the Bosches."

"If only that were true. You must promise to leave if it's clear you're in danger. If we wait for each other, both of us might get caught. Besides, it's safer to travel alone. I'll meet you at Gabrielle's. There's an envelope on the dresser in your bedroom with ten thousand francs. You should keep the money with you at all times."

"If it's too dangerous here," Sophie said, "why would it be safer in the south with Gabrielle?"

"In the beginning, it will. Later, it might not."

"Where would we go then if there's no place safe in France?" Sophie asked.

"Italy perhaps," Charles said, "unless that weasel Mussolini joins the Bosches. In that case, we'll take a ferry from Marseille to Tunisia. Your mother's cousins on the Isle of Djerba will take us in. If Tunisia becomes dangerous, we'll try to make it to Egypt where the British will protect us."

"*Sacré bleu*, Papa, you are such a pessimist," Sophie said. "You're spoiling even the little fun I had in Paris."

"You'll come with me next week for the inspection of the new army hospital in Verdun?" Charles asked. "Please. It will only be for the day and back that evening."

Sophie thought about the offer but said nothing. She had rarely seen her father so passionate about anything.

Charles added, "Mama came and worked as a nurse beside me in the first war."

Sophie smiled. "Mama told me many times about how she left me with Grandma so she could assist you. I'll come."

Charles smiled. "Thank you for not arguing."

"I could argue, but if I do you'll just say that I remind you of Mama," Sophie said, pretending to zip her lip.

Chapter Six

May 10, 1940
Verdun, France

With Sophie sitting in the passenger seat, Charles drove up to a monolithic bunker. He had on the green medical tunic he wore in the first World War, complete with a *kepi*, the French military cap that showed his rank as a major. Sophie wore a simple, blue, floral day dress.

From the window of the car, Charles and Sophie saw soldiers, nurses, and medics screaming at one another as they ran helter-skelter around the entrance, loading supplies into trucks.

"This is unusual," Charles said. "I have no idea what's happening."

"We'll find out soon enough," Sophie said.

They exited the car and stopped a soldier carrying a large trunk.

"What's the commotion?" Charles asked.

"Sir. The Huns invaded Belgium and the Netherlands today," the soldier said. "General Gamelin has ordered all divisions north, before the German army gets to the sea."

Charles ran into the building, followed by Sophie. The chaos inside echoed the chaos outside. They turned into an office, barreling past a flustered secretary and into the private office of General Maurice

Leveque. They found Leveque talking on the phone, looking miserable. A heavy-set man with a trim beard that hid his jowls, Sophie estimated him to be a bit older than Charles. Leveque held up a hand for Charles and Sophie to wait.

"Goddamn it, General," Leveque screamed, "I said we'd have two mobile hospital units functional in Belgium by fourteen hundred hours tomorrow. One at Charleroi, the other at Condé-sur l'Escaut. If you idiots had any idea that the Huns would invade the lowlands, we'd have been prepared."

Leveque slammed the receiver down, looked up at Charles, and came around the desk to hug Charles.

"It's been a long time, my friend, and we need you. We have less than half the physicians required for the injuries we're likely to see. The Dutch and Belgians are offering little to no resistance. This is a different German army than we faced in '14.'"

"I'm here to help," Charles said. "This is my daughter, Sophie."

Leveque greeted Sophie. "It's my pleasure. You look like your mother. We were all saddened by her loss."

"Thank you," Sophie said. "I will help however I can."

"We've a shortage of nurses and aides for sure," Leveque said.

"I'm a surgeon, General."

Leveque's eyes popped; he took a long look at Sophie.

"Can it be true?" he asked, with a look of disbelief.

Charles answered the question. "Dr. Sophie Sollar graduated medical school three years ago and has been apprenticing with me ever since,"

“Stranger things have happened,” Leveque said, turning back to his desk brusquely. “We need you both now. At least until our regular staff arrive.”

It was eleven days later in Charleroi, Belgium, when Leveque, holding a box, approached Charles outside a tent amid a cluster of tents. Both wore surgical scrubs on which the blood had not yet dried.

“What’s in the box?” Charles asked.

“An appropriate uniform for your daughter. She’ll be a captain and a surgeon in the medical corps. I’ve also brought the official papers that she’ll need.”

Charles nodded. “Thank you. We return to France tonight?”

“Yes,” Leveque said, shaking his head. “I’m afraid the radio broadcasts aren’t quite telling the full truth. The Bosches have steamrolled us to the north and yet another Bosche army has exited from the Ardennes, bypassing the Maginot Line. The entire French Army and the British Expeditionary Force are in full flight and find themselves pinched between two surgical clamps. Units from the French and British have retreated back to France, or they’ve headed to the coast near Dunkirk. They’re hoping for a miracle.”

“I so feared this,” Charles lamented.

“This is your daughter’s tent?” Leveque asked.

“Yes.”

Charles made a move to enter, but Leveque stopped him, hesitating.

“I wouldn’t have believed it – your daughter I mean,” Leveque said. “You must be proud. She operated non-stop for eighteen hours, slept three, and then went on for another twelve hours. She didn’t shy away from the most difficult injuries. Four thoracotomies, six laparotomies, two craniotomies, four above-the-knee amputations and six below-the-knee amputations. Too many lacerations to count. I watched her first laparotomy and her first amputation. I needed no more observation. Her technique is flawless. The few soldiers who died were beyond repair but she gave it her all. The medics and nurses are in total awe of her as they are of you."

Charles removed a handkerchief from the rear pocket of his scrubs and dabbed tears from his eyes. "Thank you. Sophie and I will stay with you as long as we're needed."

"This war might be over in two or three weeks," Leveque said, with a grim frown, "and the France you and I know will be no more. You know the rumors of what happens to Jews in lands the Nazis have taken. You and your daughter must escape now and head south."

"I can't believe it's come to this," Charles said, shaking his head.

The men entered Sophie's tent to find her in surgical scrubs, curled up on a cot but rolling her head and shoulders as if screaming at the world. Charles approached Sophie and nudged her shoulder.

Sophie quickly stirred awake and sat up. She saw her father. "Do they need me? I'll get up."

"No," Charles said. "I came to tell you something. Lie back down."

Sophie fell back, turning onto her side and curled into a ball.

Charles turned back to Leveque, who opened his arms. They embraced each other with a kiss on both cheeks.

"It's been an honor to serve with you in two wars, General," Charles said as they separated.

"Charles, the honor is ours together," Leveque said. "And an honor to serve with your daughter." Leveque stood back and saluted Charles, who returned the salute. Leveque about faced and exited the tent.

Charles turned back to Sophie, who was rubbing her eyes and trying to focus.

"Get up. We're leaving," Charles said. "Our unit is retreating before the Bosches arrive. Trucks hauling equipment have already departed for Verdun and then south."

"Will we stay with the unit?" Sophie asked.

"As I feared, the Bosches will likely control Belgium, the Netherlands, Alsace, Lorraine and all of Northern France in short order. It is no place for a Jew to be."

Sophie nodded.

"I'm proud of what you accomplished here, as was General Leveque. You are a surgeon despite what anyone might think. But we need to leave now," Charles said. "You'll take a train from Verdun to Paris, then south to Marseille, then on to Gabrielle in Aix-en-Provence."

"You'll come with me?" Sophie asked.

"I thought Verdun would be a quick visit and inspection. I left things at home that I need. I will take our car back to Metz and retrieve whatever valuables I can carry from our house and the office. I'll then drive south to meet you."

"I want to stay with you," Sophie said. "What valuables do you need so badly that you'd risk your life?"

"Things of your mother's that I cherish and want for

you."

"I don't need Mama's things. They're just things. I need you."

"I need them," Charles said. "They're all I have left of Mira."

"You have me. Please, let's head to Gabrielle's together."

Charles shook his head, ignoring Sophie's pleas. "Everyone in Paris will be trying to head south. I might make it to Gabrielle's house before you."

"I just pray that you make it all," Sophie said.

"Enough of this. General Leveque has officially made you a captain in the French army. He had one of the nurse's uniforms modified to include the proper insignias and ranks. He included papers giving your rank and authorizing train priority all the way to Marseille. It's all in the box at the foot of your cot."

"I don't want to leave you," Sophie repeated. "Please, Papa. I've lost my mother. I don't want to lose you as well."

"Not up for discussion. You have money enough for the trip to Gabrielle. I'll drive you to the train station, then head to Metz. You need to pack."

Sophie rose to her feet slowly and wobbled. Dark circles under sunken eyes revealed what little sleep she'd allowed herself during the past week.

Chapter Seven

Verdun, France
May 22, 1940

Dressed in civilian clothes, Charles navigated his auto within three blocks of the overrun Verdun rail station, but drew no closer. Sophie sat in the passenger seat wearing her modified nurse's uniform with three blue-striped epaulets on each sleeve, denoting her status as a captain.

Families of all sizes and ages filled the street. Confusion was etched on each face and parents ignored their sobbing children. Everyone who could walk carried sacks, bags, and valises filled with whatever they imagined they would need for the next stage of their life.

"I can't get any closer," Charles said. "Hopefully, you'll find a hospital car attached to a Paris-bound train where your services will be needed."

"I don't like leaving you," Sophie said. "We could pack those things of mother's you need twice as fast and then be on our way."

"The Bosches may have surrounded Metz already. I'll turn south if it appears there's no way to get in. You need to head south to Paris now. "

Sophie exited the car, opened the trunk and removed a small but weighty valise. Amidst the din of crying children and their parent's yells of confusion, the sounds of distant shelling and the sweet, acrid smell of cordite filled the air.

Charles rolled down his window as his daughter approached. She leaned through it and gave him a kiss on the cheek.

They said, “Be safe,” at the same time.

Sophie watched her father drive away, then turned toward the station.

It took thirty minutes for her to fight her way toward the trains. Taking in the chaos at the station entrance, she walked around the station and slipped under a fence along with a host of others trying to game the system. A policeman and two armed French soldiers met the encroachers and without listening to their protests, marched them back and under the loose fence. One of the soldiers, a corporal, separated Sophie and drew her aside.

The corporal eyed Sophie up and down. “I’ll have to arrest you for impersonating an army nurse,” the corporal said.

“You’re right, Corporal,” Sophie said, “I’m not a nurse.”

“At least you admit it.”

“I’m a surgeon and a Captain,” Sophie said, “and I may have you court martialed for not saluting an officer.”

The corporal laughed. “You must think I was born yesterday, big brown eyes and all. Don’t make it worse for yourself.”

Sophie stood her ground. “I’ll forget about the salute if you’ll take me to a hospital car heading toward Paris. I have a letter of authorization from General Leveque of the SSA ordering me to Paris.”

Sophie opened the valise to reveal rows of surgical

instruments and the envelope from General Leveque. She extracted the letter and showed it to the corporal. She hoped the sight of scalpels and clamps would help make her case.

"You're too fucking young to be a surgeon and a girl to boot," the Corporal responded. "There are none of those in the French, or any, army."

"Take me to a hospital car now," Sophie demanded. "Men are sick and we're standing here arguing. Move."

The Corporal responded, "Okay. But if you're pulling a fast one, you're going to be in a world of trouble. Give me your valise. I think you might have stolen it and those instruments must worth a small fortune. I'll keep it so you don't try to run."

"Gladly," Sophie said.

Off they went, Sophie trailing the corporal along the tracks for a quarter mile until they neared a train with four white hospital cars, red crosses covering the sides and roofs. Medics busily loaded injured men up ramps into each of the cars.

Sergeant Henri Kilie, a French medic in his late forties with a tough, pock-marked face, was standing on the end of the last car smoking a cigarette when he saw Sophie and the corporal marching toward him. Kilie ran into the car and came out with another medic. They jumped over a car railing, crossed tracks, then ran toward Sophie, ignoring the now confused corporal. The two medics stopped and both saluted, which Sophie ignored.

"Doc, you're here," Kilie shouted. "Is your father here too?"

"No, Henri. Just me," Sophie said.

"You have no idea how badly we need you. Are you coming with us?"

"To Paris? Absolutely," Sophie said.

"I could just hug you," Kilie said. "Two surgeons promised us from the 124th haven't been seen. We can't hold the train any longer. Soldiers are dying in these cars. C'mon, there's no time to waste."

"You might take my surgical instruments from this kind corporal who offered to lug them here from the station," Sophie said, smiling at the corporal.

"Thanks for helping the doctor," Kilie said. "She's a Godsend."

"Well, of course. Glad to be of service," the corporal said, clearly stunned, as he handed the valise to the medic, then watched Sophie and the medics scurry into the nearest hospital car.

Sophie quickly surveyed the situation in the first car. Twenty-four men lay on beds in various stages of misery. Ten battery-powered bulbs strung from the ceiling gave the only light, and the scent of death filled the poorly ventilated car.

"What's in the other three hospital cars?" Sophie asked.

"The same. A few of the men in each car have already died. We've nowhere to put them," Kilie said.

"Can we move corpses between cars once we're underway?" Sophie asked.

"Not easily, but yes."

"Assuming we don't stop, it'll be a six-hour journey. At some point I'll want the soldiers who have died away from those living. Let's make the front car the mortuary," Sophie said.

"Done," Kilie said.

"Let's start with the men in this car," Sophie said as she approached the first bed, which held a man with a bloody head bandage. She picked up a piece of cardboard with the soldier's name handwritten on it, then moved to the right side of the bed. The wounded soldier, watching her closely, attempted a smile.

"Private LeClerc, I'm Dr. Sollar. When were you injured?"

"Three, four days ago. Shrapnel took off my helmet and that's the last I remember until waking up maybe yesterday in the field," LeClerc said. "I haven't seen a doctor yet. They just bandaged my head and sent me off."

"Let's have a look," Sophie said, as she slowly unwrapped the blood-soaked bandages with Kilie's help. Sophie and Kilie's heads popped back an inch when they discovered a jagged, four-inch piece of German shell protruding from the middle of a wide laceration in LeClerc's scalp. Their looks frightened LeClerc, whose eyes opened to their fullest.

"Am I going to live?" LeClerc cried.

"Absolutely," Sophie said, "and half a kilo lighter too."

Her smile calmed her first patient. She worked tirelessly, seeing to every wounded soldier in all four cars. She pronounced thirteen men dead, and had the first of the four rail cars divided in half with drapes to cordon off the corpses. Not all went well. She performed an abdominal exploration to remove a shell fragment while the train moved. Absent blood or serum for transfusion, the soldier succumbed to blood loss from his injuries.

"We tried," Sophie said. Without hesitation, she moved to the next patient.

An hour out of Paris, the conductor hid the train in a tunnel for thirty minutes as the Luftwaffe circled overhead, giving her the time and stillness she needed to drain a subdural hematoma from the brain of a man who had been comatose for three days. He awoke twenty minutes after the procedure.

By the time the train pulled into the Gare du Nord in Paris, Sophie had worked non-stop for more than seven hours. Medics were already emptying the car using stretchers. She sat on a stool next to an empty hospital bed covered with bloody sheets. She leaned back against the wall of the train car and closed her eyes. Sergeant Kilie, her assistant and anesthetist the entire time, slid down against the wall of the rail car next to Sophie's stool and offered her a sip of water from his canteen.

"Doc, I can't believe what you accomplished today," Kilie said. "I don't know how you did it or what medals are given in the medical corps, but you deserve whatever they can pin on your chest. We lost only three men out of twenty-three who would have died, had you not been here. Had we had proper equipment and blood, no one might have died."

"You kept count?"

"Yes. I have two daughters in Lyon and I will tell them of your heroism under the most terrible of conditions."

"What we did, Henri," Sophie said. "You worked just as hard and I couldn't have done a thing without you."

"Thank you. That means a lot to me," Kilie said.

"Today, thank God, I had to concentrate on helping these men. Otherwise, I would have been worrying about my father."

"How so?" Kilie asked.

"Against my wishes and pleas, he headed back home to retrieve things from our home and office," Sophie said. "I should have gone with him."

“Where’s home?”

“Metz.”

“I wouldn’t have let him go. The Bosches control much of the Lorraine already.”

“I tried, I even got angry with him,” Sophie lamented. “But he said he’d be careful. He wants memories of my mother. Photographs, jewelry, things like that. They were so in love every day of their lives after meeting. Mama was killed in an avalanche in Champe de Feu eight years ago. I would catch him on occasion looking at photographs or holding her jewelry with tears in his eyes. He couldn’t bury her completely.”

“It’s hard to bury love, I guess,” Kilie said.

“I love my father and I loved my mother,” Sophie said. “That’s as close as I’ve gotten to some kind of love. I just hope he’s okay.”

”Love usually comes when you least expect it. I know you’ll find it. It’s not the same as the love of a parent but you’ll know it when it arrives,” Kilie said.

“Something to look forward to.”

“Working with you and your father this past week in Charleroi, I couldn’t help but notice how much you two are alike.”

“Is that good or bad?” Sophie asked.

“Mostly good, actually. The passion you showed with each injury and surgery.”

“What was the bad?”

“The passion you showed with each injury and surgery,... sometimes too much.” Kilie laughed to himself. “The medics and nurses would agree.”

Sophie smiled, thinking about her father. “I hope he’s okay.”

"As do I."

Sophie and Kilie sat quietly for a moment, sharing slurps from the canteen.

"I have to get these men off to the hospital or morgue," Kilie said, rising to his feet. "We can handle things from here. I had the medics wash your instruments. Everything is in the valise."

"Thank you, Henri."

"I hope we meet again," Henri said.

"As do I, in a free France."

"*À votre santé*," Kilie said as he stood, toasting Sophie with his canteen.

The Gare du Nord train station was quiet compared to Verdun, which surprised Sophie. The stationmaster told her that everyone was trying to get to Paris from the north, not leave it.

Once on the street, chaos resumed. Families burdened by belongings and distressed children lumbered from hotel to hotel, trying to find temporary lodging. Few had success. While lugging her forty-five-pound valise of surgical instruments, Sophie searched for a vacancy herself, standing in queues outside various hotels. After two hours of fruitless hunting, she gave up and went to a small bistro and had a light meal, then taxied to Gare de l'Est for the trip to Marseille. Fortune finally found her and she secured a sleeper car for that night. Sophie purchased a glass liter of mineral water, a croissant, and an egg salad sandwich from a station vendor. The train departed at eleven p.m.

Once in her sleeping car, she nibbled on her food then tried to sleep in her uniform, the only clothing she now possessed. Every time she closed her eyes, she saw

Nazis descending on her father or massive, gaping wounds in need of repair. When the train stopped in Marseille twelve hours later, she struggled to get off the train in time and nearly missed her connection to Aix-en-Provence.

Chapter Eight

Northeast France
May 1940

After dropping Sophie in Verdun, Charles drove south instead of east. He reasoned that the German army might not have blocked access into Metz from that direction. During the drive, he encountered an occasional shower from the cloud-laden skies. He ended up in Pont à Mousson in the late afternoon. He asked a gendarme and two civilians if the road north to Metz remained open and all three thought so. He motored north slowly along the road beside the Moselle river, stopping every mile or so to ask a farmer or pedestrian about the road. None had any knowledge of access issues into Metz.

Within a mile of Metz, Charles encountered the first uniformed Nazis at a checkpoint as well as a summer thunder shower, pelting his Citröen and the guards with rain. One guard carried a Lugar pistol; two others had automatic rifles. As he approached, all three guns were pointed at him.

In flawless German, Charles said "Heil Hitler," and explained that he was a doctor who'd just made a house call to a patient in Novéant-sur-Moselle and was now returning home to Metz. He showed the Germans his doctor's bag, but the sentries searched his car anyway, though quickly, given the rain. During the search, Charles put a death grip on the steering wheel with both hands not wishing to reveal how badly he was shaking. When the guards found no weapons, they let him through.

Once clear, Charles pulled his car to the roadside, opened the door, leaned out, and vomited.

He arrived at his secretary's house at six in the evening. Louise LaFleur screamed when she saw him at the front door; she was certain he'd been captured or killed. Once restored to her senses, she surveyed the neighborhood to see if anyone had eyes on their front door. Seeing none, she pulled him into her house and closed the door. Charles greeted Louise's husband, Paul, and together they went into the kitchen and sat.

"Where is Sophie?" Louise asked.

"She's on her way to Aix-en-Provence to stay with my sister. I left her at the train station in Verdun. She's now a captain in the French army so I don't think she'll have trouble getting on the train … I hope."

"Why didn't you go with her? Paul asked. "It's too dangerous for you here. Jews are already being targeted."

"We went to Verdun for a tour of the facilities. We had no idea the battle had begun," Charles said, with a heavy sigh. "We expected to return to Metz that evening. But they needed both of us and we were sent into Belgium the next morning. By the seventh day, the French and British armies were in full flight. Our General, a friend from the Great War, told us to get away before the Bosches surrounded us. I sent Sophie south, but I needed to retrieve a few important valuables first."

Both LaFleurs shook their heads in disbelief.

"What?" Charles asked.

"Charles, this is insanity," Louise said, her arms shaking. "Pure insanity. You should have gone with

Sophie. You're not thinking clearly.

"Louise is right. What are your exact plans?" Paul asked. "We're under curfew after six p.m. and anyone outside for any reason might be shot."

"I'll go to my house first thing in the morning," Charles said, "then my office to gather surgical instruments, then south to Aix and Sophie. I'll be here no more than an hour."

"Nazi sympathizers have already painted a Jewish star on your office building. They might be watching," Paul said.

It's not safe to go there," Louise insisted.

"I'll wait outside until I see no one around. Go in and out," Charles said.

"If I were you I'd just leave Metz now and hope to make it out safely," Paul pleaded. "Sophie needs you. She's lost her mother and doesn't need to lose her father too."

"When it's safe," Louise pleaded, "I'll gather your valuables and keep them for you."

"I'll be fine," Charles said. "I'm usually the worrier, but I'll be quick."

Louise made the sign of the cross. She and her husband exchanged looks.

Charles left at the break of dawn and drove to his house, parking far down the street. As planned, Paul LaFleur followed behind, parking his car at an eighth-mile distance, with Charles' car still in view.

Charles saw no one on the street. He walked to the rear of his house, unlocked the back door, and entered. In his hallway closet, he found an empty suitcase. He went into his study, removed a picture from the wall and opened his wall safe. He removed Mira's jewelry and forty thousand francs in cash and put it in the suitcase. From his bookshelf, he added a photo album. He locked the back door, walked the perimeter of the property to the front and stood behind a hedge, peeking out to the street. He watched an elderly neighbor walk her poodle to the curb and then back into her house. Seeing no one in the street, he hurried to his car, put the suitcase in the trunk, signaled Paul, then drove away.

Charles and Paul repeated a watch and wait not far from his office on Rue de la Cheneau. This time the street was filled with people, most walking to and from the nearby hospital and clinics. Paul LaFleur parked on a side street, exited his car, and stood in front of a pharmacy across the street to watch Charles. For fifteen minutes, Charles sat in his car, staring at the large, yellow Star of David roughly painted on the front door of his office building. He couldn't see anyone who seemed to be watching, so at last he exited his car, walked to his office building, unlocked the front door, entered, and climbed the stairs to his office.

Within ten seconds, two men exited the building across the street, only a door from where Paul watched. One wore the knee-length black overcoat and officer hat of the Gestapo. The other man, quite large, wore street clothes. They strode toward Charles' office, drawing their Mauser Lugar pistols as they neared the front door. Finding the door locked, the larger of the two stood back and kicked the door open, shattering the door and frame. Within moments, the Gestapo officer had walked back out the front door to survey the street. People either stopped walking or crossed the street to avoid the armed German. The second man soon exited with Charles in tow, a Luger pressed into the base of the helpless surgeon's skull.

The three men continued stiffly down the street as everyone around them froze. The Gestapo officer crossed the street toward the building from which he had emerged, then turned and waved his companion to follow with Charles. At the same time, a lone automobile drove down the street, apparently unaware of what was transpiring. Spotting Charles and his captor, the driver jammed on his brakes, stopping only a few feet from Charles and causing the plainclothes henchman to release Charles' collar and lower his gun.

Seizing the moment, Charles began to run around the car and up the street. In a single, fluid movement, both officers proceeded calmly into the street and emptied their pistols into the fleeing surgeon. Gripping his jacket so tightly his knuckles turned white, Paul watched his friend collapse, watched as the two Gestapo officers approached Charles' limp body where it had fallen in the middle of the street and kicked him to ensure he was dead. The officer in uniform then ejected his Lugar's seven-shot magazine, pulled a new magazine from his coat pocket, reloaded his Luger and shot Charles point blank in the head for good measure.

By the time the last shot rang out, Rue de la Cheneau had emptied. Paul was shaking as he returned to his car. Hoping to leave quickly, he had difficulty putting the key into the ignition. He wiped tears from his eyes with the sleeve of his shirt then pounded the steering wheel with both hands. Finally able to start the car, he drove off without looking back.

Chapter Nine

Aix-en-Provence, France
May 23, 1940

Four years had passed since Sophie and Charles visited Gabrielle and her family in Aix-en-Provence, the summer before Sophie's last year in medical school. Nevertheless, Charles and his sister were close. They'd spoken on the phone once a week ever since Germany had invaded Poland the previous September. Seven years earlier, after Mira's untimely death, Gabrielle had moved in with Charles and Sophie for a month. Her presence allowed Sophie to return to medical school only two weeks later. Before returning to Aix-en Provence, Gabrielle talked Charles into buying Sophie an automobile, so that Sophie could drive home from Strasbourg every two weekends during the school year.

Sophie, agitated with worry and exhausted from travel, hoisted her heavy valise and found a taxi outside the Aix-en Provence Centre rail station. She directed the driver to Gabrielle's house near the Parc Gilbert Vilers. When the taxi turned onto her aunt's street, she felt herself begin to relax for the first time since the day she and her father drove up to the Verdun medical facility, unaware that the war had begun. She exited the taxi, carried her valise to the front door and knocked. This sense of relief lasted less than ten seconds after a strange woman, mid-40s, too nicely dressed to be housekeeper, answered the door.

“How may I help you?” the woman asked.

“Where is Mrs. Cohen, Gabrielle Cohen, my aunt?”

“The Cohen family departed two days ago.”

“Departed to where?”

“South Africa. You must be Dr. Sollar. I’m Juliette LeBlanc, the new owner. My husband, Jacques, worked with Mr. Cohen.”

Sophie, confused, tired, hungry and dehydrated, began to sweat, then wobble. She dropped her valise to the ground, turned and sat hard onto the door threshold. “I need to sit. I’m not feeling well.”

Juliette lifted Sophie to her feet and walked her into the house.

Thirty minutes later, Sophie found herself lying on a couch in the living room. A cool towel had been placed on her forehead and her feet, sans shoes, were elevated on a pillow. She blinked a few times, then picked up her head to figure out where she was. She turned to Juliette who sat nearby on a chair. Atop a coffee table next to the couch sat a tray with sweet rolls, a pitcher of iced tea and an empty glass.

“You’ve rested for thirty minutes,” Juliette said.

Sophie sat up and placed the moist towel on the side of the tray. “I feel better. Thank you.” She drank a glass of tea and took two bites from one of the sweet rolls.

“Gabrielle expected your father and you to arrive at any moment,” Juliette said. “She left a letter for your father to explain everything. Read it first and then we’ll talk.”

Juliette handed Sophie a sealed envelope and left the room.

May 20, 1940

Dear Charles,

Europe is not a place for Jews now. Jacob and I have decided to move to South Africa with the children. Jacob has a sister in Cape Town and we've booked passage on a ship that leaves Marseille on May 21.

We discussed this move briefly during our last phone conversation on May 9th. The war has gone so badly for the French that we didn't feel safe waiting. As of now, Jews are accepted in South Africa.

We've sold the house to Jacques and Juliette LeBlanc. Jacques and Jacob worked together and we considered them amongst our dearest friends. They will help you and Sophie as much as possible without putting themselves at risk from the Nazis.

I expect that you will head to Tunisia to be with Mira's family. My sister-in-law's address in Cape Town is below. Please write and tell us of your safe exit from the war and an address in Tunisia so that we might stay in contact.

Expecting that you might have left in a hurry, we've left a box of extra clothing for you and Sophie. Everything will require some tailoring.

Love,

Gabrielle

Juliette returned and poured another glass of tea from the pitcher.

"Have you heard from my father?" Sophie asked. "He thought he might be here before me."

"No. We've heard nothing."

“I need to stay until I hear from Papa,” Sophie said. “He went to Metz to gather some valuables, then he was going to drive here. I pleaded that he not go home but he refused to listen. He wouldn’t let me go with him either.”

“Let’s pray that he’s okay,” Juliette said. “The Bosches control all of the Alsace and Lorraine now. Before leaving, Gabrielle tried calling your home and your father’s secretary without success. Maybe you’ll have better luck writing.”

Juliette put Sophie in a basement guest room and gave her a sewing kit to refit Gabrielle’s clothing.

The next morning at ten a.m., Sophie walked into the kitchen and brought in a plate of half-eaten food which she laid in the sink.

Juliette greeted Sophie with a hug. “ You look exhausted and I know you’re scared. I would be too. Jacques heard you crying in the middle of the night.”

“I’m sorry,” Sophie said. “I couldn’t sleep. I can’t stop worrying about my father or remembering horrors of the front. I see dying men in my nightmares. I see my father being taken by the Nazis.”

“What can I do to help?” Juliette asked.

“Nothing more. You’ve been beyond generous. I don’t want to bother you or your family,” Sophie said.

“You’re no bother,” Juliette said, “and Gabrielle was my friend. What you need now is sleep and a lot of it. My uncle traveled to the United States last year on business and was given a sedative to sleep. You’re a doctor, so I don’t want to tell you what to do.”

“I need to write letters to my father’s secretary and to other neighbors first. Let me see the drug.”

Sophie wrote the letters, had Juliette post them, then took one-hundred milligrams of secobarbital from

Juliette's medicine chest. Sophie slept soundly for eighteen hours. When she awoke the next day at noon, she found herself curled on the small floor rug next to her bed.

After a hearty breakfast, Sophie took a goodly portion of her ten-thousand francs and purchased clothing and shoes.

After countless, failed attempts, Sophie gave up trying to reach anyone in Metz by phone. She wrote a letter a day to Louise LaFleur and waited anxiously for a quick response. None came.

Sophie continued to sleep poorly, but as the nights went on, her nightmares and daytime thoughts shifted exclusively to her father. She continued, on a daily basis, trying to reach Louise and any known contact in Metz by mail. As day after day passed with no news, Sophie's hopes of seeing her father again started to fade.

Twelve days after separating from Charles, the answer arrived on June 4th, in a letter which had been placed in the LeBlanc's mailbox addressed to Dr. Sophie Sollar. Absent a stamp, Juliette assumed someone had hand-delivered the letter.

Sophie ran down to her quarters in the basement, slammed the door, opened a window for air, and laid on her bed, hoping for the best but expecting the worst.

She received what she expected.

June 1 1940

My Dear S,

I am hopeful you will receive this letter. This is the fifth I've sent to your aunt's address. The Germans control all the Alsace and Lorraine now. Assuming the mail was not being delivered, I pleaded to a friend of my husband who planned to sneak past the German lines to return to his parent's home in Toulon. He said he would hand deliver my letter. I've omitted our names but I think you know who it's from.

The news is not good. The Germans were waiting for your father at his office. I'm so sorry to tell you that your father was murdered by the Nazis.

Charles returned to Metz the same day he left you at Verdun and.....

The letter fluttered out of Sophie's hands and the color drained from her face. She squeezed her fists hard into her temples, shook her head violently as she stared into the ceiling and screamed, "Papa, NOOOO! NOOOO! NOOOO!"

A gust of wind came through the window and blew hair into her face. She swept back the hair over her forehead and without thinking, she twirled the locks with her index finger before yelling, "Papa, NOOOO!" once more.

Chapter Ten

France to Tunisia

June, 1940

Sophie lay on the bed for an hour, crying. Juliette heard her sobbing, came down, and tried to offer some comfort. Sophie pleaded that she be left alone and stayed in her room until the next morning, forgoing dinner.

Day after day, Sophie found herself unable to function. She ate little, spent most of the time in her room crying, and went outside rarely.

News of Jews being rounded up in Paris had already filtered down to Aix-en-Provence. Italy had declared itself on the side of Germany, Switzerland had closed its borders to Jews, and Francisco Franco ruled Spain and had close relations with Hitler. Tunisia, a French colony, remained Sophie's one viable option.

Sophie's nightmares continued. She blamed herself for not demanding that Charles come with her to Aix-en-Provence, or at least, let her accompany him back to Metz.

...

Each day, the war news worsened. By the twenty-fifth of May, the Germans had captured Boulogne and secured the French coast. Three days later, the Belgians surrendered to the Germans. On June ninth and tenth, the Germans launched their offensive on Paris. Feasting on vulnerability, Mussolini and the Italians declared war on France. The Germans entered Paris on June fourteenth. On June sixteenth, the French WWI war hero Marshall Henri-Phillipe Petain became prime minister of France, and asked Germany for armistice terms.

World War I had seen France last four years of trench warfare stalemate. Twenty-two years later, the country had capitulated in five weeks.

...

Juliette LeBlanc finally gave Sophie some logic that gave her comfort.

"Stop blaming yourself for things out of your control," Juliette said. "None of this is your fault. If your mother had still been alive, your father would have returned to Metz and he still would not have allowed you to go with him. Your father returned to Metz to retrieve your mother, plain and simple."

When France formally surrendered, Sophie had run out of time in which to do nothing. Jacques, speaking without Juliette nearby, reminded Sophie of the deal struck by her Aunt Gabrielle. Sophie could stay as long as it did not put the LeBlancs in possible jeopardy for hiding a Jew. Jacques said that time had come. Sophie had to leave, and soon.

Juliette hoped being among her mother's family in Tunisia would give Sophie some semblance of peace and harmony.

It was a warm spring morning when Sophie stood in the doorway of her aunt's former home and thanked Juliette and Jacques.

"I will avenge my father's death," Sophie said, gazing unseeingly down the street. "If I can find any part of the French army or any army that is still fighting the Nazis, I will help however I can."

Sophie set off for Marseille and the ferry to Tunisia. From there, she would find her way to the Isle of Djerba, where both she and her mother were born.

The following day in Marseille was overcast with gusts coming from the south-east. Other than the wind-generated chop, the eight-hour boat ride from Marseille to Tunis was uneventful until the HMS Wryneck, a British destroyer patrolling the Mediterranean Sea, intercepted the ferry and boarded it, looking for any sign of Nazi support. When a two-hour inspection of the ship's hold, as well as passenger interviews, revealed nothing of interest, the ferry went on her way.

On deck, Sophie saw a man wearing a kippah, the Jewish skull cap, marking him as a Jew. Sophie's first thought is why would anyone bring attention to being Jewish given the antisemitic climate in which they lived. The kippah also provided Sophie with a small touch of comfort that she was not alone and she smiled. A woman and three children stood close to the man. Sophie thought the oldest child, a girl, must be around thirteen or fourteen. The man showed a great deal of attention to the older daughter, who looked unhappy. The man brushed her hair back off her face, then kissed her forehead. The girl remained unhappy, but the man smiled. Touched by the father's obvious love for his daughter, Sophie felt a pang of sadness. She approached the man and woman and introduced herself to the man in French.

"Excuse me, sir, are you staying in Tunis?" Sophie asked.

"Yes, we are," the man said, looking surprised by the stranger's approach. The woman standing with the man turned to listen.

"I'm trying to get to the Isle of Djerba. I'm not sure how I might do that," Sophie said.

"Djerba. That's a good distance from Tunis," the man said.

"I was born there," Sophie said, "as was my mother. Our family left when I was four. Our home had been in Metz. Sadly, my mother died eight years ago. I'm going to stay with her family."

"Are you married?" Avram asked.

"No. I've never married."

"You're traveling alone?" the woman asked.

"Yes. My father was killed by the Nazis," Sophie said, with visible effort. "I saw your husband's kippah and..."

The woman bowed her head in acknowledgement of Sophie's loss. "May his memory be for a blessing," she said.

"Thank you," Sophie said.

"To lose two parents is very hard," the man said, "We are sorry to hear it."

"Thank you," murmured Sophie.

"I'm Avram Benoliel," the man said. "This is my wife, Jeanne, my daughter, Laila ..."

Sophie was introduced to all three children, who smiled shyly.

"Do you think Tunisia will be safer?" Sophie asked the Benoliels.

"Time will tell," Avram said. "I sold my importing business in Marseille to my partner. We'll move again if need be."

The dinner bell sounded.

"You'll eat with us," Jeanne insisted. "This boat and

the city of Tunis are nowhere for a single Jewish woman to be alone."

"We have a home in Tunis," Avram said. "You'll stay with us tonight and I'll help you arrange a train to Djerba. It's an all-day trip to Gabes and then a taxi to the ferry to Djerba."

"I was younger, but I remember the ferry. Thank you so much for your kindness. All I have is an address," Sophie said. "These are cousins I haven't seen in years."

"How's your Arabic?" Avram asked. "On Djerba, many won't understand French."

"Fair. Words my parents would utter when angry or flustered, or when they didn't want me to know what they were talking about," Sophie answered. "Later, when I was older and understood more Arabic, my father and I would alternate English and Arabic when we didn't want people to know what we were saying."

"I have an idea," Jeanne said. "You could stay with us for a bit. Write your cousins that you're coming and brush up on your Arabic. We've plenty of room."

"You are too kind," Sophie said. "I can't impose on you."

"It's no trouble at all," Avram said. "You'll stay with us until you know where you're going. It's not an imposition and someday you'll do something kind for another Jew."

"I have to ask, what did you do in Metz?" Jeanne asked.

"I'm a surgeon," Sophie said. "My father and I had our practice in Metz. We served together in the French army medical corps until the debacle in Belgium."

The answer stunned Jeanne and Avram, followed by

huge smiles.

"A surgeon! Now we have much more to talk about," Jeanne said.

Sophie stayed with the Benoliels and wrote to her mother's brother-in-law, Moise Sarfati, in Djerba. In the letter, she recounted her father's death and the events of the past two months. While awaiting a response, she learned to keep her head covered when in public and quickly picked up the modest amount of conversational Arabic she had forgotten. She felt safer now that she had departed France and for the first time since Verdun at the beginning of the war, she was sleeping through the night.

During Sophie's stay with the Benoliels, Laila followed her around, asking questions about her life, and demanding to sit next to her at meals. The fourteen-year-old teen saw the respect her parents and their friends gave Sophie. After dinner one night, three weeks after meeting Sophie, Laila declared that she wanted to be a surgeon.

The Benoliels, caught unaware, turned to Sophie. Avram had a quizzical smile and Jeanne showed a look of disbelief.

"I didn't say anything," Sophie said.

"I like how people look up to you," Laila said.

"It's a long, tough road to be a doctor, let alone a surgeon, let alone for a woman to do it. But yes, it's a wonderful profession and it comes with a lot of respect."

Laila smiled.

"You want to hear the downside before you make such a big decision?" Sophie asked.

“I’d like to hear it,” Jeanne said.

“Hours and hours of study for years and years. I didn’t finish medical school until I was twenty-four and then years of training to be a surgeon. It’s not for everyone.”

“I don’t mind hard work,” Laila said.

“Honestly,” Jeanne said. “Tomorrow, you and I will scrub the kitchen tiles.”

“Be nice. Laila is an excellent student,” Avram countered.

“There’s another thing,” Sophie said. “I’ve had lots of boyfriends and dates. I was even engaged for a few months when I was in medical school in Strasbourg. He was a young dentist I had seen for a toothache. Many of the men I’ve dated, and liked, were, I think, intimidated by me being a doctor, especially a surgeon. A banker, a stock broker, an insurance agent, a chemist and the dentist I wanted to marry – all the same. They wouldn’t come out and say it but I think they were jealous of the respect I got from others.”

The dinner table became quiet for a moment until Sophie added, “Maybe I’ll never find a husband.”

Avram and Jeanne exchanged looks once again, but Leila cried out spiritedly, “I don’t want a husband! Do you really think I could become a surgeon?”

Sophie laughed. “Of course,” she said, smiling. “The thing is, you can be anything you want to be if you’re willing to put in the work. But as a woman, you can’t just be good. You need to be better. It’s hard.”

Avram stood, walked around the table, brushed Laila’s hair off her face and planted a kiss on her forehead. Laila seemed annoyed by the show of affection. Sophie smiled wistfully.

“My father did the same,” she said. “He would twirl

my hair over his index finger then kiss me. Like this."

Sophie rolled her hair over her finger like Charles used to do.

"He did it all the time for as long as I can remember. Sometimes I thought he did it just to annoy me. I was wrong. He did it because he loved me and it was his unique way of showing that. I couldn't have been a doctor and a surgeon without the support of my father."

The Benoliels were silent, watching Sophie remember.

"I would give a million francs," Sophie said, "to have Papa twirl my hair and kiss my forehead once again."

...

In July 1940, the conquering Germans divided France in half. The southern half of France and all of the African Colonies were controlled by a puppet government, called Vichy France. To appease the Germans, the Vichy government created laws and policies just as egregious as the antisemitic laws mandated by the Germans for northern France and the countries of central Europe that they controlled. Jews in Vichy were excluded from civil work and professions as well as losing French citizenship. Blacks and Muslims living in Vichy France did little better.

The Vichy governor of Tunisia, Jean-Pierre Estéva, a Catholic, thought the new laws regarding Jews to be immoral and were not in the best interests of Tunisia. Despite pressure from the Vichy government, Estéva did not enforce the edicts. The local Tunisian rulers, Ahmed Pasha Bey and later Moncef Bey, also agreed that the persecution of Jews did little to benefit Tunisia, which had a centuries long history of tolerating all religions. Of all the Vichy France colonies, Tunisia fared best for the Jews, but only for a while.

Chapter Eleven

The Isle of Djerba, Tunisia
Summer, 1940

Sophie had seen too much in France not to be wary of how the winds of war and antisemitism could blow in her direction at a moment's notice. She kept a valise packed with surgical tools and some money by her door. She had now spent half the ten thousand francs her father had given her. She needed stability and she needed a job.

A response letter from Sophie's Uncle Moise, finally arrived two weeks after she landed in Tunis. Moise's letter did not include a surprise that would not be revealed until they met. Sophie posted another letter to Moise with her arrival date at the Gabes train station.

Sophie said her goodbyes to the Benoliels and boarded a train east at seven in the morning. After an all-day journey, Sophie, valises in hand, exited the train in Gabes. She had no difficulty finding her cousin, Moise, because behind Moise stood his niece, Hélène, whom Sophie hadn't seen since her last year in medical school. Sophie assumed Hélène was still on the Isle of St. Martin in the Caribbean delivering babies. Both women screamed in delight upon seeing the other. Bypassing Moise, they wrapped arms in a tight hug and jumped up and down together in a tight circle.

At forty-two, Moise had a full beard but looked

skinny enough that a stiff desert wind might blow him over. Hélène towered over Sophie and stood even a bit taller than Moise.

"I'm so sorry about your father," Hélène said. "May his memory be a blessing."

"I have no family anymore," Sophie said. "You are my sister now."

"Yes," Hélène said, "and you are mine."

Moise stood discreetly to the side for a while before interrupting. "We'll miss the ferry if you two don't stop hugging."

Sophie and Hélène started to laugh, broke their embrace, and followed Moise to a cab.

On the ferry, Hélène told Sophie all about her life since they'd last seen each other. Both women apologized for not writing as they promised. After the visit to Strasbourg, Hélène had gone to the Isle of Saint Martin in the Caribbean. Her skills as a midwife were in demand on both the French and English sides of the island. Besides honing her midwife skills, Hélène learned to speak English.

Just before the war started in Europe, Hélène's mother, Moise's sister, became ill from the effects of childhood rheumatic fever. Hélène closed her practice and returned home to Djerba to care for her. Her mother died just as the Germans invaded France. Given the turmoil, Hélène decided to stay in Djerba. By the time they reached Moise's home near the Djerba synagogue, Sophie and Hélène had hatched a plan to open a medical clinic.

Sophie spent her first week meeting three generations of cousins. Most of the cousins spoke passable French and occasionally Ladino, a Spanish dialect brought with them while fleeing Spain during the Spanish Inquisition. Sophie, determined to master Arabic, made sure the conversations remained in the local language. At night, she and Hélène plotted their practice's future. They found an empty store near the only hospital on the island. Knowledgeable of the local politics, Moise stopped them from signing a lease until both Sophie and Hélène could obtain local licenses to practice. Sophie thought Moise silly as she had a license to practice in France and Hélène had her midwife certificate, however Moise's advice prevented a catastrophe.

Sophie and Hélène met with the hospital council, which was comprised of men and Muslim clerics. All were suspicious of Sophie's qualifications. The president of the council and the sole surgeon on the island, Abdel Gharbi, M.D., whose wife had a thriving midwifery practice, grilled both women. At some point, Gharbi reduced Hélène to tears, which angered Sophie enough that she questioned Gharbi's qualifications in return. By the end of the four-hour meeting, the council told Sophie and Hélène they would consider their applications but gave no date as to when that decision would be made.

Three days later, signs were posted throughout Djerba of the Vichy French rules which prohibited Jews from public service. The hospital council sent a notice to Sophie and Hélène that the edict from the Vichy government precluded them from practicing on the island. The winds of war had once again blown into the face of Sophie.

On learning the news, Sophie remained sullen all day, snapping at Moise and Hélène with little cause.

"Will the Nazis follow me to the ends of the earth," Sophie complained. "There's nowhere for me to go."

That night, Sophie's nightmares returned with

visions of her father being murdered by the Nazis on the streets of Metz.

Moise knew one of the council members personally and approached him with gifts in hand. Moise asked why the rebuke should stand, given the fact that the Vichy governor of Tunisia, Estéva, and the Tunisian ruler, Ahmed Pasha Bey, had specifically not enforced the edicts. His friend gave an honest answer – Gharbi and his wife did not want competition, especially from two Jews. Moise's friend suggested that Sophie and Hélène hide their religion and look for a community in need of their services.

The reasoning calmed Sophie.

Moise encouraged Sophie to adopt a more typical Arabic name in an attempt to hide her heritage. For a few hundred French francs, Sophie Sollar became Safiyah Shaloub, complete with a new Tunisian passport. Sophie and Hélène then sent letters to smaller communities throughout Tunisia, looking for medical and midwife vacancies.

A month later, Sophie received a letter from the mayor of Fériana, a village in the Kasserine Governate in the southwestern regions of Tunisia near the Algerian border. The mayor wrote that his village had been without a midwife for over a year, adding that an older physician remained in the village who refused to treat women for any malady. The medical clinic in Fériana had everything each would need to practice medicine and midwifery, including a bedroom, kitchen, bathroom, and a root cellar. The mayor offered the clinic building free of charge to Sophie and Hélène if only they would come.

Sophie and Hélène wrote the mayor to expect their arrival in two weeks. Moise knew no one who had been to the Kasserine Governate, so he couldn't tell the women what political or religious mores they might expect. On Djerba, most women wore simple head scarves. Smaller villages in the remote areas tended to be more religious.

To be safe, Sophie and Hélène, with the help of a Muslim friend, bought a few black *burqas* and a variety of white *abayas*, a kind of loose, full-body robe covering the arms and all the way down to the feet. Both garments would cover their bodies for the next three years. They also purchased *hijabs*, a headscarf that left the face uncovered, and *niqabs*, a scarf that covered the entire face save for the eyes, but without the mesh of the *burqa*.

Moise loaded his car with Sophie and Hélène and their tools of trade, and set out for Fériana at dawn. The trip would take ten hours. Moise was dressed in typical Arab garb, with a flat, red woolen hat he called a *chachia*, and a short-sleeved robe from Morocco known as a *gandora*.

That day, September 13, 1940, Italy invaded Egypt from its bases in Libya. World War II had come to North Africa.

Chapter Twelve

Fériana, Tunisia
September, 1940

The village of Fériana, set against the dorsal ridge of the Atlas mountains to the north, was comprised of drab, stone-and-mudbrick houses, most with mud floors. The streets were narrow and twisting without addresses or street signs. Some of the houses were surrounded by plain, windowless walls with a single door which would open to a courtyard filled with colorful tiles and plants. On the town's periphery, groups of tents of various sizes housed poorer families.

A single mosque sat in the town's center, surrounded by a large open-air market and a series of water fountains.

"Algeria is just over these mountains," Moise said, slowing his car.

Hélène and Sophie covered their entire faces with *niqabs*. But as Moise kept driving, some of the village women came into view.

"It's about half wearing hijabs or head scarves and half with niqabs, said Moise. "Only the rare burqa."

Moise looked to his right and saw that Hélène, sitting in the passenger seat, had already removed her niqab. Behind him, Sophie wore only a head scarf and a large smile.

Moise stopped the car and asked a man for

directions to the mayor's office. After a few wrong turns and a dead end, he asked two more men. The last man asked if the two women in the car were the new doctors. Moise said yes. The man said, "Follow me" and ran three blocks to a simple building with the Tunisian flag waving. The man didn't wait for a thank you, sprinting off at a gallop.

"This must be it," Hélène said. "No other building has a flag." Hélène turned to the back seat to see Sophie turning her head right and left. "Are you excited?"

"Excited?" Sophie replied. "It's a hundred degrees outside and my teeth are chattering. I'm scared."

"Let's go meet the mayor," Moise said. "What's the worst. We head back to Djerba."

Minutes later, Moise, Sophie and Hélène stood in front of an elderly bearded man in a small office.

"Shut the door, please, and take a seat," the man said in Arabic. "I'm Abdel Bahoul, "the mayor of Fériana. You must be Hélène and Safiya, yes?"

Hélène and Sophie answered "Yes," in unison.

"I called a friend in Djerba," Bahoul added. "You didn't mention in your letter that you are both Jewish."

A moment of tense silence followed. Sophie started breathing heavily and the teeth chattering restarted.

"Is that a problem?" Hélène asked.

"Maybe. Small villagers have a natural distrust of strangers, which include any other religion. I'd say it would be a problem if we didn't need your help," Bahoul replied. "The women of Fériana and the few left in Thélepte are forced to go to Kasserine for health care. An hour by car, longer if they ride a donkey or even walk. I'll say nothing as long as things go well. Besides,

I'm considered a hero now for finding the both of you."

"Good," Hélène said. "And you're our hero for hiring us."

Moise nodded agreement and Sophie stopped hyperventilating.

"Your clinic is around the corner. Follow me." Bahoul opened the door to his office and walked by a secretary wearing a full burqa. The secretary let out a high-pitched grumble of disgust that sounded like a hissing snake causing Moise to jump away. Bahoul suppressed a giggle.

Once outside the front door, Bahoul said, "She doesn't like anyone without a full face covering. Disregard her. If you need something done, come covered in a full burqa."

Hélène and Sophie followed Bahoul out of the building. Moise got into his car and followed slowly behind them.

As they walked, Bahoul kept talking. "The villagers are poor but proud. Payment for services may be in money, food, gifts, an animal, or help around the clinic. Payments might not arrive for months, but it will come."

As soon as the group turned the corner, they encountered a line of ten women standing in front of a modest stone building. More women could be seen streaming toward the same destination. As Sophie and Hélène passed, the women held their hands out while repeating the word, "*Shukran*".

In turn, Sophie and Hélène responded, "*Ahlan wa sahlan*," a familiar form of 'You're welcome.'

"They're very grateful," Bahoul said, unnecessarily.

Sophie and Hélène stopped to hold the hands of a few the women for a moment as they walked by. Two of the women were heavily pregnant. Sophie turned to Hélène and said, "At least you'll be busy."

Bahoul said, "Wait here. I need to start the generator."

"We might as well follow him," Sophie said. "We'll need to be able to start it was well."

With that, the two women followed Bahoul around the building and started the generator.

The main room of the clinic measured twenty-five by twenty feet, with a ten-foot ceiling. Three large posts supported the ceiling and roof. Bahoul flipped a switch and bulb lights every five feet gave adequate light, aided by the ambient light from four three-by-three-foot windows with shutters. In the corner was a kitchen with a sink and running water, a wood-burning stove, and a small round knee-high, dining table with four flat cushions. On the opposite side of the room sat two examination tables, a birthing bed, three stools, and two bassinets. Two large cabinets near the beds had an ample supply of sheets, pillows, and blankets. Another cabinet held an array of simple bandages, tapes, and gauzes. Another had piles of paper and folders for patients' charts. Two other cabinets were empty, and two more were padlocked.

Sophie rattled the key ring Bahoul had given her but he just shrugged, as if to indicate that one of the keys might, or might not, open the locks.

A door to the side of the large room led to a windowless bedroom with an overhead light, twin mattresses rolled up against the wall, a large chest of drawers, and an armoire. A kerosene lantern sat between the mattresses. A second door led to a squat toilet, and a third door led to a small, tiled bathing room which consisted of a stone-slab stool, a floor drain, a wooden bucket, and a water nozzle eighteen inches off the floor. Showering would require sponge-bathing, or else the cousins would have to fill the bucket and pour the water over their heads. A twelve-inch square window above eye level provided the only light.

"It's not Paris," Sophie whispered in Hélène's ear. Hélène in turn nudged Sophie in the chest with her elbow.

Near the kitchen, Bahoul showed the women a trap door under a Persian throw rug, leading to a root cellar. He pulled it open with some difficulty, revealing a gaping black hole.

"I'm not sure what's down there," Bahoul said. "You'll need a lantern to see."

Bahoul shut the cellar door. "Another thing. There's a hospital in Kasserine, but it's an hour away by car. The only phone in the village is in my office, so here's a key if you need to make a call for help. Can one of you drive a car?"

"We both can," Hélène said.

"Good. There are keys to my Citroën in my desk, which I keep parked next to the city building. You may use it only for emergencies or necessities. Understood?"

"Absolutely," Sophie said. "Thank you."

While they were viewing the premises, Moise had brought in all the valises and boxes and placed them in the bedroom. He returned to the main room.

"All unloaded," he said.

"It's late and you won't get far tonight if you want to be safe," Bahoul said. "There is a clean, small hotel in Kasserine where you can stay the night. It's too late for you to go food-shopping, so I've asked my wife to make dinner for three more – if you'd like to stay."

"Yes, thank you," Moise said.

"Normally we have pork, but knowing what we know, we'll have chicken," Bahoul said with a huge smile.

"What?" Moise said, "Muslims don't eat pork."

"Just testing you," Bahoul said as all four started to laugh.

"We knew things would be different," Sophie said. "We'll eat what we're served for as long as we're here in Fériana."

Hélène nodded assent.

"Good," Bahoul said, taking out his pocket watch. "It's five p.m. now ... let's say eight. Our house is four doors past the city center building."

"Perfect," Hélène said. "Thank you for everything."

Sophie, Hélène and Moise moved to follow Bahoul out, but immediately the women waiting outside the clinic surrounded them, shouting. Sophie held her hand up until the women quieted.

"We've not unpacked and haven't eaten since this morning," she shouted in Arabic. "The clinic will open tomorrow morning, an hour past sun-up. I'm sorry, but we cannot see anyone today."

Looking disappointed but accepting, the women slowly dissipated, all except for one clearly pregnant woman holding her stomach.

Hélène approached the woman and repeated Sophie's announcement. "We cannot see anyone until we have unpacked. You'll have to wait until tomorrow morning."

The woman grimaced, fear and determination shining in her eyes. "The contractions have been coming every three minutes and I can feel the baby's head. Please. My first child was stillborn and my husband will leave me if I have another dead baby."

"I guess we start the clinic now," Hélène said to Sophie.

Moise understood in a flash.

"I'm going to find the hotel in Kasserine," he said, "after I tell the mayor you may not make dinner."

He kissed the girls goodbye and headed off.

While Hélène attended to the woman in labor, Sophie unpacked their valises and boxes and inspected the cabinets. Every time she found something of interest or unusual in the locked cabinets she'd say, "Look what I found," and hold it up like a trophy. Her finds included an axe, a carved chess set, a bicycle tire inner tube, bottles of perfume, a series of books on gynecology, and a *Tarzan of the Apes* novel by Edgar Rice Burroughs, translated into French.

An hour later, Hélène made her first delivery in Fériana, with Sophie assisting. The woman kept thanking Allah for Hélène's expertise and asked her to name the baby girl out of appreciation.

"Name her Safiyah," Hélène said. "It means your daughter will be intelligent and wise."

Sophie leaned over and pinched Hélène on the butt as both laughed.

"You realize that you'll need to be my assistant," Hélène said, "and I yours."

Sophie laughed. "I'm a nightmare with babies. The only one I delivered in medical school slipped through my hands and was caught by a nurse. I swore I'd never deliver another."

"Better start un-swearing then," Hélène said.

It turned out they didn't have to forgo dinner – the

mayor's wife, Layla, a delightful woman at least twenty years younger than the mayor, brought a sumptuous feast of chicken shawarma, olives, tomatoes, pita and hummus, along with a locally produced wine. Bahoul noted that Muslims aren't supposed to have wine but somethings were too good to pass up.

The new mother lay recovering on a cot with the baby on her breast, praising the mayor and Allah, again, for bringing Hélène to their village. Before the mayor's wife left, she said she'd be over the next day to help the Hélène and Safiyah learn the ins and outs of local shopping.

In their bedroom that night, Sophie said, "A good day, actually."

"A very good day," Hélène replied.

Sophie turned off the room light, found sleep quickly, and slept through until the next morning.

At sunup, a loud rap on the door awakened the thoroughly fatigued women. Entering the main room, they found the new mother dressed, sitting on a floor cushion, and breastfeeding her baby.

"It's my husband," the mother said.

Sure enough, a young man breezed through the door, straight past Sophie. Sophie and Hélène immediately covered their faces with a scarf. Without a word, he carried a large basket of apricots which he laid on the table, then went to his wife. He seemed happy enough, but when she offered him the baby to hold, he shook his head and walked out.

"I need to go home and prepare his food," the mother announced. "He's not happy. He expected a son. You'll need to dry the apricots or they'll spoil. Wash them, cut them in half, remove the pits, and soak them in lemon water. Then cover them with a light cloth and put them in the sun for two or three days." She turned and walked out, baby in her arms.

A half hour later, the queue of women seeking attention started to form. At sundown, the last patient exited the clinic. The day's tally included seventeen pregnancies, two congestive heart failures, one breast mass, probably cancerous, three with stomach reflux, two incontinent women, one cataract, one hemorrhoid, and two abscesses drained, one on the buttock, the other on an elbow.

That night over dinner, Sophie and Hélène toasted their success with tea and honey. Dinner, provided by two of the grateful patients consisted of a large bowl of 'koski bil ghalmi,' which is fine-grained couscous, topped with lamb.

"Have you ever had patients, one after the other, who were so appreciative?" Hélène asked.

"Never," Sophie agreed. 'Thank-yous' fell like rain in a thunderstorm. My father and I had patients in Metz whose lives we'd saved and they didn't say thank you."

"However," Hélène said, "we didn't collect a single franc."

"At least we're eating like kings," Sophie said as she picked up, then kissed, a piece of lamb with her fingers.

The next day, Sophie borrowed the mayor's car and went to Kasserine. She applied for surgical privileges at the hospital and ordered a variety of medicines for the clinic, including cocaine as a local anesthetic, morphine, tincture of iodine, sutures and ethyl alcohol. While there, she introduced herself to the two surgeons in Kasserine, Drs. Mansour and Abid, as well as the anesthetist, Dr. Farhat. As she expected, all three doubted her credentials. The letters from General Leveque and a ten-minute conversation pacified their concerns. She explained that the distance to the Kasserine hospital made anything but outpatient surgery impossible in Fériana. She would refer all major surgeries to them.

Sophie had more experience with trauma than either of the Tehran-trained surgeons. She offered to assist them if something arose for which she might be of help. The surgeons did not block her privileges.

That night, a Friday, Sophie and Hélène sat for dinner. For the first time since arriving in Fériana, Hélène had shuttered all the windows. Hélène then brought out two handmade candelabras, two books of matches and two candles. Sophie, surprised, smiled broadly and nodded.

"I am so thankful that you are back in my life," Hélène said.

"Me too. It's been a while since I've had any good luck. I'm happy I'm here and happy that it's with you," Sophie said.

Each woman lit a match and then a candle. Together they closed their eyes and waved both palms over the flame and said the Jewish Sabbath prayer.

> *Barukh ata Adonai Eloheinu, Melekh ha'olam, asher kid'shanu b'mitzvotav v'tzivanu l'hadlik ner shel Shabbat.*

Two weeks later, Sophie returned to Kasserine. Dr. Abid had a diabetic patient who had lost circulation to his lower left leg. Sophie came to show both surgeons the latest techniques in amputation, adding that she was available to help with more surgeries if either Mansour and Abid left town on vacation or were ill. With that, Sophie achieved both respect and friendship as well as a promise from Mansour and Abid to take care of Sophie's patients post op in Kasserine if ever they needed to stay in the hospital. Sophie began performing more complicated procedures in Kasserine.

Chapter Thirteen

Detroit, Michigan
July 1941

Daniel 'Danny' Booker sat in his hallway office at the firm of Goldstein Booker and Gordon, a mid-sized law firm on Woodward Avenue in downtown Detroit. Danny's father, Martin Booker was one of the firm's named partners. GBG, as it was known, specialized in litigation involving the automobile industry. Out the window of his office, Danny could see a corner of the J.L. Hudson department store down the street. Danny wore a pinstriped Brook Brothers suit that hid his muscular physique but set off his blue eyes, light brown hair, and fair complexion. There was a subtle scar through his left eyebrow dating back a decade, recording a fall off his Schwinn bike.

After high school, Danny entered the School of Engineering at the University of Michigan, having no interest in following his father into law. He'd watched the construction of the Ambassador Bridge, which spanned the Detroit River into Windsor, Canada. Completed in 1929, it was the longest suspension bridge in the world at the time. Danny longed to build bridges, big bridges.

It took Danny one semester and an advanced calculus class to decide he had made a grievous error, and he switched his major to History. Always a good athlete, he found himself on the practice squad of the Wolverine football team but never played a minute.

Much to his parents' displeasure, Danny had joined the U of M Flying Club his junior year, and flew airplanes at least once a month. Along with most of his friends, he joined ROTC as another European war became likely. He and those same friends felt confident they would never see action given the isolationist stance the United States had taken since the Great War of 1914-18. Not for a moment did Danny believe his prowess as a pilot would dictate his role in the Army Air Force. He simply enjoyed flying.

In the middle of his junior year, Danny fell in love with a girl from the Upper Peninsula of Michigan. Suzie Cornelius was a blonde, blue-eyed Catholic who'd slipped on an icy sidewalk outside the library and twisted her knee. Danny carried her and her books a half-mile to her sorority. To each, their romance seemed dangerously wicked. Before Suzie, Danny had only dated Jewish girls, and Suzie had never met a Jew until coming to Ann Arbor. Suzie knew her father had antisemitic leanings. They kept their tryst secret.

Before long, Danny was thinking about marriage. He knew he'd have to tell his parents at some point. The confession didn't go well. Marty and Linda Booker assured Danny that such a marriage would be doomed. Danny listened to their reasoning, but said he would continue to see Suzie. Though disappointed, his parents did not forbid him from continuing the relationship.

That summer before senior year, Danny worked as a mail clerk, delivery boy, and all-purpose gofer in his father's law firm. Much to his own surprise, he loved the hustle and intensity of the lawyer's life. He made a deal with his parents. "Don't pester me about flying or Suzie, and I'll go to law school and join dad at GBG."

Danny and Suzie's relationship ended abruptly the first semester of their final year when a sorority sister of Suzie's saw the two kissing in an alcove on campus. The sister told the house mother who, in turn, informed Suzie's parents. Her father pulled her from the university the next week, only a semester before graduation.

Danny contemplated sneaking up to the Upper Peninsula over Thanksgiving. However, Suzie's house mother delivered a note to Danny from Suzy's father telling Danny he'd be shot if he came within a hundred miles of his daughter. A .30-06 bullet from a Winchester rifle was included in the envelope. Danny spent Thanksgiving in Detroit and never heard from Suzie again.

Danny graduated from the University of Michigan Law School at the age of twenty-five, passed the Michigan State bar, and joined his father's firm.

On Danny's desk sat piles of legal documents relating to Smith v. Harding, a three-year-old lawsuit filed before Danny had become a lawyer. Harding, a wealthy, car dealer and amateur pilot based in Detroit, had crashed his WWI biplane into the barn of Mr. Smith, a farmer near Pinconning, Michigan. The barn caught fire and burned to the ground, destroying the structure, a tractor, and other equipment. Smith's wife and son rescued Harding from the conflagration, dragging him to safety. Harding suffered mild burns to his hands and legs and bruises to his head, arm, and ego. Unfortunately, the Smiths' insurance refused to pay for the barn and tractor, believing that Harding should be liable. Danny's father Marty had wanted Danny included on the legal team because of his experience as an amateur pilot.

Marty entered his son's office. "How's the research going on Smith?" he asked.

“Good,” Danny said. “Not a lot on airplanes and responsibility, but we can draw from automobile liability where there’s ample law.”

“We’re having your grandmother over for a birthday dinner on Saturday. You and Sheri are invited,” Marty said. Danny’s parents didn’t think much of his current girlfriend, Sheri Friedman, a cocktail waitress at a popular bowling alley. But, she was Jewish and that’s all that mattered. Anything was better than Suzie Cornelius. Truth be known, Danny didn’t think much of her either, but she did like flying.

“I’ve got my Michigan National Guard meeting this weekend in Lansing,” Danny said. “I’ll call Grandma and tell her I’m sorry.”

Marty nodded and left Danny to his work.

A moment later, the secretary Danny shared with two other junior lawyers knocked on his door.

“Yes, Jenny, what is it?” Danny asked.

“There are two Army officers here to talk to you,” Jenny said.

“It’s not on my schedule,” Danny said.

“No ... They just walked in and said it was important.”

“Show them in, then.”

Danny closed the folders on Smith v Harding and cleared his desk just as the officers entered his office.

An hour later, Danny knocked on the door of his father’s office. He stood in the doorway.

“Dad. I’ve some news for you.”

“Later. I’m busy,” Marty said.

“I just got activated by the Army. I have to report to

Ft. Benning, Georgia, in two weeks."

"What the hell. That can't be," Marty said, angrily. "I'll call Representative Gordon and get it fixed."

"I was in ROTC and now the Michigan National Guard. FDR himself couldn't fix it."

After unsuccessfully attempting to calm his father, Danny went back to his own office and called Sheri Friedman.

"How stupid were you to have joined ROTC?" Sheri said.

"It's done," Danny replied.

"How long will you be gone?"

"I have no idea. The U.S. isn't in the war yet."

"What if?" Sheri asked.

"If we go to war, it could be for a long time."

"Dumb. You're so dumb," Sheri said and slammed the phone down.

By the end of 1941, the United States was again drawn into a world war.

Chapter Fourteen

Fériana, Tunisia - March 1942

Hélène and Sophie lay in bed, looking up at the ceiling. Neither woman liked the floor mattresses used in most Arabic village homes. Six months after arriving, Moise returned to Fériana with elevated wood frames on which the mattresses fit.

Earlier that evening, they'd spent an hour at the mayor's house after dinner, listening to the BBC.

"It's so peaceful in Fériana, as if the war didn't exist," Hélène said.

"Be thankful they're fighting in Egypt and not here," Sophie said. "I've had enough Bosches for a lifetime."

"The Americans have been in the war since December. Why do you think they're only fighting the Japanese?" Hélène asked.

"I don't know. My dad said the Americans turned the tide in the first war. They have more men and don't need to import steel or oil like the European countries. So we wait for them to come to Europe, I guess."

After a moment of thought, Sophie changed the subject. "What will we do after the war, if it ever ends?"

"I'd like to find a partner and adopt children," Hélène said. "And I love the work here. The villagers couldn't be nicer and more respectful. Nothing at all like Saint Martin."

“Yeah. We’re treated like goddesses. Never in France did I feel that way. But we’re not saving any money. If we’re to leave after the war, baskets of vegetables and a goat won’t buy much.”

“I’d find a partner and come back, if I could,” Hélène said.

“And when they find out your partner is Jewish, what then? Two’s company, three’s a crowd.”

“C’mon. They know. They all know we’re Jewish. What’s one more. We’re not being invited over for the Muslim holidays.”

“I suppose,” Sophie said, then got out of bed and turned off the lights.

Eight months swiftly passed. Sophie was finishing the last suture on a sliced index finger of a village woman when Hélène ran into the clinic. “I just talked to the mayor. He’s been listening to the BBC all morning.”

“And?” Sophie asked.

“The Americans landed in Morocco and Algeria and the Bosches now occupy all of France.”

“Finally, the doughboys are here. That’s what my father called them,” Sophie said with a little laugh as she taped the gauze.

"And the Brits have the Bosches on the run and are chasing them through Libya toward Tripoli.”

Sophie looked up at the woman and gave instructions. “Keep this hand dry until I see you in two days to change the dressing. Try to keep it elevated as much as possible. Your husband won’t be happy, but he’s going to need to do the cooking and cleaning. Do you understand?”

“Yes. Thank you,” the woman said. She stood and

walked out of the clinic with her hand up on her chest. Sophie knew from experience that the husband would neither cook nor clean.

"Neither of you ever listens," Hélène said.

"All we can do is try," Sophie said. "A hand infection would be devastating."

"I'm talking about you!' cried Hélène. 'Are you even listening to me? The Bosches have occupied all of France. Vichy France is dead! Could Tunisia be next?"

Sophie waved her hand dismissively. "Vichy France was dead on the first day. What does the mayor say about Tunisia?"

"He said if the Americans come from the west and the Brits are pushing the Bosches from the east, Tunisia is in the middle."

Sophie kept her face neutral. She said lightly, "I hope they're just interested in Tunis. I'm running out of places to hide."

...

In November 1942, Operation Torch began. The U.S. Army landed in Morocco and Algeria with plans to advance five-hundred miles eastward to the valuable Tunisian ports of Bizerte and Tunis. With the British pushing west from Egypt toward Tripoli and Libya, the Allies hoped to control the entire North African coast of the Mediterranean sea. This would allow Allied shipping unfettered lanes to provide materiel to the Allies in Europe and airbases to bomb Italy.

As soon as the Allies landed in Morocco and Algeria, the Axis armies (German and Italian) landed in Tunisia in force to counter an Allied advance. By the end of December 1942, the Axis armies, already veterans of war, with better air support and logistics, stopped the Allies' Operation Torch short of their Bizerte and Tunis goals.

The Allies also sent forces toward the south of Tunisia through Algeria. They stopped near Tebessa, Algeria, west of the Atlas Mountains, where they set up headquarters.

Meanwhile, the Germans, now in control of Tunisia, began rounding up Jews and putting them into labor camps.

Chapter Fifteen

Fériana
January 1943

A backfiring engine awakened Sophie and Hélène at dawn. They sat up, heard nothing more than a motor and laid back down. Moments later, they heard men yelling at each other. Immediately, both sat on the edge of their beds.

"What's that?" Hélène asked, rubbing her eyes.

A distinctive shout immediately nullified the question.

"*Seig Heil!*"

Without saying a word, Hélène jumped out of bed, shuffled in the dark to the bedroom door, and slid the bolt to lock their door. She flipped the switch on the bedroom light, but nothing happened.

"Is the generator off? Hélène asked.

"It was working when we went to bed," Sophie replied. "Someone must have turned it off."

Sophie, her hands shaking, sat on the edge of the bed, trying to light the lantern with a match. It took four attempts to strike the match and two attempts to get the match to the wick. Once lit, she checked her wrist watch – 6:15 a.m.

"What should we do?" Hélène asked.

"Get dressed," Sophie said. "We listen, act dumb,

speak Arabic and only a few words of elementary French if anyone comes."

"Should we see patients today?" Hélène asked.

"Hopefully everyone will stay indoors today, but we can't have someone pounding on the door and not answer. We'll have to wait and see. Put on your burqa. We don't want them seeing any part of us. Trust me."

Three years had passed since the cousins had arrived in Fériana. In all that time, they'd only worn their burqas once, when obtaining the signed license they needed to practice and a rental agreement from Mayor Bahoul's office. At first, they approached his burqa-clad secretary wearing only head scarves, but she refused to even look at them. Remembering the mayor's admonition about how to dress if they ever needed something from his secretary, they returned an hour later covered from head to toe in black with mesh slits covering their eyes. Fifteen minutes later, they walked out with the papers they needed.

The burqas, stashed at the bottom of a trunk, smelled musty. Under lantern light, the two women helped each other into the black, constricting two-piece wear. The black abaya covered their entire lower body from the neck down and a head piece concealed the entire face, expect for a small horizontal slit for their eyes, covered with mesh.

Once dressed, Sophie confirmed the electricity was also out in the clinic. She went to the front door and saw no lights on anywhere in the village. Fériana and the neighboring villages would have no gas for generators or electricity until the end of March, but she didn't know that yet. She went back inside the clinic and opened the shutters. As Hélène started a fire in the stove, Sophie went down into the root cellar with the lantern and returned with a loaf of bread, jam, and dried apricots. By the time she'd ascended the ladder and shut the cellar door, Hélène had water heating on the stove for coffee.

As Hélène made coffee and Sophie covered the root cellar door with a rug, a door knock stopped both women in their tracks. The wall clock read 7:10 and patients wouldn't be expected until 9 a.m. Their heads swiveled toward one another. Hélène seemed unable to move. Sophie went to the door and opened it slowly.

A pregnant patient of Hélène's, Fatima Abadi, stood with her back to the door, fixated on troops of German soldiers winding along the clinic's street then branching toward the mayor's office. Troop trucks and a fancy German sedan were parked at the rear of the troop formation that extended north to the edge of town.

The soldiers stood rigidly at attention, eyes forward, rifles on their shoulders as an officer barked orders. Sophie rested her hands on Fatima's shoulders and gazed hard. This would be the first time that Sophie, Hélène, or Fatima had actually seen Nazi troops in the flesh. At her touch, Fatima glanced backward.

"Are they alive?" Fatima asked, her body shaking. "They don't move or breathe."

"Yes, they're Germans and alive. I wish they weren't," Sophie said. "Come in quickly."

Fatima Abadi was a fourteen-year-old newlywed in her sixth month of pregnancy. She'd visited Hélène every week for the past four months. Fatima's father, Mohammed Aziz, absent a wife who had run off, had sold Fatima to Mansour Abadi for six goats and two sacks of flour. Aziz then sold the goats, the flour and his house, took a bus to Tunis, and was never seen again.

"I could just kill Fatima's father for selling her," Hélène said to Sophie after meeting Fatima for the first time. "She's a baby."

Mansour Abadi, fifty-six, had never been married and didn't think he could father children. He married Fatima so someone would cook for him, clean the house and assuage his masculine needs. In need of motherly comfort, Fatima had adopted Hélène. After cleaning Abadi's house, she'd come to the clinic to clean but mostly to talk to Hélène. If Hélène was busy, Fatima would talk to Sophie.

"Why are you dressed like that?" Fatima asked.

"I'm showing respect for Allah while the Germans are here. You shouldn't be out with all these soldiers around," Sophie said. "You should go home."

"I was alone. Mansour went to his shop to protect it. I got scared," Fatima responded.

Hélène, hearing the conversation, came to the door. "I'm scared too, and I hoped you'd come," she said. "We're just about to have breakfast. Will you join us?"

Fatima nodded eagerly, rushing inside to hug Hélène.

Before Sophie could close the door, it was kicked open by a German soldier pointing a rifle.

"*Beweg dich nicht*," he yelled.

Sophie stumbled backward. She was fluent in German and knew the soldier had ordered her not to move, but she pretended not to understand, instead moving quickly to join Hélène and Fatima in the middle of the room. A second soldier entered, also pointing a rifle.

The two soldiers began rummaging through the clinic shelves as the three women stood in shock, holding each other's hands. One of the soldiers kicked the rug covering the root cellar door to the side, opened the door and went down with a flashlight. He returned with a jar of homemade jam.

A very large and muscular Arab soon came after them, wearing typical dress. Sophie thought the Arab's neck was larger than her chest.

"Are there any weapons in this building?" the new man asked in Tunisian Arabic.

Sophie and Hélène shook their heads.

One of the soldiers smelled the coffee that had been poured into a cup on the table. He gulped it down in two swallows, while the other soldier pocketed all the apricots. Together, the soldiers sauntered out.

The Arab man put his hands on his chest, nodded, and greeted the three women with, "*Asalaamu alaikum.*"

Still huddled, the three women could barely nod.

"My name is Omar Sader. I am from Tunis and I translate for the Germans. What are your names?"

"I am Safiyah Shaloub."

"Hélène Al-hadef."

"Fatima Abadi."

"Don't move," Sader said, then walked out of the clinic.

Sophie then heard Sader say in German, "It's safe. Only three women."

Sader returned to the clinic, followed by a tall, broad-shouldered German officer. His fair complexion was sunburnt, and a scar ran under his left eye to the front of his ear. Every time the officer blinked, his left lower eyelid would pull toward his left ear, leaving a small gap in the lid closure. A loose tear would often hang in the opening.

Colonel Gregor Gunther wore a black Waffen-SS uniform with a Swastika arm band and carried a Lugar pistol holstered on his belt. He had the double SS patch on one collar lapel and four silver pips centered on the other collar patch. A large German cross medallion hung between his lapels.

"I'm SS-Standartenführer Gunther. I've talked to the mayor. Someone here is a doctor."

Sophie played dumb and looked to Omar.

"He said the mayor told him that someone here is a doctor," Omar said in Arabic.

Sophie spoke to Omar. "I am Dr. Shaloub. I am a doctor of women only. My cousin is a midwife, and this young girl is pregnant and a patient."

Omar translated accurately.

"Where did you study medicine?" Gunther asked. Sophie waited for Omar to translate.

"My father was a doctor in Algeria," Sophie lied. "He taught me. That's it."

"I wouldn't trust you with a toothache," Gunther said.

"He said congratulations," Omar said.

Sophie knew then that Gunther didn't understand a word of Arabic and Omar would translate as he thought best.

Gunther approached Fatima, who was wearing only a head scarf. He pulled the simple scarf down behind her head and grabbed her face in his hand, staring her coldly in the eyes. Tears poured down her cheeks. Roughly, he felt her abdomen through her loose-fitting garment.

"How old is she?" Gunther asked, and Omar translated.

"Fourteen," Hélène said.

"Barbaric cretins," Gunther said, shaking his head.

Everyone looked to Omar, who said, "She's very young."

"May she go home to her husband?" Hélène asked.

Omar translated, and Gunther nodded yes.

"Go home, quickly," Hélène said to Fatima. "We'll see you tomorrow."

Holding her stomach with one hand and wiping tears with the other, Fatima ran from the clinic.

Gunther took a step toward Sophie and Hélène and attempted a smile. He looked directly at Sophie and said, "Take off your head covering so I can see your face."

A bolt of pure terror darted through Sophie. Buying time, she looked at Omar, watched his mouth shape the words. She steeled herself as Omar translated the directive.

"I cannot. It is improper and impure," Sophie said, shaking her head.

Omar explained to Gunther, "Respectful Muslim women cannot remove their coverings in front of men who are not in their family."

"I wasn't asking," Gunther said. "Take it off."

Omar, shook his head, but repeated the demand, "Take off your head scarf."

Sophie shook her head and said, "*No.*"

Gunther didn't need a translation. He removed the Lugar from his holster. He grabbed Hélène by the throat and held the Lugar to her temple. "Take it off, or your cousin dies."

As Hélène grimaced in pain from Gunther's squeezing hand, Omar translated Gunther's demand, adding, "He means it. Take off your head covering."

Sophie slowly removed her head covering. Gunther let go of Hélène and approached Sophie, who looked away. His free hand brought Sophie's face back to front. Gunther smiled, but when he let go, Sophie turned away again. His hand moved down to Sophie's neck then slid slowly down, lingering on her breasts, then down to her belly.

"Nice," Gunther said. "A pretty one finally, in a race of ugly and stupid people."

Sophie looked to Omar. Her cheeks were flushed with anger and her heart was racing.

"He says you're pretty."

Gunther turned to Hélène and repeated the demand as he spun his hand around his head as a clue. "Take off your head covering."

Hélène understood and slowly removed her covering.

Gunther watched. "Not as pretty." Just as he'd done to Sophie, Gunther's hand moved down Hélène's neck then slid further, onto her breasts and then her belly. He then stood back and faced Omar. "Tell these women that the Americans are coming through the mountains in the next few days. They will come into the valley and we will kill each and every one of them. They do not understand the might of the German army."

Omar translated accurately.

"If anyone helps the Americans," Gunther said, "in any way, we will find out and kill them and their family and a hundred villagers for good measure."

Again, Omar's translation was precise.

Sophie said, "I am obliged to help any person who is sick. It is a medical oath. I swore it to my father."

Omar translated to Gunther.

Gunther smiled. "It is my oath to kill you, your cousin, your family and a hundred villagers if you disobey my orders."

Omar translated as Gunther, smirking, pointed his Lugar at Hélène, then Sophie. Gunther then holstered his gun. He turned toward the door, but stopped suddenly, gesturing to Omar.

"Remember this house," Gunther said. "After we defeat the Americans, I will return and take the pretty one. The other one my officers can have."

Omar met Sophie's eye just as she winced. Fear once again darted through her. Had Omar seen? Had she just given herself away?

"What did he say?" Sophie cried out.

"He hopes you do not help the Americans, but wishes you the best. He'll not bother you again. He's sorry he made you remove your head coverings," Omar said.

"Thank you," Sophie said.

Gunther exited. Omar stopped at the door, turned to Sophie and put a finger over his mouth. He then turned and followed Gunther out the door. Sophie couldn't be sure what the gesture meant. Omar seemed observant and had grasped, probably, what Gunther had not – her slightly accented Arabic, her European features. That wince.

Sophie ran to the door, locked it, then waited until she heard Gunther's vehicle leave. Anger flashed in her eyes.

"I need a gun. If that German returns, I will kill him, I swear."

"Tell me what he really said," whispered Hélène.

"Think of the worst thing he and his men could do

to you and me," Sophie said. "I will kill him first."

Hélène collapsed in a chair and started to cry. Sophie had never seen her cousin so rattled. She decided she needn't tell Hélène that Omar Sader probably knew that she understood German.

That night, Sophie's nightmares returned. Visions of Gunther's eyelid haunted her. Even though Hélène must have noticed her writhing and crying in the night, neither one of them mentioned it in the morning.

The Nazis had vanished from Fériana by two p.m. the next day, heading east to their base in Faid Pass a hundred kilometers away. Everyone in the village sensed that they would soon return.

Sophie went to Mayor Bahoul's office and found him at his desk. Over the three years in Fériana, Sophie, Hélène, and Bahoul, the only three people in the village with an education, had learned to trust each other. Bahoul remained a hero in the eyes of the villagers for bringing and keeping Sophie and Hélène in town. Bahoul insured that the women had fuel for their generator and anything else, within reason, for their clinic. At least once a week, they would break bread together and listen to the BBC broadcasts.

Mincing no words, Sophie said, "They are sons of dogs and don't deserve to live."

Bahoul sighed heavily. "One must tiptoe around the devil. Luckily, they didn't find my radio. The BBC says they are not happy to have lost Libya and the port at Tripoli to the British."

"I need a gun. Can you find me one?" Sophie asked.

"The few rifles in town from the First War were confiscated by the Germans," Bahoul said. "The commander in the black uniform threatened to kill everyone if we did not bring all our weapons to him. Do you think you can defeat the Germans yourself with a single gun?"

"Of course not. But I'll kill the officer in the black uniform if given the chance. He held a gun to Hélène's head, made us remove our head coverings and then violated our bodies with his hands."

Bahoul shook his head. "I'm sorry."

"Not as sorry as I am." Sophie turned and walked out.

Chapter Sixteen

Fériana, Tunisia
February 1943

Three days after Colonel Gunther and his SS storm troopers left the village, Sophie, Hélène, and Fatima sat inside the clinic having a lunch of lablabi, composed of shredded stale bread, a garlicky, cumin-laced broth with chickpeas, poached egg, and spicy harissa chili. Turning their heads to the open door, they detected a slow and steadily buzzing sound.

"Are the lifeless men back?" Fatima shouted, as she raced to the door and then out into the street.

"Men and trucks and many strange things with long noses are coming! Too many to count," she called from the doorway.

Sophie went to doorway. "The Americans are here," she said. "The strange long-nosed things are called tanks and artillery. They're powerful guns."

Hélène joined them at the doorway and watched.

The American troops walked by the clinic as the women watched from the doorway. The men, rifles slung over their backs, were laughing and waving as they paraded by. The drivers and riders of the troop trucks waved, as did the men sitting above the turrets of the tanks or on the ends of the 105 mm howitzers.

“They’re different than the German soldiers,” Fatima said. “They breathe and smile.”

“The Germans have been fighting for three years,” Sophie said. “The Americans haven’t fought anyone yet. They don’t know what’s about to happen. The battles to come will stop the smiles and laughing.”

The convoy of troops coming through Fériana lasted for hours. Few patients came to the clinic that day. Sophie and Hélène stood at the door, waving at the troops. Most of the men waved back, and many screamed funny things.

“Will you marry me?” “What’s for dinner?” “You need a real man.” “I’m in love already.”

Sophie’s English allowed her to respond.

“Good luck,” she called, and “Thank you! Come back. Who are you?”

Who are you? elicited a range of responses. The answers varied from “Americans”, “First Infantry”, “Yanks”, or “Kraut Killers”. Sometimes they simply said their names: “Rocco DeVito”, “Robert Layne”, “Billy Jones.”

By dinner time, the convoys had passed through, leaving only clouds of dust on the windows and doors and a gritty taste in the mouth. Hélène closed the clinic door and joined Sophie at the table for a cup of sugared tea.

“I’ve never been close to war before, not like you. What will happen?” Hélène asked.

Sophie shook her head. “It’s more terrible than you can imagine. Many of those young men will die or suffer terrible injuries. They’re so young and innocent. That innocence will evaporate when they see their friends die in front of their eyes.”

Two nights later, flashes of artillery began to fill the

sky to the east near Faid, Tunisia, one-hundred kilometers to the east. Every night after closing the clinic, Sophie and Hélène would often go to the Abdel Bahoul's house for dinner and sit with him and his wife, listening to short wave broadcasts from the BBC. Bahoul's wife was a fabulous cook. They supped on *tajine (*a crustless quiche filled with eggs, cheeses, vegetables and meat), felfel mahchi (peppers filled with lamb and covered with a spicy *harissa* sauce), and chakchouka (a ratatouille-like vegetarian dish with tomatoes, peppers, garlic, onions and chickpeas). After dinner, they'd consume baklawa, the sweet, flaky pastry with nuts and butter dipped in honey.

Gregor Gunther, the SS colonel who'd harassed Sophie and Hélène, accurately predicted the outcome. The American 1st Armored division entered the fray and destroyed a few tanks. They followed the enemy into Faid Pass, thinking the Germans were retreating and fell into a trap laid by deadly German '88' antitank guns. Tank after American tank was destroyed. Even tanks at the rear of the column couldn't maneuver back fast enough under the unrelenting fire of the German artillery. German Panzers followed the retreat, and every place the Americans tried to make a defensive stand failed miserably. Gunther was right – the Americans did not know how to fight.

The following week the Germans routed the Allied stronghold at Sidi Bou Zid. The Americans retreated quickly to Fériana, Kasserine, and Sbeitla, hoping to make a defensive line between the villages.

Sophie and Hélène finished supper of lamb stew at the clinic and worked together to clean the kitchen. They hadn't heard artillery for ten hours, the longest lull in a week. The rumble of vehicles, voices, and marching men brought both women to the windows.

A different American army straggled through Fériana. Covered in dust and grime, heads low, the American soldiers had lost their swagger. Many fewer 'things with long noses' rolled through town.

"We should see if they need help with the injured men," Sophie said.

"Don't you dare," Hélène demanded. "You're not worried about the German colonel's threat?"

"I suppose. Maybe we were lucky and he was killed by a stray bullet."

"He didn't look the kind of person who would get his clothes dirty fighting."

I'm sure you're right," Sophie sighed. "It's dark and I'm exhausted."

The next morning, Sophie went out the front door only to find the streets empty of all soldiers. Only later in the day did she learn from Mayor Bahoul that the Americans had already retreated into the Kasserine Pass toward Algeria. Everything felt oddly normal, other than the clinic had no fuel to run the generator. Patients came and went, Fatima stopped by to help clean and have lunch, and Sophie shopped for fruits and vegetables while Hélène prepared dinner.

As they got into bed that night, Hélène seemed happy. "Pretty normal day for a change. I could get used to it."

"Surgeons are a superstitious lot," Sophie said. "So why would you tempt the Gods by saying that?"

"I'm sorry," Hélène laughed. "I was just saying, that's all."

Sophie's fears became reality in a matter of days –

Hélène had tempted the Gods, and the Germans returned to Fériana.

At night, Sophie and Hélène shuttered and locked the clinic. The Germans had placed a sundown curfew on pain of death. On the first night of the curfew, the German patrols shot a man dead who was out looking for his dog. After that, no nighttime emergencies came knocking.

A German patrol again searched the clinic, finding nothing. They stole all the food they could carry from the root cellar.

Each day that passed without a visit from SS-Standartenführer Gunther was a relief to both women. They did not speak of it.

Chapter Seventeen

Tebessa, Algeria – First Army Headquarters (HQ)
February 13, 1943

Major Cap Teller, head of 1st Army Intelligence, Captain Danny Booker, intelligence officer and sometime-pilot of an L-4 Grasshopper reconnaissance plane, stood in a command tent in front of Major General Lloyd Fredendall, Major General Orlando Ward and Major General Terry Allen. The three generals led First Army. The five officers surrounded a table on which a large map of Kasserine Pass had been laid out.

"I hate to say it, but the Brits were right," Ward said. "We weren't prepared to fight these guys. We're getting slaughtered."

Allen added, "They use air, artillery, armor and infantry in sync with each other. They showed that in Poland in '39 and France in '40 and we didn't learn a goddamned thing. If we can't figure it out, Ike is gonna can all of us."

After a pregnant pause, Teller asked, "What do want from us?"

"We need eyes in the air," Fredendall said. "We need to make a stand at Kasserine Pass to protect Tebessa, or they'll push us back to Morocco."

"As long as they're putting up Messerschmidt-109 fighters in numbers, our Grasshoppers are sitting ducks," Danny said. "We've lost six of our nineteen already."

"Major, Captain, we need eyes on the pass now. We have to know if they're coming and with what," Ward stated.

"Our intercepts decrypted from Enigma suggested they're not following in strength," Teller said.

Fredendall replied, "And the intercepts were dead wrong about Faid and Sidi Bou Zid. We can't trust what we're intercepting. It's up to you guys flying intel that means a damn. Got it?"

Teller and Danny stood and saluted.

Danny, knowing he'd be the one flying, added, "Got it."

Outside the tent and their Jeeps, Teller put his arm around Danny. "I don't have to tell you how important this is. You know the risks."

"I understand, Sir," Danny replied and saluted.

An hour later, Danny and his co-pilot, Lt. Nick Pascavage, a stick-skinny, twenty-two-year-old from Denver, hopped in a jeep and headed toward the Youk-les Bains airfield, twenty kilometers northwest of Fredendall's headquarters. They had two hours until the sun set.

"I'm guessing we've got an hour, no more, of flying the pass," Nick said. "I'm not at all keen about trying to find our base when it's pitch dark."

"I'd be more worried about running into ME-109s than the dark," Danny said.

"Do we have any cover?" Nick asked.

"Nope. We lost six P-40s, three P-38s, and four

loaner Spitfires today. We can't afford to lose any more until we get replacements ferried in from Casablanca. Maybe two, three days. Grasshoppers, however, we got plenty of."

"Shit," Nick said. "Flying in the dark sounds better and better."

"Yeah."

Forty-five minutes later, Danny and Nick had climbed their Grasshopper to five thousand feet and could see the western entrance to Kasserine Pass in the distance and the peaks, Jebel el Chambi to the south and Jebel Semmama to the north, which provided bookends to the pass. At its narrowest, the pass was a mere mile from side to side. Snow and jutting rock formations on the top half of both mountains gave a false sense of serenity. Somewhere below were American and German armies intent on killing the other.

Nick took the plane down to two thousand feet and entered the pass.

Nick, hands shaking, loaded his camera. "What do you think, one run to the east and one run back?"

"Keep flying until we can't see," Danny said. "Those were the Teller's orders."

Danny kept the plane low as he entered Kasserine Pass.

"That's our First Battalion down there, Sixth Field Artillery, and a few Free French troops," Danny said.

As they flew through the Pass, Nick kept taking pictures. He reloaded his camera and continued to shoot. "Ain't seeing much," he said.

Danny exited the pass, rose to four thousand feet and banked south toward Fériana, where they spotted German encampments in the distance between the airfield at Thélepte and the outskirts of Fériana. A few German patrols saw the American markings on the Grasshopper, and took shots with handguns and rifles.

"Wasting ammo on us," Nick laughed as he saw the muzzle flashes of the guns a mile down.

Danny and Nick re-entered Kasserine Pass again but saw nothing different. Nick conserved his film. Exiting the pass, Danny banked over the American and French troops and re-entered the Pass.

"Last run," Danny said. "It'll be almost dark by the time I turn around."

"Roger that," Nick said with a smile.

As the plane neared the eastern end of the pass, Nick suddenly leaned forward in his seat. "Go further north. I see something."

Danny banked left and dropped to three hundred feet over the floor of the Pass.

"Shit," Nick yelled. "You see it?" He was snapping picture after picture.

"Yeah, I see 'em! Camouflaged 88s and Panzers. I can't count how many," Danny said.

At that moment, heavy gunfire from automatic weapons with tracers burst around them. Danny immediately banked right and yanked the yoke back, pulling the nose of the Grasshopper up and out of harm's way. Nick got on the radio as Danny continued to climb away from the gunfire, elevating the Grasshopper to three thousand feet above the floor of the pass.

"We got what we need," Danny said. He spoke excitedly, the veins in his temple pulsing with the thrill of their discovery and close escape. "Get on the radio and let 'em know. We're getting out of Dodge now."

“First Infantry, this is Grasshopper XJ2, do you read me?” Nick said.

Only static returned from the speaker.

Nick repeated, “First Infantry, this is Grasshopper XJ2, do you read me?”

Again only static sounded, followed by WHAP, WHAP WHAP. The plane shook.

“We’ve been hit!” Danny yelled.

“By what?” Nick screamed.

Danny banked sharply to the left, then the right. At that moment, a German ME-109 fighter passed over the Grasshopper, rose and banked hard right. The Grasshopper had now exited the eastern end of the pass. Danny tried to bank left, but the controls wouldn’t respond.

“I’ve lost control of the rudder. I can only bank right. Hold on!” Danny yelled.

WHAP. WHAP. WHAP.

“Aaaah. I’ve been hit,” Nick screamed. “I’m hit. My leg. Oh, God. There’s blood everywhere!”

Danny looked down and saw blood streaming down Nick’s right pant leg. Danny slid his belt off and thrusted it at Nick.

“Put this around your thigh,” Danny yelled, “and tighten it as hard as you can. You’ll bleed to death if you don’t.”

Nick secured the belt then slumped forward as the ME-109 passed over the Grasshopper again, rose and banked right to make another pass.

“I can’t control the plane. We’re going down,” Danny yelled. He looked over to see Nick motionless, slumped forward in his seat. Danny thought Nick might have died until he saw him take a shallow breath.

"Stay with me," Danny yelled.

WHAP. WHAP. WHAP. Flying at three hundred miles per hour, the ME-109 shot the left wheel and strut but overflew quickly, given its airspeed. Knowing the Grasshopper could glide, he quickly shut off the engine to reduce the chances of an explosion on impact. He glided at sixty knots airspeed, five hundred feet over Fériana, looking for a flat place to crash.

Darkness had just about set in when Danny's plane hit the ground and pinwheeled twice before coming to rest on a sandy knoll. The nose of the Grasshopper was buried. The ME-109 made one further pass but didn't fire. It banked left and turned toward its airbase at Faid.

Danny came to minutes later. Blood dripped down his forehead and face from a gash over his left eye. He tried moving his left arm to wipe away the blood, but the pain was too severe; the arm wouldn't budge. He used his right hand to clear his vision.

Danny turned right to see Nick slumped forward over the control panel.

"Nick. Nick! You with me?" Danny yelled.

Nothing.

"Nick!"

Nothing.

Then a slow "oooh," came from Nick's throat.

Danny unbuckled his seatbelt, using only his right arm to pull himself out of his seat. He pinched Nick's blood-soaked neck to see if he could elicit a response. When his co-pilot's head twitched, Danny had a sigh of relief.

The exit door was mangled and jammed shut. Danny squatted down and kicked the door with his heels until it opened. Once out, he scanned the horizon. He could see faint candlelight from the direction of Fériana. He estimated the distance to be a mile to a mile and a half. Danny knew the ME-109 pilot would radio the crash coordinates and a patrol would be sent to take prisoners, if any were still alive.

Danny re-entered the plane to find Nick in the same slumped position. He pinched his co-pilot's neck again and got the same guttural response. Danny unbuckled Nick's seatbelt and, using only his right arm, dragged his co-pilot out of the plane with great difficulty.

Outside, Nick collapsed on the ground. Danny inspected Nick's legs and found that much of his right calf had been shot away. Blood oozed steadily onto the ground. Danny retightened the belt-tourniquet around Nick's leg, which created another round of moans but slowed the blood flow.

"Okay. I'm going to get you up and we're gonna try to find some help," Danny said. "Stay with me."

"Uhhhhh," Nick moaned.

Using his good arm, Danny got Nick upright, then bent over and hoisted Nick over his shoulder like a sack of flour. Slowly, Danny walked his wounded co-pilot toward the dim lights of the nearby village.

Carrying Nick the mile to the edge of Fériana took an hour. All the houses on the periphery were dark, the windows shuttered. Danny lugged Nick to the first door he encountered. Rapping on the door, a man in a nightshirt answered, holding a lantern.

"We need help," Danny said in English.

Raising the lantern, the man said nothing, but his

eyes grew wide when he lowered the lantern and saw what remained of Nick's blood-soaked leg. Extinguishing the lantern, the man crept soundlessly out of the house and into the street. Still propping up Nick, Danny followed behind, a step at a time. The man stopped twenty feet down the street and pointed to another darkened house. Having accomplished this, the man ran at full speed back to his house, slamming the door shut. The sound of the slamming door signaled that the man would not reappear.

Danny headed toward the designated house and banged softly on the door. He gently let Nick's feet slide down to the ground. After a moment of no response, he kicked the door as hard as he could, waited a moment and then kicked again.

Danny heard "*Ana qadim*" from within, but had no idea what it meant. He kicked the door again once. He heard the door latch release and saw the door open a few inches. A lantern appeared in the opening at belt level. The lantern rose until he could make out a figure wearing a niqab.

"Help us, please," Danny begged.

"*Américains*?" the niqab-covered woman asked.

"Yes, Americans. We're hurt."

The woman handed the lantern to another woman and opened the door.

Chapter Eighteen

Fériana, Tunisia

February 13, 1943

Trying to support all of Nick's weight with one arm, Danny took a step through the open door, caught his foot on the threshold and fell forward, losing his grip on his co-pilot.

Sophie grabbed Nick as Danny let go. The weight of Nick's body brought Sophie down to the floor and he sprawled on top of her, motionless.

"*Lâchez-moi*!" Sophie wailed.

Hélène rushed to roll Nick off Sophie.

"I'm so sorry," Danny said, not understanding Sophie's scream. Clutching his wounded arm, he stood with difficulty. "*Anglais*? English? Do either of you speak English?"

Still on the ground, Hélène said, "We both speak English." Hélène stood and slammed the door shut. Sophie got up, grabbed the lantern and leaned over to look at Nick.

"He's hurt bad," Danny said. "A bullet tore through his leg and then we crashed. We're pilots. I thought he was dead. Where can we find a doctor?"

Nick's head swayed left and right slowly as the three looked down at him.

“I’m a doctor,” Sophie said. “We need scissors and a blood pressure cuff. Quick, Hélène.” Sophie looked at Nick’s leg again, then back up to Danny. “What’s your name?”

The American stared at her for a moment, then found his voice.

“Danny, sorry, Danny Booker. This is Nick Pascavage.”

“I’m Dr. Shaloub. You can call me Safiyah. This is my cousin, Hélène.” Sophie mumbled to herself, “Danny, Nick.”

Hélène rushed over with a large pair of scissors, a blood pressure cuff, a stethoscope and another lantern. Down on her knees next to the lantern, she took Nick’s blood pressure.

“Did you put your belt around his leg?” Sophie asked Danny.

“Yes. He was bleeding.”

“You saved his life.”

“Ninety-four over sixty. Pulse ninety-two,” Hélène said.

“We’re good,” Sophie said as she cut off Nick’s blood-soaked pant leg while Hélène unlaced his boot and removed his reddened sock. Hélène and Sophie cringed in unison as they inspected the damage to Nick’s leg.

“Ohhhh, God that hurts,” Nick moaned.

“Nick, I’m a surgeon. Do you understand me?” Sophie asked.

“Yeah,” Nick answered, eyes closed, his head rolling.

Sophie looked up to Danny to make sure she had

his attention.

"Listen carefully, both of you. It's bad. You've lost all of your calf muscles, the arteries and veins to the leg and shattered the fibula, one of the leg bones. Your foot is already black, as is the skin over the shin, which means those areas will not receive any blood even with the tourniquet off your thigh." Sophie waited a moment. "Do you understand what I'm saying?"

Nick, eyes closed, grimacing painfully, nodded. Sophie looked to Danny who nodded.

"We need to amputate your leg above the knee," Sophie said. "The belt on your thigh kept you from bleeding to death."

"Oh, God," Nick moaned. "I'm going to die, aren't I?"

"No. I won't let that happen," Sophie said.

"Where is the nearest hospital?" Danny asked. "I don't care if it's German."

"More than an hour away by car, but don't count on the Germans to do anything," Sophie said. She was thinking of the threat Colonel Gunther had made, to kill her, Hélène, and a hundred villagers if they helped any Americans. She met Hélène's eyes, and knew they were thinking the same thing. Hélène gave her a subtle nod.

"Where am I? How did I get here?" Nick shrieked, his eyes opening and closing.

Sophie went into surgical command mode.

"Hélène, cut off the rest of his pants and remove his jacket while I get an IV started."

Hélène well knew the look and tone Sophie adopted in true emergencies, and she obeyed wordlessly.

Sophie cast a hurried glance at Danny. He'd approached a stool under an exam table and pulled it free with his right arm while holding his left motionless against his side.

"Danny, is your arm hurt?"

"I'm fine," Danny said, suppressing a wince. "I'll be fine, just look after Nick."

"Hélène," Sophie barked, "stop with the pants and take off Danny's jacket. I think he's broken his arm or dislocated his shoulder. We're going to need him."

"I'm okay. Stay with Nick," Danny pleaded, then whispered, "Please don't let him die," Danny slumped over with his right hand over his eyes, hiding his tears. Hélène put down the scissors and went to Danny's side.

"Word of advice," Hélène whispered to Danny as she removed his flight jacket. "Listen to what she says and don't argue. She knows what she's doing."

Sophie hung a bottle of saline and started an IV inside Nick's left elbow crease, the only vein she could find. Once in, Sophie opened the intravenous flow to run as fast as possible. In the corner of her eye, she could see Danny wincing as Hélène pulled on the left sleeve of his flight jacket. She and Hélène switched places. Sophie examined the bruise on Danny's forehead, then felt the shoulder joint.

"I tried to brace myself when we crashed. When I came to, I couldn't move my shoulder," Danny said.

"It's an anterior dislocation. I can try to pop it back," Sophie said. "The bruise on your forehead will heal by itself.'

"You're a real doctor?" Danny asked. "Like, a *real* one?"

"Like you've got choices," Hélène scoffed, busy removing Nick's flight jacket.

"Yes," Sophie said. "I've done this before. I'd give

you some pain medication, but we have only so much and we're going to need it for your friend."

"What?" Danny asked, clearly confused.

"I've got to amputate his leg or he's going to die. He may die anyway," Sophie said.

"You can't do that," Danny said.

"Not only can I do that, I need to do it now and I need your help. So I have to get your arm back in its socket first or you're worthless. You're going to have to trust me."

Danny nodded, then tried a smile. "Like I have a choice."

Sophie shook her head at the dark humor as she removed Danny's shirt, sliding it carefully off the non-functioning left arm. "Turn ninety degrees so your right shoulder rests on the side of the exam table. Try to relax."

"Easy for you to say," Danny said, grimacing, as he turned. "How much is it going to hurt?"

"A bit," Sophie said.

Sophie flexed Danny's left elbow to ninety degrees and held it in position. She called Hélène over. "Hélène, hold his left hand in your left hand and the top of the elbow in your right. When I say push, push his whole arm down and little forward. Got it?"

Hélène nodded, "Yeah."

Sophie stood behind Danny and pushed his scapula toward his spine as she pushed down on his shoulder from above. "Ready. Push his arm down firmly and a little forward."

"Ahhh," Danny groaned, until a soft pop was heard. Hélène let go of the arm.

“I think that’s it,” Sophie said. “How does it feel?”

Danny wiggled his arm and smiled. “I think I’m good. Just a dull ache. That wasn’t so bad.”

“You can put your shirt back on, but don’t raise your arm or turn it too much or it’ll dislocate again.”

Danny stood and donned his shirt without effort.

“Between the three of us, let’s get Nick on a table,” Sophie said.

With Danny’s good hand under Nick’s head, Sophie placed the IV bottle on Nick’s chest. Sophie and Hélène picked up Nick with joined hands under his back and upper legs. They rested him on one of the exam tables.

“We need every lantern and flashlight,” Sophie said. “Nick, you with me?”

“Pain’s awful,” Nick panted.

“Danny, go over to the sink and wash your hands and face,” Sophie said.

“Then what?”

“Then come back. I need your help.” She addressed Nick next. “I’m going to put a bit of morphine into the IV.”

“Thanks, Doc,” Nick mumbled.

Sophie drew up morphine from a syringe and injected it into a port on the IV tubing. “You’ll feel better in a moment.”

While Sophie tended to Nick, Hélène gathered drapes, Sophie’s surgical instruments, sutures, chloroform and a chloroform mask for anesthesia. Hélène placed everything on the adjoining exam table. Danny stood nearby, watching.

Sophie took the mask and chloroform bottle and faced Danny. “Come here next to me and watch.”

Standing behind Nick's head, Sophie said, "Nick, I'm going to place a mask over your nose and mouth to give you an anesthetic. It's chloroform. Just breathe normally. It'll smell and taste sweet."

With Danny watching, Sophie placed the mask over Nick's face and nose and held it firmly with her left hand. She then slowly dripped chloroform onto the gauze mask.

"Just breath normally ... nice and easy ... that's it ... nice and easy ...." Sophie's lilting voice seemed to soothe Nick. Soon his head fell to the side. "He's down."

Danny, next to Sophie, awaited instructions.

"You with me?" Sophie asked.

"I'll try.".

"You're going to drip chloroform into the gauze with your left hand while you hold the mask tight to his nose and mouth with your right hand," Sophie said. "Drip only one drop at a time and only when I tell you. If you see him start to move, drip a little more. Remember, hold the mask tightly, like this with his chin back."

Danny, struggling to hold the mask over Nick's nose and mouth, asked, "Why can't Hélène do this?"

Sophie looked daggers at Danny. "I need her to assist with the surgery. Just do as I tell you. Also, don't faint. Look away if you must, but Nick needs you. Don't faint."

"Like I have a choice," Danny said.

Sophie shook her head in disgust.

Sophie stood next to Nick's leg and applied a tourniquet at the top of the thigh. She then removed Danny's belt-tourniquet and was relieved to see no significant increase in bleeding. She bent what remained of Nick's injured leg so the knee was at ninety degrees.

“Another drop,” Sophie said to Danny.

As Hélène painted Nick’s leg with iodine, Sophie taped two flashlights to an IV pole, aiming the light at the top of Nick’s knee. She then placed every lit lantern in the clinic around the table. Hélène and Sophie donned gowns and gloves and worked together to place drapes above and below Nick’s knee.

“Another drop. Don’t faint,” Sophie said. “You’re doing great. This might be a good time for you to look away.”

Sophie started the procedure with a fish-mouthed shaped incision two inches above Nick’s knee. She checked on Danny with a glance; he was concentrating on the ceiling.

Danny had seen attorneys concentrate in trials and pilots concentrate in turbulent weather, but he looked in awe as the two women, especially Sophie, concentrated fully on the task at hand, asking Hélène for the tools or sutures that she needed. Danny stopped looking at the wall and ceiling and concentrated on Sophie, even as she sawed through Nick’s femur.

Thirty-two minutes later, Sophie had Danny stop dripping the chloroform as she started to close the incision. After she placed the last sutures in the skin flap and drains, she said, “Take away the mask and let him breath air, but keep his chin up.”

Sophie wrapped the stump tightly with gauze. As Nick’s stump went down to rest on the bed, his head started to sway right and left and his body began to shiver. Sophie removed the tourniquet, watching the dressed wound. She saw no bleeding.

“Looks good, but his body temp is low. Let’s get a little more heat in the room and a few extra blankets,” she said.

Sophie and Hélène removed their surgical gowns and gloves.

Hélène went to the fireplace, stirred the embers alive and added two large sticks of firewood. She then went to a cupboard and brought out two heavy cotton blankets and placed them over the shaking patient. Meanwhile, Sophie changed Nick's IV to a fresh bottle of saline.

"Not bad, Captain Anesthesia," Sophie said, throwing a look in Danny's direction.

"Who are you? I can't believe we, you, just did that," Danny marveled. "With lanterns, flashlights, two women surgeons, in the middle of Goddamn nowhere and me giving anesthesia. It's surreal."

"It's not over. There's still a chance of infection and we don't have any sulfa or penicillin here," Hélène said.

"Plus, hiding you gets complicated," Sophie said. "We should talk about that now. The Bosches are everywhere in this village, and when they find no one in the plane, they'll start searching. They'll kill us if they find you here. But we can't move Nick just yet."

"What are Bosches?" Danny asked.

"That's our French-not-nice term for the Germans"

"We call them Krauts and the Brits call them Jerries. Whatever, they're all still assholes. So what do we do?" Danny asked.

"We hide you," Sophie said, "and hope that the Bosches leave after they chase you guys back to Morocco or, by some stroke of luck, you guys chase the Bosches back to Tunis."

"We'll figure it out," Danny said, looking around the room. "So where's the hiding place?"

“First you need a sling on your shoulder,” Sophie said.

Grabbing a clean pillowcase from a cabinet, she tore it open and fashioned a sling from the cloth. As she worked, Danny couldn’t help staring at her again. “You’ll need to wear this all the time for the next week. If you dislocate your shoulder again, you might need surgery to keep it in place.”

Facing Danny, she put the sling around his neck and tied it. She didn’t see the way Danny was looking at her, but Hélène did.

“Will you put this on me every day?” Danny asked.

Sophie looked at him like he was crazy. “No. Do it yourself.”

“Just asking,” Danny said with a grin. Hélène shook her head.

Sophie went to the pile of Nick’s belongings and took his standard issue M1911 Colt .45 pistol, embedding it among piled blankets on a shelf. Danny watched but said nothing.

“Come with me,” Sophie said.

Moving aside the floor rug, she opened the trapdoor to the root cellar and descended the eight-step ladder with a lantern. Danny followed after her, using only his right arm. In the cellar, Danny could only see shelves of preserved food, some raw vegetables and fruits, and the skinned hind leg of a sheep.

Sophie went to a bottom shelf of jars, slid them to the side, opened a small, hinged door on the back of the shelf and pulled a latch. She then pulled an entire case of shelves away from the wall, revealing an eight-by-eight room with two mattresses rolled against the wall. Sophie unrolled one of the mattresses.

“We didn’t find this room until we’d been here for

four months," Sophie said. "I'm not sure what they used it for."

"Nothing good, I bet," Danny said.

"We'll bring bottles of water, a lantern, towels, soap, a bedpan, everything you need. You'll have to help Nick with that," Sophie said.

"Of course."

"You'll sleep here tonight, and we'll move Nick down in the morning. It's warmer upstairs and he needs to get his body temperature up. The Bosches won't come around 'til after sunup," Sophie said. "But they'll come. I've bandaged a few blisters and lanced an abscess on a Bosch butt. They know we're here."

"Okay, I got it," Danny said. "But I'll need Nick's pistol back. I saw you hide it."

"I need it," Sophie said.

"I don't think so."

"I really need it," Sophie repeated.

"You even know how to use it?"

"No. I've never fired a gun, but there's a Nazi officer I need to kill if he returns."

"Not going to happen," Danny said. "Then we're all dead."

"If he returns, we're all dead anyway. He came a week ago to warn us not to help you Americans. He spoke through a Tunisian translator and had no idea that I speak German."

"And English and French and Arabic," Danny said.

"When he visited, he held a gun to Hélène's head and said he'd kill her if I didn't remove my head covering. I obeyed, and then ... then he slid his hands over our bodies." Sophie took a deep breath and went on. "Afterward, he spoke in German and told the translator that after they kill all the Americans, he would return and keep me for himself and give Hélène to his officers as a treat."

"Got it," Danny said. "I'll show you how to use the gun."

"Thank you," Sophie said. "I'll bring the lamb leg upstairs and hang it in the kitchen in case they see blood anywhere when they search. We'll wash the sheets and towels before we go to bed. Early tomorrow morning, I'll head out and make sure there aren't any blood tracks or boot prints leading here."

"Any chance there's something to eat?" Danny asked.

"I'll bring you a plate and you can open any jar on the shelves," Sophie said. "Tomorrow, after you and Nick are in the room and you close the secret shelf and the latch from the inside, you can't come out or make noise."

"A deal," Danny said. "I'm curious. Why'd you help us if you thought that SS asshole would kill you and your cousin?"

"The Bosches murdered my father. Reason enough?"

"More than enough. You're something else. Thanks for everything."

"You're welcome," Sophie said as she climbed the stairs. "One day at a time. Let's see if we're alive by the end of the week."

Danny, holding the lantern, picked out a jar of apricot preserves, opened it, and consumed half the jar before Sophie returned with a plate of cold lamb and mixed vegetables. As Danny ate, Sophie lugged the lamb leg up the ladder.

Sophie and Hélène collapsed in bed around midnight.

"Patient okay?" Hélène asked.

"Fair amount of pain. I gave him what's left of the morphine into his butt. It'll last longer than intravenous. I told him we won't have any more pain medicine after tonight. He's shivering less, so I'm guessing his body temperature is rising."

"They seem like nice guys," Hélène said. "Danny was staring at you during the surgery and again when you put on the sling. I know what that look means."

"You're crazy. I treated him like a misbehaving school boy," Sophie said, feeling sad for moment. She didn't know how to put it into words exactly, but she knew that the wounded American pilot had full view, that night, of all the power and authority she possessed – the exact qualities that had sent every other man running for the hills. Romantic love was not for her, she reminded herself. She refocused on the positives. "But he's letting me keep Nick's handgun in case the German officer comes back. I told him what happened, and he said he'd show me how to use it."

"You're not really going to shoot a Nazi officer?"

"If I have to," Sophie said.

Hélène was silent for a moment, then changed the subject. "I think we got all the blood off the floor. Good idea to bring the lamb leg up."

"Yeah, but if the Bosches come in, the lamb leg is as good as gone," Sophie said.

"They'll check the cellar, so it's gone already."

"Probably."

"I've never been one to pray," Hélène said, "but this

seems like a good time to start."

"Amen to that," Sophie said as she turned off the lantern.

Only Nick, drugged on morphine, found much sleep that night.

At four a.m., Sophie entered the secret room and shook Danny awake. She held Nick's pistol in her hand and a set of crutches in the other.

"Hélène and I are up," Sophie said. "It's still dark and I've changed Nick's bandages. He's been brave about the amount of pain he's tolerating and knows he'll need to be quiet."

"Thanks again for everything," Danny said.

Sophie smiled. "You're welcome. We'll need help getting Nick down the ladder and into the cellar. You should keep his gun for now. I can't have it upstairs if the Bosches search the clinic looking for you. The crutches are for when he's up and about. They're a bit short, but they'll have to do."

She leaned the crutches against the wall, unrolled Nick's mattress and then laid the gun on it. Danny sat up quickly and followed Sophie up the ladder.

Ten minutes later and with Hélène's assistance, they had Nick on the floor of the root cellar. Danny then helped Nick into the secret room where he curled into a ball on his mattress and fell asleep. Sophie brought down Nick's shoes and placed them against the wall.

Hélène brought down a breakfast of coffee, dried fruit, yogurt and dark bread, before removing and returning the urinal and bedpan.

"How is Safiyah?" Danny asked. "Is that even her name? You call her Sophie."

“Safiyah is the Arabic equivalent of Sophie, “Hélène said. “You should call her Saifyah, for now.”

“Understood,” Danny said. “How is she?”

“We’re frightened and I’m not used to it. Sophie went through this in France when the Bosches invaded. She lost her father then.”

“She told me about her dad. I think you and Safiyah are the most amazing, courageous people I’ve ever met.”

“For what it’s worth, I’ve seen you staring at her. Don’t. Don’t distract her. Not now,” Hélène said.

Danny nodded.

“One of us will stomp the floor twice over the cellar door to let you know when you have to be totally quiet and not move around. Tell Nick when he awakens. Three stomps mean it’s clear,” Hélène said as she turned, closed the secret door, and headed for the ladder.

While Hélène saw to the men, Sophie, lantern in hand, swept up the sandy footprints near the doorway and swept or kicked away the blood stains between their clinic and the edge of town. When Sophie returned, they buried the remnants of Nick’s leg behind the clinic in a shallow pit with lye and a cover of sand. She placed the now empty cans of gasoline for the generator over the sand.

“We’re sunk if they dig up the pit,” Hélène said.

Sophie nodded.

Both knew they had no other options.

As the sun rose above the eastern mountains an hour later, Sophie and Hélène sat for a quiet breakfast, niqabs lying and ready on the floor cushions. Knowing the day would be tense, they said little until they completed their meal.

“If Fatima shows up, we need to send her home,” Hélène said. “She’s always going down in the cellar.”

Sophie was nodding agreement when they heard a knock on the door. Both women held their breath.

Chapter Nineteen

Fériana, Tunisia
February 15, 1943

Hélène and Sophie exhaled, took deep breaths, then donned their niqabs. Sophie stomped on the cellar door twice to warn Danny and Nick, then walked with a pounding heart to the door.

A German lieutenant stood there, a scowl pasted on his face and a cocked Lugar pistol in his hand. Behind the lieutenant stood three soldiers, one carrying a machine gun and the other two with rifles. All three were aiming at Sophie. Behind the patrol stood a village man, Adbul Abdallah.

Sophie and Hélène knew Abdul from shopping in the open market at the center of town. Neither woman had ever spoken to him, but he was easy to identify thanks to marked scoliosis of the spine and a partially missing left ear. Although Abdul always seemed courteous, his presence behind the soldiers unnerved Sophie.

"Sprechen Sie Deutsch?" barked the lieutenant.

Sophie lied with a mute head shake.

The lieutenant continued speaking in German: "An airplane of Americans was shot down outside the village last night. They are not in the plane."

The lieutenant pointed his gun at Abdul. Shuffling

forward, Abdul translated his words into Arabic. After translating, Abdul bowed his head as a gesture of apology. Sophie correctly assumed Abdul was not willingly translating.

Sophie felt Hélène come beside her in the doorway.

"We have seen no one," Hélène replied in Arabic, which Abdul duly translated.

"Is there anyone else inside this building?" the lieutenant asked, through Abdul.

"No. Come look," Sophie said.

The lieutenant turned to one of his soldiers and pointed his pistol at Hélène. "You stay outside with this one. If you hear gunfire, shoot her dead."

Hélène stepped outside.

"The airmen were injured," the lieutenant said to his soldiers. "Look for blood on the floor, in the garbage, everywhere."

The lieutenant pushed Sophie into the clinic with his Lugar pressed against the back of her head. Abdul and the two other soldiers followed. Once in the middle of the room, he stopped and grabbed Sophie by the back of the neck. "Don't move." Abdul translated, but Sophie was already frozen.

The men fanned out, inspecting every inch of the floor, opening cabinets and drawers, looking under exam beds, peering down into the squat toilet, the shower room, and rifling through everything in their bedroom.

"Where is your cellar?" the lieutenant asked, gesturing impatiently at Abdul.

Sophie waited, then pointed to the small rug that covered the door to the root cellar. The lieutenant kicked the rug to the side.

"Open it," Abdul told her.

Sophie opened the cellar door and stood back. With his gun pointed into the cellar, the lieutenant peered in.

"I need a lantern," he said.

One of the soldiers lit a lantern he found in the cabinets and brought it to the lieutenant. The lieutenant pointed down into the cellar. Without hesitation, the soldier slung the rifle over his shoulder, took the lantern, and climbed down. Sophie could hear him searching the cellar.

"Nothing here but jars of food," came the soldier's muffled voice.

"Do you see any blood?" the lieutenant shouted.

"No."

"If you see anything tasty, bring it up."

The soldier climbed out with two large jars of apple preserves, which he rolled onto the clinic floor before pulling himself off the ladder.

"There are no other rooms or cellars?" Abdul translated.

"No."

The lieutenant spotted the leg of lamb hanging on a hook near the sink. "Take that. These whores don't need it."

Abdul didn't see the need to translate as one of the soldiers cut down the meat and slung it over his shoulder.

"Nothing here," the lieutenant announced. "On to the next house." He holstered his pistol and put his arm around the soldier with the leg of lamb. "Take this to the cook as a present from me to the rest of our officers."

The soldiers left and Hélène came back in, visibly shaking after enduring a gun pointed at her head for thirty minutes. She shut the door and looked to Sophie. Both heaved a breath of relief.

Sophie went to the root cellar door and stomped on it three times, then replaced the rug.

An hour later, another pounding on the door startled the women. Again, Hélène and Sophie held their breath for a moment. Hélène stomped on the cellar door twice.

BANG!

Before Sophie could open the front door, the women clearly heard something fall in the cellar. The sound froze both of them. They waited a moment, but heard nothing else. The pounding on the door resumed.

Sophie took a deep breath and opened the front door to find three very young German soldiers, all shouldering rifles. The lead soldier, a tall blond corporal, took off his hat and said, "*Sprechen Sie Deutsch*?"

Sophie expected the question, as every German she encountered had started conversations with the same one. She stared blankly and shrugged.

The same soldier then asked, "*Parlez-vous français*?"

"*Un peu*," Sophie said, then deliberately botched her follow-up: "*Ce que je veux*?"

Without answering, the soldier strode into the clinic, rested his rifle against the wall, and pulled off the shoe and sock on his right foot, showing Sophie a totally black nail on his big toe. The soldier pantomimed holding something heavy and dropping it on his foot. Sophie nodded that she understood.

Directing the soldier to an exam table, she washed his foot with a soapy, wet towel, dried it, and then applied iodine to the toe. Next she took a paper clip, lit a candle, and heated the end of the clip until it glowed red.

The soldier's eyes and mouth opened to their fullest. Shaking his head, he started to sit up.

Sophie said, "*Tout est bon, s'il vous plait.*"

The soldier laid down, closed his eyes, bared his teeth and waited. Sophie punctured the toenail with the red-hot clip. Thick purplish blood oozed from the puncture site without the soldier feeling a thing. Sophie applied a gauze pad and tape.

"*Fini,*" she said.

The soldier sat up and gingerly touched his toe. Smiling broadly, he put his shoe and sock back on, stood, and saluted Sophie with a "*Merci beaucoup.*"

The other two soldiers then put their rifles next to their friend's and rushed to jump onto the tables.

Just as the French-speaking soldier began to translate, a German officer marched into the clinic and started screaming at the three soldiers. They quickly stood to attention; heads bowed before the diatribe.

"Why are you three pieces of shit here? You're letting these daughters and mothers of cretins and whores touch you!" screeched the officer. "How many diseases do you think they carry? You put your rifles down, but they won't think twice about taking them to kill you!"

Sheepishly, the soldier with the blackened toe said, "The line for our medic was too long. Besides, he is rough and unclean. We heard these women were cleaner. She fixed my toe in a second."

"She could have killed you. Get out now before I put

all of you in chains and send the lot of you to the Russian front," the officer growled. "We've routed the cowardly Americans. We're leaving to chase them back to Morocco."

The three soldiers picked up their weapons and ran out.

The officer turned to Sophie, wagged his finger and sneered in German, "Do not allow my men in here again."

Sophie kept her face blank and ignorant.

"Do not allow my men in here again!" screamed the officer.

Sophie shrugged and said in Arabic, "I don't understand."

The officer shook his head in disgust and yelled, "Idiots, all of you."

He stomped out. Sophie closed the door and turned to Hélène. Together they laughed heartily. It had been a long time since either had laughed so much.

Sophie waited thirty minutes before giving the all clear three-kick sign to Danny and Nick. A half hour later, she went down to the cellar.

"Sorry about the noise," Danny said. "Nick knocked over his crutches which fell on the bedpan. I can't imagine that it didn't' scare you and Hélène."

Sophie accepted Danny's excuse but only glared at the two Americans.

The afternoon after the German search for the American pilots ended, Sophie came down to the secret room. Danny showed Sophie how to load and cock Nick's Colt .45 pistol.

Sophie learned the loading maneuvers quickly.

"Good hands, Doc," Danny said. "You're going to

need to hold the gun in both hands to shoot it. It's got a helluva kick."

"Kick?"

"Isaac Newton's third law. For every action there is an equal and opposite reaction. You shoot that way and the gun wants to kick back the other."

Danny showed Sophie a two-handed stance, then gave the gun to Sophie. He walked behind her and put his arms around hers to demonstrate. "Aim at that hook on the wall." He expected her to turn away, but she didn't, letting him demonstrate.

"Thank you," Sophie said. "I hope never to use it."

"That would be best," Danny said. On a roll, Danny tried to learn more about Sophie by telling of his past.

"I'm from Detroit, Michigan. My parents and my brother are there."

"I know Detroit," Sophie said, with a slight smile. "My father spent a year in Ann Arbor. That's where I learned English."

"I went to college there," Danny said. "Where are you from?"

"Metz, France," she said.

"I don't know it.

"It's near the German border, in a region called the Lorraine."

"You left?"

"Yes. When the Bosches invaded Belgium and the Netherlands in 1940, I worked with my father for the French Army, operating on wounded soldiers. The Bosches turned south and the French Army collapsed. I fled to the south of France and then finally to Tunisia."

"You still have family in Metz?" Danny asked.

"No. My mother died six years ago in an avalanche while skiing. There was only my father. The Nazis killed him when he tried to return home. I think and dream of it often and it disturbs me. I don't want to talk about it.

A switch had been thrown. Sophie's jaw tightened and she turned away.

"I'm sorry," Danny said. "I didn't know."

"No, you couldn't have known. End of discussion. We don't have the luxury of idle talk. The Bosches could walk in at any time." She turned, didn't say a word, took the pistol, now loaded, up the ladder, and closed the trap door.

Sophie hid the pistol behind sheets in a cabinet.

After the warning from the German officer, no more soldiers came to the clinic. Fearing the Germans, few villagers came to seek medical attention either, although the number of Germans soldiers in Fériana fell each hour as they were deployed to follow the retreating American Army. Neither Sophie nor Hélène were sleeping well, but Sophie was anxious even during the day. Staring at the wall, she would sit in a chair for hours, twirling her hair with her finger. At night, she would check and recheck if the door was locked, and check and recheck if Nick's .45 was loaded and in the cabinet.

"You okay?" Hélène asked each night before turning off the lantern.

"Every time I close my eyes, I see that Nazi officer's eye staring at me. The one with the distorted eyelid," Sophie said. "Every door knock, unusual sound, or even silence, I think he's outside our door."

"We'll be fine. I just feel it."

"I'm jealous," Sophie said. "I don't."

By the third day post-op, Nick seemed to have tolerable pain levels and was able to eat, albeit sparingly. Daily, his pain continued to dissipate and his appetite increased.

Talking to other villagers at the market, Sophie confirmed that the Germans had stopped searching for the downed pilots. Still, sporadic patient visits always risked discovery, which weighed heavily on Sophie and Hélène. They insisted that the two pilots spend all day, every day in the cellar. It was rare for patients to come after six p.m., but a German patrol could arrive without notice. Only after Sophie or Hélène stomped three times on the cellar door could Danny come upstairs to pick up food or return dishes, urinals and bedpans. Sophie would make him retreat to the secret room immediately.

On the fourth day, Hélène returned from the open-air market and dropped the bags of food on the table. Sophie was heating a pot of water for tea.

"We may have a problem," Hélène said.

"What?" Sophie asked.

"Mr. Habib, the butcher, asked why we're buying more meat."

"Oh. What did you say?"

"I was tongue-tied for a moment," Hélène said. "I finally said that so few patients are coming that we're cooking more."

Sophie shook her head. "That's what you said? Did he believe you?"

"I don't know. After I thought about it, I told him the Bosches had taken all our meat.'"

"Should have said that first."

"I suppose. I didn't expect the question," Hélène said. "You think he could turn us in?"

"For enough money," Sophie said, "anyone in this village would tell."

"There's nothing we can do about it now," Hélène said.

The fifth night was a Friday. Sophie checked and re-checked the door locks, then moved the rug and stomped three times on the cellar door. Danny, always quietly careful, got to the top step, lifted the door a few inches and with his eyes just above the floor, scanned the room.

Danny saw Sophie and Hélène sitting at the edge of the kitchen table lighting two candles. They waved their palms over the candles, and whispering to each other.

"What are you doing?" Danny asked, surprising both women.

Sophie wheeled around to the cellar door. "Nothing."

"We do this once in a while," Hélène said. "For luck."

Danny climbed out and approached the table. "What did you whisper?"

"A prayer for luck," Hélène said.

"Is it Friday night?" Danny asked.

"Yes," Sophie said, looking at Danny curiously.

"I know what's going on."

"You don't," Sophie said.

"I do, actually. Do it again, please." Danny kneeled on a cushion.

Sophie hesitated then looked at Hélène, who shrugged.

"Okay," Sophie said.

The candles remained lit, so Hélène and Sophie waved their hands over them and started singing the Sabbath prayer very softly.

"Barukh ata Adonai ..."

To the astonishment of both women, Danny joined in the singing.

"...Eloheinu, Melekh ha'olam ..."

Together they finished the prayer.

"... asher kid'shanu b'mitzvotav v'tzivanu l'hadlik ner shel Shabbat."

"You're Jewish?" Sophie asked.

"Why not?" Danny said.

"I wouldn't have guessed," Hélène said. "Booker isn't a Jewish name, is it?"

"My grandfather's real name was Baronofsky. U.S. immigration got it wrong in 1894. For that matter, Shaloub and Al-hadef aren't Jewish either."

"Actually, they are," Sophie said. "We're Sephardic Jews. The ones kicked out of Spain in the 1500s. during the Spanish Inquisition. Our family moved to Tunisia."

"We were both born on the Island of Djerba off the Tunisian coast," Hélène said.

"I learn something every day about you two," Danny said. "I wish you'd tell me all your stories. I've got the time."

"Is Nick Jewish too?" Hélène asked.

"No. Good Christian kid from Denver, Colorado."

After the prayer, Sophie didn't ask Danny to return to the cellar immediately as she normally would. She stowed the candelabras in a cabinet, then went to prepare the dinner plates for Danny to take down to the cellar.

Hélène watched as Danny, head atilt, gazed at Sophie as she worked. Hélène took Danny by the arm and walked him into the bedroom.

"You know how precarious our situation is, right?" Hélène asked. "Today, the butcher at the market wondered why we're consuming more meat. The Bosches are still in town and could knock on our door at any time."

"I don't understand," Danny said.

"I'm not blind or jealous," Hélène continued, "but I see the way you look at Safiyah. We don't need that now. We cannot be distracted, even for a moment. Leave her alone. Do you understand?"

"I'll try, but finding out you two are Jewish just made it impossible," Danny said. "Sorry. I'm human."

"Try harder," Hélène implored as she pushed Danny back to the main room.

Undaunted by Hélène's pleas, Danny asked, "Maybe I could stay upstairs for a while after we eat?"

"No, absolutely not, for as long as any of the German Army remains in town," Sophie said. "It's time for you to head down."

"You didn't know that before the war, I was an attorney."

Sophie laughed. "That explains the arguing. Please don't ask again. I'm having enough nightmares as it is without worrying you'll be up here if the Bosches knock on the door."

"Okay then," Danny said. "Two stomps and three stomps, I know. But you never know when you might actually need me. How about five quick stomps means danger, come now?"

"No," Sophie replied immediately. "It's too dangerous."

Hélène thought for a second then added, "I guess I'd feel better knowing we could call Danny if we need him."

"Okay, five stomps," Sophie said, then pointed to the cellar door. "Now get back down in the cellar."

"Be nice," Hélène said.

"I'm sorry. It's the stress," Sophie said.

"Agreed," Danny said as he stood, gathered the full dinner plates, then headed back to the cellar ladder, one plate at a time. Once the plates were down, Danny climbed up, grabbing the inside cellar door handle to shut it.

A knock on the door froze everyone.

Chapter Twenty

Fériana, Tunisia
February 21, 1943

The soft knock came again.

"Uh oh," Sophie muttered.

Hélène and Sophie quickly ran to put on their niqabs.

Danny stayed at the top of the cellar ladder as Hélène ran to the window, opened the shutter, and said, "There's a car outside. I can't see anyone."

Loud knocking on the front door followed.

"Knock on the window and see if someone comes," Sophie said.

Danny pulled down the cellar door until it was only a few inches from shutting and watched.

Hélène knocked on the window and waited. After a few seconds, Omar Sader, the Tunisian translator for SS Colonel Gunther, appeared in the window, his nose to the glass.

"Open the damn door," Omar yelled in Arabic.

Hélène nodded, slammed the shutter closed and turned to the room. "It's him, the translator from Tunis. I can't see anyone else."

With Danny watching, Sophie went to the cupboard and grabbed Nick's Colt .45 from under the sheets. Danny closed the cellar door and disappeared.

“I said open the damn door now,” Omar yelled once again from outside the window.

Hélène went to the door but watched Sophie lift her abaya, put on a belt, then tuck the Colt .45 into her belt, dropping the abaya to cover herself and hide the gun. Only then did Hélène open the door a few inches.

Omar, looking anxious, stood in the doorway. “Colonel Gunther needs to talk to you.”

“We were about to go to bed. Can’t it wait until tomorrow when the clinic is open?” Hélène asked.

“No. Now!” Omar yelled.

“Open it,” Sophie said. “Or he’ll bash the door in.”

Hélène opened the door halfway. Omar stood at the door. Behind him was Colonel Gunther.

“Is that the terrible man who made us remove our headcovers?” Hélène asked Omar, pointing at Gunther.

Before Omar had the chance to translate, Gunther pulled out his Lugar and pushed Omar away. He forced the door wide enough to raise his pistol to Hélène’s forehead and screamed, “Open the fucking door!”

“You’d better let him in,” said Omar.

Hélène stepped back and Gunther kicked the door open. He entered the clinic, gun raised, followed by Omar. Hélène and Sophie retreated all the way to the kitchen and stood behind the table, holding each other’s hands. Gunther holstered his gun. Omar moved closer to the table.

“Tell them we need them to come with us,” Gunther said.

Sophie released her grip on Hélène’s hands and clenched her hands inside her abaya to stop them from trembling.

Omar translated and Hélène and Sophie shook their

heads.

"We will not come with someone who has defiled a Muslim woman," Sophie said, shaking her head.

Gunther looked to Omar. Omar shook his head.

"If I tell him that he'll kill both of you," Omar told Sophie.

"If he kills us, then we're no good to him. I don't think he'll kill us," Sophie said.

"He'll kill you, trust me," Omar said, as Gunther started to fume.

"Listen, you son of pig-dung," Gunther demanded, swiveling his gun so that it was now aimed at Omar, "what are they saying? Tell me now."

Omar said, "They say you defiled them when you took off their head coverings. They don't want to go with you."

Gunther laughed then aimed his Lugar at Sophie, who froze in position. "One way or another they're coming. My men are waiting for the tall one. Grab her and put her in the trunk of the car so she won't run. Then come back."

Without hesitation, Omar grabbed Hélène by the arm and waist and hoisted her over his shoulder like she was a bag of potatoes. Despite her kicking, screaming, and pounding his back with both fists, he proceeded out of the clinic.

Gunther approached Sophie along one side of the table. Sophie started screaming, "Yabtaeid," (go away) over and over. She moved to the other side of the table, then moved to stand on the cellar door, stomping her foot as hard as she could five or six times. She continued to scream until her voice became hoarse.

"You think you can run, you stupid whore,"

Gunther laughed with a sneer. “Stomping your feet won’t awaken any of your worthless Muslim gods.” He moved quickly trying to trap Sophie in to a corner.

Sophie ran into the bedroom and shut the door, which had no lock. She rushed to a dark corner behind the second bed, frantically grappling under her dress for the .45. She could hear Gunther’s forceful footsteps thundering toward her, and with shaking hands, she cocked the gun just as Danny had shown her. Disengaging the safety on the side of the gun, she raised it up with two hands just as Gunther kicked the door open.

“Where are you?” he shrieked. “You cannot escape!”

The force of the blow shattered the doorframe but also let in light from the main room. Sophie could see her assailant perfectly, from the Lugar in his hand to the snarl on his face to the wild juddering of his eye. Draped head-to-toe in black and with no light source behind her, Sophie hoped she was as good as invisible.

In perfect German, she shouted, “Here, you pig. For my father!” and fired two rounds into Gunther’s chest. He dropped to the floor.

“Safiyah!” shouted Danny from the other room. “Are you okay?”

“In the bedroom,” Sophie yelled. “I shot him!”

She dropped her gun on her mattress and ran out of the bedroom. Crying, she fell into Danny’s arms. “I think I killed him.”

“Where’s Hélène?” Danny asked, embracing Sophie without letting go of his own .45.

“The translator forced her into the trunk of the car.”

“He must have heard the shots. He’ll be back,” Danny said, suddenly stiffening. “Was he armed?”

"I don't know, I never saw him with a weapon," Sophie said.

"Go stand behind the table," Danny said. "Hurry! I'll be in the bedroom."

Sophie ran to the table as Omar ran through the door. He saw Sophie immediately and shouted.

"I heard gunshots! Where's the Colonel?"

"He's dead. I shot him," Sophie said in Arabic.

"Now we're all going to die," cried Omar. "They'll come and kill us on the spot. I've seen them do it for no reason at all."

Danny came out of the remnants of bedroom entry with his .45 trained on Omar. Omar's mouth and eyes opened as if he'd seen a ghost.

"Tell him not to move," Danny said. "Or I'll kill him."

Sophie started translating into Arabic, but Omar stopped her.

"I understand English and German as well as you do," Omar said, speaking in a pronounced British accent. "Who is this?"

"Captain Danny Booker of the United States Army Air Force," Sophie said.

"Ah, yes, the missing pilot. Don't shoot me," Omar said quietly. "I worked for the Germans under duress. I don't want to die for those crazy monsters. I can help you."

"We need to kill him," Danny said, his eyes darting to Sophie. "He'll turn us in."

"I need to think," Sophie said, still shaking. "He said he knew I spoke German and never told. Didn't you, Omar?"

Danny gave Omar a hard stare and kept the gun

pointed at him. Omar's head snapped back and eyes, fully opened, were no longer on Danny, but beyond him.

"Behind you!" Omar shouted, diving to the ground.

Danny wheeled around to see Gunther, ten feet away, staggering out of the bedroom, holding his right chest with one hand while waving his Lugar wildly in the other. Without hesitation, Dany fired two rounds at the SS officer, one to the chest and one to the head, and killed him.

Sophie, Danny, and Omar stood motionless for a long moment until Sophie spoke.

"We've got to get Hélène out of the trunk."

Omar said, "I don't think she'll come easily if I go. I forced her with difficulty, as I was ordered. I'm sorry for it."

"I'll go," Sophie said.

First checking that her face was covered, she exited the clinic. As Sophie approached Gunther's car, she heard Hélène screaming in Arabic for anyone to help her. The trunk of the 1939 Mercedes-Benz 230 SV opened easily; Sophie dodged her cousin's kick.

"Stop, It's me," Sophie whispered. "Get out and get back into the clinic! The Nazi is dead."

"And the translator? I will kill him," Hélène hissed, clambering out of the trunk.

"We may need him," Sophie replied, trying to close the trunk as quietly as she could. "He knew I understood German and said nothing. I believe he follows their orders but he's not on their side."

Sophie took Hélène's arm and hurried back into the clinic. They locked the door. Danny stood ten feet from Omar, his finger still on the trigger but the gun at his side. Hélène turned toward Omar who went down to his knees, bowing to Hélène, whose fists were clenched and revenge filled her eyes.

"Surely Allah loves those who always turn to Him in repentance. I am truly sorry for what I have done," Omar said.

"He means it," Sophie said.

Hélène relaxed. "Okay, for now. You're lucky I don't know how to shoot a gun." She then kicked Omar in the side as hard as she could. Omar barely budged but he accommodated Hélène's residual anger by rolling over and pretending to gasp. He sat up and held his side.

"English is the only language we all understand. We need a plan and staying here isn't one of them," Sophie said.

"How many people will fit in the car outside?" Danny asked.

"We're good. Four comfortably," Omar said.

"There are five of us," Hélène said.

"I see only four. Who else?" Omar asked.

"My co-pilot is in the root cellar," Danny said. "His leg was amputated five days ago."

"Who amputated his leg?" Omar asked.

"I did," said Sophie.

"And the Germans didn't find you? Hard to believe. Can he travel?" Omar asked.

"Yes," Sophie said.

"We're wasting time. We need a plan," Hélène said.

"The Germans are here and in Thélepte still in great numbers," Omar said, "and in Majel Bel Abbes to the south. Plus the car eats gasoline like my brother's camel eats grass. Maybe enough left for seventy kilometers."

"The Germans emptied all of our generator gas cans the first day they arrived," Sophie said.

"Tebessa is the major base for our troops. It's eighty kilometers away," Danny said.

"Can we even get past the German sentries on the roads?" Sophie asked.

"Never, on the roads, but I have an idea," said Omar. "I interrogated a goat herder two days ago. He said there's a goat track through the Atlas Mountains. It starts between Fériana and Thélepte. It's marked on the highway with a pile of stones and ends in a valley. It's on the way to the village called Bou Chebka. If we can get past the guards outside Fériana, there are no checkpoints until the airfield at Thélepte.

"Can we get through the checkpoint in Fériana?" Danny asked.

"Most of the guards know me and will let me pass," Omar said. He looked at his new friends meaningfully. "If I'm alone, the ones that don't know me will stop the car. With the colonel, no one stops us for long."

Sophie gasped with comprehension. "Danny, you're about the same size as the colonel and the trunk is big enough for Hélène and me to curl up. Can we hide Nick in the back seat?"

"Actually, the other man will be fine sitting up in the back," Omar said. "The colonel took prisoners all the time for interrogation. He would sit in the back of the car with a gun pointed at the prisoner's head. I would drive. I was always scared that if I hit a bump or the brakes, he'd kill the prisoner."

"I can't speak a word of German if they ask me anything," Danny said.

“It might be a problem,” Omar said. “But I have no other ideas.”

“It could work,” Hélène said.

“Whatever, we need to move before someone comes looking for the Colonel. We’ll need to clean his jacket,” Sophie said.

“The Major had a trench coat in the back seat,” Omar said. “He’d wear it over his SS jacket at night.”

“Good,” Danny said, “One less thing to do.”

Sophie took Danny to the side of the room. “Should Omar have Nick’s gun, just in case?”

“Absolutely not. I’d feel more comfortable with Nick carrying his own gun,” Danny said. “He’s alert enough and wouldn’t hesitate to shoot a Kraut.”

Sophie nodded in agreement.

“Omar, help me get my friend out of the cellar,” Danny said. “Safiyah, Hélène, grab water, food, and whatever you really need and nothing else. Wear layers, it’s freezing on the mountain passes. We need to act fast.”

Chapter Twenty-One

Atlas Mountains
February 1943

Sophie threw jars of preserves, bags of nuts, and glass bottles of water into the trunk of the Mercedes, then climbed in, careful to make room for Hélène.

Hélène looked at the trunk and said, "I swore I'd kill anyone who ever made me get into a trunk again, and here I'm doing it on my own."

Omar shut the trunk and climbed into the driver's seat. Danny sat in the back on the right side, wearing Gunther's hat and overcoat over his USAAF uniform.

Nick sat in the opposing back seat in his own uniform, the crutches on the floor board of the back seat. Hélène had reconstructed his pants, which had been cut off when he first appeared. He wedged his .45 Colt into his belt. As they drove off, Danny aimed Gunther's Lugar at Nick's head.

Omar said, "Danny, listen. When we reach the sentries on the outskirts of town, we should be able to drive straight through. If it looks like they want to talk to you or Nick, say '*gahen*,' which is pronounced like 'gain.' Say it with conviction, but don't scream. It means 'go.'"

"*Gahen*," Danny repeated.

"That'll do," Omar said.

Driving through Fériana was uneventful until they

reached the edge of town where the sentries waited. Two Germans with machine guns stood at guard and a third sat in a makeshift booth at the roadside. A railroad-crossing type gate blocked both sides of the road to Thélepte. One of the Germans, a tall and muscular sergeant, held up a Lugar pistol for the car to stop. In his other hand, he raised a flashlight.

"I know this guard. His name is Oskar," Omar said. "We're in luck, I hope." Omar pulled to a stop and rolled down the window.

"Oskar, good evening," Omar said with glee. "It's too cold to be standing outside, my friend."

"Yes, cold enough to freeze a polar bear's dick," Oskar said.

Omar laughed. "The colonel is taking this prisoner to the airfield at Thélepte. He's flying him to Tunis for further interrogation. Then they'll kill him. He doesn't speak a word of German."

Oskar flashed the light at Nick, who squinted when the beam hit his eyes. Danny kept his pistol aimed at Nick's head the whole time.

"Oskar," Omar said, "don't shine the light in the colonel's eyes. He's had a headache the whole day. He might shoot you."

Oskar hesitated, the beam of his flashlight wavering.

"*Gahen*," Danny said.

Oskar retracted the light, stood back, saluted, and waved the Mercedes on. The other guard raised the gate and Omar drove through.

Once past the gate, the three men in the car simultaneously heaved a gigantic sigh of relief.

'Please, God, no more sentries," Nick said.

Fifteen minutes and seven kilometers later, the five-foot-high stone marker identifying the goat track into the Atlas Mountains came into view. Parked next to the marker in the middle of the goat track stood a Volkswagen Type 82 Kübelwagen, the equivalent of an American Jeep. Inside was a soldier asleep behind the wheel.

"This doesn't look good," Omar said. "That soldier shouldn't be here."

"What if we drive past him?" Danny asked.

"He'd probably wake up, see us, and report it. Then they'd send a patrol out," Omar said. "Worse, we could get stuck in the loose sand off the side of the road."

"For starters," Danny said, "tell him to move on."

"I'd better ask why he's there first," Omar said.

"You do that," Danny said.

"I agree," Nick said. "Maybe he's got mechanical trouble."

"C'mon. He's asleep," Danny said.

Omar took a flashlight from the Mercedes, exited the car, approached the Kübelwagen, and turned on his flashlight. Between the soldier's thighs on the seat sat an empty bottle of French wine. The soldier remained asleep, snoring loudly.

Omar returned to the Mercedes.

"He's drunk on French wine," Omar said. "Even if I wake him, I'm not sure he's able to drive."

"Can we push that thing off the side of the road?" Danny asked.

"We can try," Omar said.

Danny yelled toward the trunk. "Safiyah, Hélène, can you hear me?"

“Yes,” came back from both women.

“We’ve got to move a car with a drunk soldier,” Nick said. “If he wakes up, he’s dead.”

Danny turned to Omar and asked, “You okay with that?”

Omar nodded and shrugged at the same time.

Danny switched to his .45 Colt and followed Omar to the Kübelwagen. The soldier didn’t stir. Omar released the handbrake, turned the steering wheel to the left and joined Danny at the front of the Kübelwagen. The car moved slowly at first, then progressed steadily off the side of the road until there was enough space for the Mercedes to pass.

“Drive our car past and let’s see if he stays asleep,” Danny said.

Omar got into the Mercedes, drove slowly by the Kübelwagen, stopped and rejoined Danny. Danny nudged the soldier’s shoulder and he started to stir.

“He doesn’t have to die,” Omar said.

“I agree,” Danny said. He removed the soldier’s helmet and knocked him firmly on the head with the butt of the gun. “He won’t wake up for a while.”

“Thank you,” Omar said.

“You think he’ll mind if we take his rifle and ammo?” Danny asked.

“Not at all,” Omar laughed. “He won’t find himself in worse trouble. If they don’t execute him his next stop will be the Russian front.”

Omar and Danny returned to their car and drove off. When the lights of Fériana and Thélepte faded to twinkles, the men pulled over to let Hélène and Sophie out of the trunk. The women stretched their legs, then Sophie climbed between Danny and Nick in the back while Hélène sat in the front opposite Omar.

"Omar, any chance we'll run into German patrols out here?" Danny asked.

"It's possible," Omar said. "But I don't think they'd shoot us without checking who's in the car. It's German and used only for important officers."

"Don't bet on it," Danny said grimly. "We have about six hours, I'd say, before they find the dead colonel in our clinic and see that his car missing. Probably best that we keep the head and tail lights off."

"Our biggest problem right now may be that this path is for goat herders and not automobiles," Omar said. "Ruts, washed out areas, and boulders aren't an issue for the goats. I have no idea how far we'll get in six hours at night."

"Where does the track lead?" Nick asked.

"Into a valley. On the other side of the valley and over another pass is Bou Chebka, a nothing village," Omar said. "It's on the Algerian-Tunisian border on the way to Tebessa. If General Rommel is meaning to run the Americans back to Morocco, they'll head to Tebessa. That might be a problem."

"If push comes to shove," Nick said, "and we have to walk, then I'm a liability. I understand and ..."

"We're not leaving you," Sophie interrupted. "No matter what."

Nick nodded with a faint smile and looked out the window as the hills of the Atlas Mountains approached. Danny said nothing but reached over and squeezed Sophie's hand. She looked at Danny who mouthed, "Thank you."

"In a few minutes," Omar said, "we'll start climbing. Be prepared that someone will need to walk in front of the car with a flashlight. Gunther kept extra batteries in the trunk."

"Got it," Danny said. "I'll go first."

"I can go second," Sophie said.

"I'll go third," said Hélène.

By six in the morning, the sun had begun to show over the eastern ridges. The fugitives had traveled four miles and reached the crest of the first mountain pass. Light snow covering, jutting rocks, and a few leafless plants filled the clear, cloudless, and frozen landscape. Omar and Danny estimated the outside temperature at twenty-five degrees Fahrenheit.

All except Nick clambered out of the Mercedes to look down into the valley. It was two miles across, with another set of hills visible past the valley.

"Doesn't look too far," Sophie said tentatively, shivering in the cold. "You think Bou Chebka is on the other side?"

"I was told it was," Omar said. "We should get going."

"Wait," said Danny. "Do you hear something?"

The four fugitives froze. The faint roar of airplane engines was clearly audible in the distance. Everyone looked up and scanned the skies.

"There they are," said Hélène, as she pointed northeast. "Three of them."

"They're 109s," Danny said.

The three planes split, each flying parallel a mile apart a few thousand feet off the ground.

"That's a search pattern. They're looking for us," Danny said. "Quick, let's pile plants and dirt over the car and windows then get back inside. Anything that will reflect light might give us away."

They frantically gathered leafless desert plants and placed them over the Mercedes' windows. Running out of nearby plants, they covered the chassis with dirt and snowy mud. Breathing heavily from the exertion, Hélène and Sophie tumbled into the car next to Nick. Omar and Danny positioned the last pieces of camouflage as the roar of the three engines grew louder.

"No time to get in!" Danny hissed.

Omar ran to the driver side door, shielding his body with a plant. Danny joined him, crouching next to the back door. One of three search planes flew directly over their car. Danny and Omar sat immobile until the airplane engine sounds diminished.

Danny opened the door and spoke to everyone. "We can't travel until nighttime. Not with the planes searching. We need to move the car next to a large boulder and get more plants to cover the top and open side. I'm going to walk back a few hundred yards and see if any German patrols are coming up behind us."

Danny left on foot while Omar moved the car next to a bus-sized boulder on the side of the path. Omar, Hélène and Sophie gathered plants frantically to cover the Mercedes' windows and caked dirt and mud over the rest of car's body. By the time they had covered the car, dusty sweat poured down their faces and neck, their hands caked with mud, and scrapes from the plants could be seen on their hands, arms, and faces. No one complained.

Danny returned twenty minutes later to report he'd seen no one trailing them. Even with the sun out, the temperatures remained cool, so the five fugitives sat in the car with the windows closed and supped on jars of apricot and apple preserves. Every two hours or so, they heard the sound of search planes overhead.

The searches stopped as the sun set. Danny had the plants covering the windows put into the trunk to use again. Omar got back in the driver's seat and Sophie walked ahead as they descended the mountain. After thirty minutes, Danny had Omar stop the car and he got out and approached Sophie.

"I'll take over," Danny said. "It's too cold for you." He put the back of his hand on Sophie's face and shook his head.

"I'll be okay," Sophie said, her lips blue.

"In the clinic, you were the boss. Not here. Get back in the car," Danny said.

"Thank you," Sophie said, only too happy to warm up.

By two a.m. the group had descended only halfway down the far side of the mountain pass. The trail narrowed and rocks blocked the path, requiring help from everyone but Nick to proceed. Danny then came upon a hurdle that seemed insurmountable.

"Stop," he yelled and raised his hand.

Omar stopped the car and rushed out. Ahead of them, a large, irregular washed-out ditch extended across the entire path.

"We're not driving over this," Danny said.

"Indeed not, my good fellow," Omar said.

Hélène and Sophie joined the men to survey the obstacle.

"That's not good," Hélène said.

"Unless you're a goat," Sophie added.

"We'll build a bridge," Danny said.

"With what?" Omar said.

"Rocks," Danny said. "There are millions of them. Just enough to get over."

"It's pitch dark," Sophie pointed out.

"Let's do what can tonight with the flashlights," Danny said. "We'll finish tomorrow during the day when the planes aren't looking for us. With luck, we'll get down to the bottom and across the valley tomorrow night."

"Can a stone bridge support a car?" Hélène asked.

"It should work. It only has to hold for a few seconds," Danny said. "How much water do we have left?"

"If we ration, enough to get through today," Hélène said. "There's one jar of olives and a bag of almonds left. That's it."

By the morning, the fugitives had managed to throw only a few nearby rocks into the ditch, but the Mercedes remained covered from head to toe with dirt and mud and the windows were, once again, covered in leafless plants. At six-forty-five in the morning, the first group of ME-109s came through the valley looking for the fugitives. They returned at noon and four p.m. In the intervening time, the four able-bodied workers had the ditch filled with two piles of rocks a bit wider than the width of the tires on the Mercedes. A short distance away, Nick practiced using the too-short crutches. As the sun set, Omar got in the driver's seat, ready to try the rock bridge.

"We're out of water and food," Hélène announced. "This better damn well work."

Omar and Danny stood at the side of the car surveying the situation. Just a touch of daylight remained.

"We've got one try," Danny said. "If the car falls into the ditch, we're not getting it out."

"No," Omar agreed.

"You can't accelerate while you're on the pile," Danny said, speaking with careful intensity. "Spinning the rear wheels will throw the rocks off. That said, the quicker you're over the better. Maybe back the car up and get a head of steam and try to coast over the rocks. It should work."

"From your lips to the gates of heaven," Omar said.

Danny stood at the far side of the ditch, equidistant between the two piles of rocks and waited. Omar backed up thirty feet, put the car in forward gear and lurched forward, trying to keep the center of the car in line with Danny.

Sophie and Nick watched as Hélène closed her eyes and crossed her fingers.

"He's going too fast," Sophie cried.

As the front tires hit the piles, Danny jumped out of the way. The rocks let out a strange, gut-crunching sound.

"Oh God," Hélène yelled, her eyes popping wide open.

The front tires cleared the opposite side easily just as both rock piles started to separate and crumble. Omar had speed on his side and kept his cool. The rear wheels hit the edge, bounced hard, then up. Omar timed the bounce and put the car in gear. The Mercedes leaped forward and over the edge and into safety.

Omar turned off the engine, and jumped out of the car, as the four observers shrieked with joy. Danny turned to Sophie and hugged her, perhaps a bit longer than a congratulatory hug. Sophie didn't pull away.

Hélène hugged Omar. "This erased all my thoughts of wanting to shoot you," she said.

Everyone laughed at Hélène's dark humor.

She then added, "For now."

"I'm guessing we have very little gas left," Omar said. "I think I can coast close to the bottom with the engine off so long as we encounter no more ditches. I pray we've enough gas to get across to the next set of hills."

Everyone settled in the car except Danny who would lead the way down on foot. By the time the Mercedes had reached the bottom, the sun was rising. The goat path had ended; no discernible path existed to the other side of the valley.

"The goatherd told me this valley is where his goats would graze. He knew nothing of the other side," Omar said. "But it appears to be flat."

"Do we try and get across now, or wait until tonight?" Nick asked.

"We're out of food and water," Hélène said. "Another full day and then we don't know what, or if, a path exists on the other side. I vote to press ahead now before we get too weak to walk. The Bosches haven't spotted us for two days, why will they look in the same place for a third?"

"Because they're vindictive assholes," Danny said. "If we're stuck in the middle of the valley because we have no gas, or an impassable ditch, swamp, or stream, the Krauts will have no difficulty killing all of us. We've come too far to let that happen."

"I'd say go now and not waste another twelve hours," Sophie said, looking at Danny beseechingly.

"You can go on without me if need be," Nick yelled through the open car window.

"That's not happening," Danny said. "We're all getting through."

"I agree," Sophie said. "All or none."

"Let's vote," Hélène said. "I for one want to push ahead."

"Stay 'til night," Danny said.

"Go," said Omar.

"Danny's gotten me this far, so I'll side with him," said Nick.

Everyone looked to Sophie. Sophie met everyone's eyes and shook her head softly. "Let's go. I'm already dehydrated and feeling weak."

Everyone entered the car as an edge of sun crested the eastern edge of the Atlas Mountains.

The Mercedes started with a pop and a plume of exhaust smoke. Omar put the car in gear and drove onto the valley floor. Every fifty yards or so, the rear of the car would sink into the soft sand. At a half-mile, the car's weight sunk so deeply that the rear wheels spun and the car burrowed further into the self-made rut.

"We're too heavy," Nick said. "We all need to get out."

The car emptied of everyone including Nick, who stood to the side as Danny, Sophie and Hélène pushed. The Mercedes rocked up then back, up and back. On the third try, the car exited the ditch and found level ground.

Everyone entered the car and off they went at a slow and steady rate. By nine a.m. they had crossed two-thirds of the valley.

"I think the ground is firmer now," Omar said. "I'm going to try increasing our speed."

Just as Omar delivered this good news, the five fugitives heard the muted roar of an airplane engine above the putter of the Mercedes. The sound increased steadily and fifteen seconds later, the distinctive roar of a lone Messerschmidt ME-109 passed over the car at two thousand feet above the valley floor.

Danny got out of the car and watched the German fighter rise above the valley floor and bank left around. Twenty seconds later the fighter flew at five hundred feet to get a better look at the Mercedes. The fighter rose again and banked right.

"Get out, he's coming back!" Danny yelled. "Get away from the car!"

Everyone jumped out as fast as they could. Nick fell to the ground and crawled as best he could manage away from the Mercedes. The first pass of the fighter left a trail of bullets starting thirty yards from the side of the Mercedes to thirty yards past it, scoring direct hits on the mid-chassis and demolishing the side windows, the left rear door and the roof of the car. The fighter rose and banked left, coming back for another pass as the fugitives scrambled even further from the car.

As the plane closed in, Nick and Danny prepared to empty their pistols in its direction. Suddenly, before it reached the Mercedes, the ME-109 banked hard right and rose.

"There," Nick yelled, "Behind the German, a P-38!"

Chasing the German fighter was an American Lockheed P-38 fighter. Its four cannons let loose a volley of 50 caliber bullets. The Messerschmidt, wanting no part of a dog fight, revved its engine and rose toward the southern peaks.

The P-38 followed the ME-109 then disappeared, returning a minute later. Danny and Nick held up their flight jackets and Omar, Sophie and Hélène waved with both hands. The P-38 flew over, tipped its wings, then banked right and disappeared to the north.

"Do you think he saw us?" Sophie asked.

"Definitely saw us, but has no idea who we are," Danny said. "The German saw us too and they could be back in numbers. We gotta get out of here."

Omar needed no prodding and jumped into the Mercedes, which miraculously started.

"There's glass everywhere but I think we need to push on," Omar yelled.

Everyone slid slowly over glass shards onto the seats of the Mercedes. Once all were seated, Omar pulled away. Only few hundred yards from the rise of the far side of the valley, the Mercedes sputtered, lurched, and died.

"Out of gas?" Danny asked.

"Afraid so," Omar said. "We got farther than I thought we would."

"Everybody out now. We walk," Danny said.

"Or hobble," Nick added.

"We're all together," Sophie said. "The Musketeers."

Nick looked at Sophie and mouthed, "Thanks."

The five fugitives exited the Mercedes and headed toward the hills to the north, hoping that Bou Chebka could be reached but uncertain how far or difficult that trek might be. Danny had the stolen German Mauser rifle over his shoulder, his .45 Colt on his belt and Gunther's Lugar in his pocket. Nick carried his own .45. As the sun began to set, the fugitives reached the edge of the far side of the valley, dehydrated and exhausted from walking through soft sand. They scanned for possible trails.

"Don't see where we'd go," Danny said.

"Nor I," Omar added. "Maybe we should rest a while ..."

Just then, the familiar sounds of unfriendly airplanes interrupted Omar's hopes. An ME-109 swooped into the valley, two more circling above as escorts and lookouts for enemy aircraft.

"Everyone find a rock or bush and don't move," Danny yelled.

Without hesitation, the fugitives scurried to the edge of the hills and hid behind plants and rocks. Nick used his crutches before realizing that hopping allowed him to move more quickly. From their hiding places, the five watched the ME-109 strafe the Mercedes repeatedly, even after it had rendered the automobile useless.

"There's no gasoline, so it won't explode," Danny yelled. "It's pissing that pilot off."

After the strafing, the ME-109 circled the valley, looking for the fugitives. The pilot did three runs over the valley and foothills, but didn't spot them. He exited to the southeast with his two watchdogs. When all seemed quiet, the fugitives came out of their cover to figure out their next steps.

Hélène, sitting on a rock, was looking back over Danny's shoulder to the opposite side of the valley and the mountain pass they'd already traversed, when she suddenly stood up and screamed," I see movement coming down the other side!"

Everyone turned. German soldiers and half-track vehicles were pouring down the mountain.

"We gotta move," Danny said. "Once they're down at

the bottom, those halftracks will come across the valley in thirty minutes."

"Which way?" Sophie asked.

"Right here is as good a guess as anywhere. If they've spotted us, we're cooked," Danny said.

With Danny and Omar helping Nick, the five moved up the mountainside around boulders, loose rocks, soft sand, and sagebrush. After an hour, darkness had set in.

"No flashlights," Nick yelled. "They'll spot us. They've spread out on the valley floor not knowing which way we've headed. In the morning, our footprints will give us away."

"Can we stay here?" Sophie asked.

Danny said, "I think so. We'll head out at first light."

"Danny's right," Nick said.

As nighttime set in, the temperature dropped to well below freezing. Despite the layers of clothing they wore, the cold, dehydration and lack of food affected Hélène and Sophie to the point that neither could stop shivering.

To make an intolerable situation worse, it started to snow.

"Safiyah, come here," Danny said, propped up against a rock.

"I'm okay," Sophie said.

"You're not, now come over here," Danny demanded.

Sophie didn't like Danny's tone and folded her arms.

"We had this discussion last night. In the clinic, in

no uncertain terms, you told us what to do," Danny said.

"You fought me," Sophie said.

"But in the end, I listened," Danny retorted. "You knew what you were doing. Out here, I know what to expect. I can't have you immobile because you have frostbite or your body temperature is too low. Come over here."

Sophie, reluctant, stood and walked over to Danny.

"Sit between my legs," Danny said.

Too weak to argue, Sophie did as she was told. Danny encircled her in his arms. Over Sophie's head scarf, he placed his USAAF B-2 flight cap with its leather outer cover and sheepskin inner layer. Danny folded the outside sheepskin flaps over her ears.

"I'm *so* cold," Sophie said, her teeth chattering.

Danny hugged Sophie tighter.

"Thank you," she said after a few minutes. "I'm warmer now. I'll listen. I'm sorry."

Danny smiled and continued to hug Sophie, who'd stopped shivering.

"Won't you be cold?" she asked.

"You're keeping me warm," Danny said.

"Please. Don't do that," Sophie said.

"I'll be fine." Danny said then turned to Omar and Hélène. "Hélène, don't argue. Omar, get Hélène in a bear hug and give her Nick's flight cap."

Nick extended his hat to Hélène, who moved into Omar's arms to mimic Danny and Sophie. When Sophie's head fell backward under Danny's chin, he knew she had found sleep. He thought of Columbus who said upon landing in Hispaniola, *'I claim this land for Ferdinand and Isabella of Spain.'* Would it be possible to stake a claim on a woman like Sophie? He had no idea how Sophie felt about him but hoped to find out. He whispered, "I claim you."

Within twenty minutes, all five fugitives had fallen asleep.

Sophie woke first. The sun sat just below the mountains to the east, but there was enough light to see. Danny's arms remained wrapped around her chest and his flight cap sat askew on her head. She slowly removed his arms, slid forward and stood up. She removed the flight cap and put it on Danny's head with the flaps down. She stood for a moment watching Danny and smiled.

Sophie looked down the mountain. She could see the Germans bivouacked below and starting to stir. Glowing campfires sat on the edge of the bivouac. As she stared, worry growing in her stomach, Danny approached and looked down the mountain over her shoulder.

"They're making breakfast. They won't move 'til everyone's eaten," Danny said.

Sophie nodded. "We best be moving, eh?"

"Yeah."

"Thanks for last night," Sophie said. "I was so cold."

"I know."

Sophie awakened Hélène and Omar while Danny got Nick up as the edge of sun cleared the mountains. With the sun out in a cloudless sky, the temperature rose to the mid-forties. The snow on the trail melted quickly.

"Hopefully, the melted snow will hide our tracks.

Let's see how far we can get," Danny said.

With nothing more to say and nothing to eat or drink, the five started to climb. Looking back, they could see the Germans dividing into multiple squads, each taking a different path up the mountain.

An hour later, Sophie and Nick had come close to a breaking point.

"I've got to stop for a few minutes," Sophie said.

"Me too," Nick said. His hands blistered to bleeding trying to use the ill-fitting crutches.

"Omar," Danny said. "If you want to keep going, be our guest. Sophie, against my better judgement, had you figured out pretty good. You're all right."

"Maybe I can find help," Omar said, shrugging.

"Maybe," Danny said. "Go."

With that, Omar headed up the hill at double pace and didn't look back.

After a few minutes, Sophie looked over to Nick. "Want to try?" She asked.

"Sure," Nick said.

"I wish I had something for your hands," she said.

Nick nodded. "I know." He then stood up with his crutches and took a step up the hill.

Sophie, Hélène and Danny followed.

Twenty minutes later, Sophie again reached her limit. "I can't move," she said, gasping for air and collapsing on the side of a large boulder. "I'm so sorry. I wanted to be stronger."

The group stopped.

Danny helped Sophie to the ground. He saw dry and cracked lips, sunken eyes, sadness and fear.

Danny turned away and started to cry.

Nick had lagged twenty yards behind throughout the ascent and had finally reached the limits of his strength as well. He sat down. The silence of the mountain allowed them to detect German voices below them.

Danny wiped the tears with his sleeve. “Might as well make our stand up there,” Danny said, pointing up the hill about fifteen yards. “I see some large rocks right and left of the path that will give us some cover. We’re not going to be able to outrun them.”

Everyone looked up the hill at two large boulders bracketing the path. Hélène, without being told, headed up.

“Can you manage another fifteen?” Danny asked Nick.

“Yes. You get Sophie,” Nick said.

Danny went down to Sophie and scooped her up in his arms. “Put your arms around my neck,” Danny said. Sophie, breathing heavily, complied without hesitation, then laid her head on Danny’s shoulders as he climbed.

“Thank you,” Sophie whispered.

As Hélène waited, Danny put Sophie down to the left of the path behind a huge boulder. Nick followed as quickly as he could on the crutches.

“Nick, you’ll be there,” Danny said, pointing to the boulder on the right of the path.

“I’m good,” he said, drawing his .45. He stood on one leg, looking over the boulder with his back against the hillside.

“Can I have the pistol?” Sophie asked.

Danny took the .45 pistol from his holster and

handed it to her. “The clip is loaded. You know how to use it and what to do. Don’t let them take either of you. Understood?”

“Understood,” Sophie said. Hélène nodded.

“As long as they’re talking loudly, they don’t know we’re here. When they do,” Danny said, “they’ll send men right and left to surround us. Keep watching our flanks.”

Using the massive boulder as protection, Danny climbed to the top with the German Mauser rifle and the SS colonel’s Lugar in his holster. He laid prone on the top of the boulder and aimed down the hill with the German rifle and kept the Lugar an arm‘s length away. Nick, ten feet lower, stood ready with his .45 Colt, balancing against one crutch. Sophie, her .45 held in both hands, sat below Danny’s boulder with Hélène, both looking right and left.

“We tried,” Hélène said. Sophie squeezed her shoulder.

“We’re still trying,” Sophie said. “Don’t give up.”

“If I’ve not said it often enough, I love you.”

“And I love you back, my only sister.”

Minutes later, Danny and Nick saw their first glimpses of German helmets climbing up the hill between rocks. A single German helmet, rifle at the ready, advanced until Danny could clearly see him from the waist up about thirty yards downhill. Danny took aim and fired one round, hitting the man in the chest and knocking him backward.

“Halt,” came the German yell.

The German voices stopped immediately.

“Keep looking right and left,” Danny whispered to the two women.

Sophie turned to her left and Hélène turned to her right and watched.

Moments later, something flew through the air toward Danny.

“Grenade!” Danny yelled.

Danny and Nick ducked, but the grenade fell far short, landing between the rocks fifteen yards below. The detonation raised dust and small rocks. A second grenade again fell short, with the same result.

Danny stared down the hill where he had shot the first German. Two shots sounded behind him as Sophie fired the .45 Colt to her left. He looked to see Sophie on her knees, the .45 in both hands.

“I ... saw ... a ... helmet,” Sophie stuttered. “It disappeared.”

“Keep looking.”

Nick fired his pistol twice, yelling, “Fifteen yards down. I don’t think I hit him.”

A voice from downhill cut through the air.

“*Erge Sie sich jetzt, sonst töten wir Sie.*”

“What did he say?” Danny asked.

“Surrender now or we will kill you,” Sophie replied.

“They’ll kill us anyway,” Danny said.

Hélène, looking the opposite way from Sophie, screamed, “Soldier there.”

Sophie spun around and saw a German soldier from the waist up, twenty yards away and slightly above them to the right, standing on a rock. He pulled the cord on a potato-masher-looking hand grenade and cocked his arm as Sophie, using both hands, brought her gun to chest level over Hélène’s shoulder. Before she fired, a short burst of gunfire erupted above them and blood exploded across the soldier's chest, throwing him backward. The grenade detonated harmlessly next to the fallen German.

Danny, wheeling his rifle toward the downed man, yelled, "Good shot."

"I didn't shoot," Sophie yelled.

"I didn't either," cried Nick.

"What? They killed their own guy?"

Just then, automatic gunfire erupted from above.

Danny screamed, "Get down."

The four fugitives ducked to the ground. Rock chips and dust flew in the air from the area where Danny had shot the first soldier. Danny raised his head and saw the German soldiers running pell-mell down the hill. Looking up the hill behind him, he saw five U.S. Army soldiers with automatic rifles firing intermittent bursts down the hill at the fleeing Germans. Between the soldiers, waving his arms, was Omar Sader.

"It's Omar with our guys!" shouted Danny.

Danny slid down the boulder to join the women. He hugged a smiling Hélène first. He then turned his head to Sophie, who was sobbing and struggling to breathe. He let go of Hélène and took the .45 Colt from Sophie's clammy, shaking hands and holstered it. He then wrapped his arms around her.

Danny pressed her head to his chest and planted a kiss on her temple. "You're safe now. Everything will be okay."

"I've been so scared for so long," Sophie said, her chest heaving. "... ever since that German colonel ... came to the clinic. I couldn't breathe ... and I couldn't tell anyone ... how I felt."

"I'm here now," Danny said.

“I’m not so tough,” Sophie whispered. “Thank you for getting us through.”

Sophie continued to hug Danny and he kissed her temple once more.

Together, they watched as a tall, handsome, chiseled U.S. Army lieutenant, Richard ‘Dickie’ Port, strides down to greet the fugitives with Omar and five infantrymen trailing. Three other men in Port’s squad remained above with automatic weapons pointing down the hill.

Danny released Sophie and opened the SS overcoat to reveal his USAAF jacket. He turned to Lieutenant Port and received a salute as Sophie moved to hug Omar and Hélène.

“Captain. Good to see you,” Port said. “Lieutenant Dickie Port from Uniontown, Pennsylvania, at your service.”

“Daniel Booker, Intelligence. You saved our bacon.”

“Hope so, but I think we need to get back down the other side as soon as we can,” Port said. “They could come back up with more guys.”

“I’ve got a wounded co-pilot, Lieutenant Pascavage,” Danny said, pointing to Nick, now standing on his one leg against the rock that had protected him.

“We’ll get him down,” Port said. “How’d that happen?”

“In a Grasshopper doing recon for Fredendall in Kasserine Pass, a week ago. An ME-109 shot us down. Bullet tore Nick’s leg apart. We crashed outside Fériana and I carried Nick into town. We found these two, Sophie and Hélène, in a women’s clinic.”

“With Krauts everywhere?” Port asked.

“Yeah, but it was pitch dark,” Danny said. “The

women hid us in a secret room off a root cellar."

"Who took his leg off?" Port asked.

Danny pointed to Sophie. "She did, at night, under a lantern. Fuckin' amazing."

"No shit," Port said. "There's a story. We need to get him back to base and have our surgeons see to him."

"How'd you find us?" Danny asked.

"A P-38 coming back from a run over Thélepte yesterday saw you guys being strafed by a Kraut One-Oh-Nine down in the valley. He had no idea who you were but assumed the Krauts didn't like you, so we must. We're in the Big Red One with General Allen holding Bou Chebka on the other side of the pass. He sent squads out looking and we ran into Omar here running down the mountain. Lucky we didn't shoot him."

"I'm gonna buy that P-38 pilot a jug of whiskey and another for you guys in the 1st," Danny said.

Port turned to two infantrymen and pointed to Nick. They understood exactly what to do.

Sophie approached Port with Hélène trailing. "Do you have any water?" Sophie asked. "It's been a couple of days."

Port took a canteen off his hip and handed it to her. She gulped half the canteen, then gave it to Hélène who finished it off. Danny and Nick drained other infantrymen's canteens.

"Let's move out," Port yelled. "Ladies first."

The two remaining infantrymen shouldered their rifles and aided Sophie and Hélène by the arm following Lieutenant Port up the hill.

Chapter Twenty-Two

Atlas Mountains
February 1943

The fugitives and the infantrymen reached the summit of the second hill and had started down. They could see Bou Chebka in the distance. Walking with Lieutenant Port, Danny asked, “Been out of it for a week. What’s happening?”

“They beat the shit out of us in Kasserine Pass, just like they did in Faid and Sidi Bou Zid. After that, I ‘spose they thought they’d drive us all the way back to Kansas. But Big Red with the help of the Brits, some Frenchies and General Robinett in the First Armored stopped ‘em cold, then kicked some Nazi ass real bad at a place called Djebel. They’re licking their wounds now and hightailing it back toward Tunis.”

Danny smiled. “Good news for a change.”

Sophie, feeling much restored after water and two chocolate bars, caught up to Danny and Port.

“Feeling better?” Danny asked.

“Oh yes,” Sophie said. “Can I keep you two company ‘til we get where we’re going?”

“Didn’t have to ask,” Danny said.

When Port went back to relieve one of the men helping Nick, Danny took Sophie’s hand and held it the rest of the way down the hill.

Danny, Sophie, and Hélène sat in front of General Terry Allen, the Commanding Officer of the First Infantry. With him were four others: Allen's chief of staff, a captain from the intelligence group, Lieutenant Port, and a stenographer. Danny, Sophie and Hélène had eaten but remained, unbathed, in their clothes from Fériana.

Allen, a thin, tall, angular man in his mid-fifties, listened to Danny explain his mission and the aftermath.

"You may be the luckiest son-of-a-bitch I've ever met, Captain," Allen said.

"Not one of the luckiest, Sir, the luckiest," Danny said.

Allen laughed. Allen then turned to Sophie and Hélène.

"Sophie and Hélène deserve all the credit," Danny added. "They risked everything for us without hesitation."

"Which one of your fixed the Captain's arm and amputated Lieutenant Pascavage's leg?" Allen asked.

"I did," Sophie said.

"And you're ... midwives?" Allen asked.

"Hélène is," Sophie said. "I was a surgeon in the French Army in 1940 when the Bosches invaded Belgium and Holland. I went to medical school in Strasbourg."

"Where'd you learn to speak English?" Allen asked.

"Michigan while my dad did surgical training," Sophie said.

"Are there many female surgeons in the French

army?" Allen asked.

"No, sir. A bit of a story. My father, also a surgeon, and I were merely touring the medical facilities on the Maginot Line near Verdun when the war broke out. The French were missing more than half their medical team and the general, a General Leveque, asked my father and me to stay and help. We stayed until it was obvious that the French would lose."

"Where's your father now?" Allen continued.

"He died," Sophie said with difficulty. "He tried to return to Metz to gather valuables before heading south. When he returned home, our office had already been desecrated with Jewish stars by local French antisemites. Dad was arrested at his office by the Nazis who were waiting for him. When he tried to run, they murdered him. I had already fled to the south of France. When the Nazis came south, I headed to Tunisia."

"Sorry for your loss," Allen said. "You're Jewish? Why the Arab outfit?"

"When in Rome," Sophie said with a shrug.

Allen laughed again.

Just then, Nick Pascavage and Colonel James 'Jimmy' Gaspar, M.D., head of the 1st Infantry's Medical Corp, entered the room.

Nick stood in front of General Allen on a new pair of crutches and saluted, as did Gaspar.

"Have a seat, Lieutenant," Allen said.

Nick took a seat next to Hélène.

"Jimmy," Allen said looking at his notes, "This is Captain Booker of the AAF, Dr. Safiyah Shaloub, and midwife Hélène Al-Hadef."

Gaspar tipped his hat to the women.

"How's Lieutenant Pascavage doing?" Allen asked.

"Lucky as hell," Gaspar said. "He said the lady here took his leg using lanterns for light with the help of a midwife. His wounds are healing nicely. Looks like a pro did it."

"I am a pro," Sophie said.

"Jimmy," Allen said, "Dr. Shaloub was a surgeon with French Army in Belgium in '40 when the Krauts invaded. Got out by escaping to Tunisia."

"Still, she's got to be a magician. Surgery in the dark, assisted by a midwife, and Captain Booker here doing the anesthesia with a dislocated arm."

"No, not a magician," Danny said. "She's an incredible surgeon."

"Agreed," Gaspar said.

"Amazing saga," Allen said. "I'm guessing, they'll need a shower, some grub, and a good night's sleep."

"Thank you, General," Sophie said. "Maybe some clothes too."

"Doc," Gaspar said, "I like you to tour our medical facilities when you have a chance. People are already talking about you. They're calling you the 'Angel of North Africa.'"

"I'm no angel," Sophie said.

"Actually, she is," Danny said.

"Stop it," Sophie said, with a shake of her head.

"Tomorrow," Allen said, "Intel will formally debrief you four and your interpreter. Then we'll ship Lieutenant Pascavage back stateside with a Purple Heart."

That night, after a shower and a small meal, Sophie

and Hélène slept for twelve hours in the nurse's quarters. The nurses loaned them clothes and toiletries. Sophie had lost seven pounds and Hélène eleven.

At lunch the next day, Hélène and Sophie sat alone in the mess area.

"Did you know I told Danny to leave you alone more than once?" Hélène said.

"You did?"

"He kept staring at you like a puppy. I told him to stop. You had too much on your mind. He still did it."

"He got us through," Sophie said. "For that we'll always be grateful."

"That he did. But unless I'm reading the tea leaves wrong, he wants more."

"Oh, come on," Sophie said. "He's probably got a girl back home."

"He might have once," Hélène said, "but not anymore. Trust me, now he's only got eyes for you."

Sophie looked down at her food to hide a smile.

That day and night, the military intelligence officers grilled Sophie and Hélène about anything and everything they had seen from the time the Germans arrived in Fériana. After evening mess, Sophie told Hélène she wanted to see Nick, but she actually wanted to see Danny. She headed for the medical tents.

Arriving at the medical facilities, a private with a log book gave Sophie directions to Nick's tent.

"Tent 4, Bed 6," the private said.

As Sophie turned to head off to see Nick, the private asked, "You that 'angel doctor' that saved the lieutenant after he crashed?"

"I suppose I am," Sophie said.

"You're a hero to all of us, ma'am," the private said. "We all hope you stay with the First. Need all the help we can git."

"Thank you, Private. I might just do that."

"Lieutenant's probably getting flown out tomorrow afternoon," the private said. "Casablanca, then ship home. I think a Captain Booker is with him now. Came by twenty minutes ago." He then stood stiff, shoulders back, and gave Sophie a formal salute. Sophie saluted back, then ran to look for Nick's tent.

Six beds in the eight-man tent held injured soldiers. Nick lay in far bed with Danny sitting on a stool at the bedside. Nick saw Sophie first and announced to the tent, "Ten-hut. Here she is, the 'Angel of North Africa!'"

Danny turned around, stood and smiled as three of the injured men sat up to better see Sophie. Two others, too injured to move, only lifted their heads. Sophie had no choice but to spend a moment with each of the injured men individually, which she did with a smile. One of the men, a young private from Sioux Falls, South Dakota with burns to his chest and neck, became tongue-tied and could barely speak to her. He whispered something and Sophie leaned over and kissed him on the cheek. He started to cry.

Danny stood and stared at her the entire time she rounded. Eventually she made it to Nick's bed on the opposite side from where Danny stood. Only then did the man from South Dakota yell through his tears, "An angel kissed me. I'm gonna be okay."

"Doing okay?" Sophie asked Nick as she held his hand.

"No discomfort at all," Nick replied. "Just wished I

had a leg. But I'm alive."

Sophie turned to Danny. "Where've you been?"

"Same as you," Danny said, "Intel had me until thirty minutes ago. They'll grill Omar for a week."

"Hélène and I missed you at dinner."

"Didn't know we had a date."

"Just saying."

"Sit here. I'll get another stool," Danny said.

Sophie came around the bed and sat on the now vacant stool next to Nick as Danny went searching for a folding chair or stool.

"No damn chairs here," Danny yelled, darting out of the tent.

"Off tomorrow, I hear?" Sophie asked.

"Yeah. First boat back home leaves from Casablanca," Nick said.

"Can I look at the stump?"

"Who else but you? The docs here are impressed as hell with your technique. No one could believe it. Thanks again."

"You're welcome."

Sophie pulled back the covers. Nick's stump rested on a pillow, undressed and looking clean and healthy.

"I'd leave the sutures in for another week," Sophie said, smiling at her work. "For now, keep it elevated as much as you can. Six to eight weeks before you should be fitted for a prosthesis."

"I've gotta tell you something before Danny returns," Nick said.

"Okay."

"He's in love with you."

“Please.” Sophie scoffed at the suggestion. “How do you know?”

“He told me on the walk down the hill after we were rescued and again ten minutes ago. He doesn’t know how to read you.”

“That’s good. I don’t know how to read me. I’m still processing everything I’ve been through, which started long before you knocked on our door,” Sophie said.

“Don’t hurt him too badly. He’s a good guy, kept you warm, and got us through.”

“That he did. We all owe him for that.” Sophie trembled slightly as Danny re-entered the tent with a folding chair.

The next morning, Colonel Gaspar gave Sophie and Hélène a tour of the medical facilities. Both Sophie and Hélène wore borrowed nurse’s uniforms. By this time, the legend of the ‘Angel of North Africa’ had spread to everyone: doctors, medics, nurses, technicians and patients. They were just nearing Gaspar’s office when Danny ran over, saluting Colonel Gaspar and facing Sophie.

“What are you doing today?” he asked, slightly out of breath.

“Just finished a tour of the facilities,” Sophie said, unable to fully repress a smile at seeing Danny. “We were just wondering how Hélène and I could best help.”

“I pulled strings,” Danny said, “until they agreed to let you and me escort Nick to Casablanca, transfer him to medical, then enjoy a few of days of R and R. You’re the air transfer doc and I’m co-pilot.”

A look of bewilderment crossed Sophie’s face.

“Uh ... Hélène, too?” she asked.

Danny looked down, at a loss for words. “No. Just us.”

Sophie glanced at Hélène to judge her feelings.

“I hate planes. They scare me,” Hélène said. “Man wasn’t meant to fly. You guys go.”

“Really?” Sophie asked.

Hélène winked, then resumed a serious face. “Yes. Really.”

Sophie turned to Danny. “When would we leave?”

“An hour ago. They’re holding Nick in an ambulance at the airbase. They’ll give us thirty minutes to pack.”

“Uh, I don’t know,” Sophie said, hesitating.

“Go, damn it,” Hélène said. “You could use a little holiday.”

Sophie turned back to Danny and nodded yes. He grabbed her hand and together they ran out of the office.

Gaspar looked at Hélène and asked, “Are you really afraid of airplanes?”

Hélène smiled and said, “Absolutely not and she knows it.”

“I wouldn’t have thought so,” Gaspar laughed.

“You know, I’ve seen her in the operating theater with blood and guts going in every direction,” Hélène said. “She makes decisions in a second, without hesitation. When it comes to emotional stuff, she’s stuck in the mud. She keeps scaring men off.”

“She is impressive,” Gaspar said.

“That she is.”

“They good together?” Gaspar asked.

“Oh, very good,” Hélène said.

Chapter Twenty-Three

Morocco
March 1943

A team of medics loaded a dozen injured soldiers, including Nick, into the cargo bay of a C-47 transport plane, affectionately nicknamed the 'Gooneybird' by the Americans. The inside reminded Sophie of childhood pictures of Jonah inside the whale's cavernous stomach. She laughed at herself, realizing that from the inside of any stomach, one wouldn't see the ribs. The C-47 structural ribs were in clear view and ran the gamut, nose to tail, of the aircraft.

Three of the injured men remained on stretchers. Two of the three had intravenous fluids running. The twelve-hundred-mile flight to an airfield outside Morocco's capital would take seven hours. Sophie, as was her position, examined each wounded soldier.

After takeoff and before his co-piloting duties started, Danny came back to talk, but actually yell, to the injured soldiers. The thin skin of the C-47 made the engine noise close to oppressive.

Each of the men enjoyed Danny's presence and some had already heard of Sophie's reputation. Sophie stood back and watched until he'd finished talking to each soldier.

Halfway through the flight, Danny and the pilot switched places. The pilot came back to talk to the men as well. He told Sophie to head up to the cockpit and join Danny.

"Ever flown a plane?" Danny asked, as Sophie sat in the vacated pilot's seat.

"You know I haven't," Sophie said.

"Didn't stop you from asking me to give Nick's anesthesia."

"Different," Sophie said.

"Not really. Grab the yoke, that's the steering wheel."

Sophie put her hands on the vibrating yoke. Danny released his grip on the copilot's yoke.

"The plane is yours, Captain Shaloub," Danny said. "The panel in front of you shows everything you could imagine – airspeed, altitude, compass, pitch, yaw, yadda yadda."

"Huh?" Sophie asked. "Pitch and yaw?"

"Pitch is up and down; yaw is right and left. We've got jargon too."

Sophie smiled and nodded.

"Thanks. Something new. My real name is Sophie Sollar, by the way. Not Safiya Shaloub."

"Hélène had told me it's Sophie but thought I should still call you Saifyah. Why the different name?"

"Sophie's uncle thought an Arabic name would be a better disguise in Tunisia. Shaloub was my mother's maiden name. Safiyah is the equivalent of Sophie."

"Sophie Sollar?"

"Yes. I'd like you to call me Sophie."

"Aye, aye, Captain. I love it. Although Safiyah Shaloub did sound exotic and mysterious to a Michigander." Danny drew "Sa-fi-yah Sha-loub" out in long syllables.

"It did, didn't it," Sophie said with a little laugh. She pulled the yoke a little to the right and the plane banked. "Wow, this is so amazing." She pulled the yoke to left and leveled the plane, laughing. She had a smile from ear to ear. There was a strange new feeling of freedom inside her. Then the plane began to shake.

"What's happening? Did I do something?" Sophie cried out.

Danny grabbed his yoke as Sophie let go of hers, panic written on her face.

"You did nothing wrong. It's just turbulence," Danny said. "It'll pass. Put your hands back on the yoke and don't faint."

Sophie laughed, regrabbed the yoke, and a moment later, the turbulence subsided, and the concentration on Danny's face melted into a smile.

"See. All smooth," Danny said. "I'd never let anything happen to you."

"I'm sorry," Sophie said. "I feel like I'm always on edge. I want to apologize for how short I've been with you."

Danny shrugged, waiting for her to go on.

"I was so scared by that Bosch SS officer who threatened Hélène and me. When you knocked on our door, I thought it was him. Then with you and Nick in the cellar, I thought the Bosches would find you and kill all of us. During the escape, I didn't think we'd make it to the American base. I was in a never-ending, multi-chapter, revolving nightmare."

"It makes sense," Danny said.

"Adding to that was running from the Nazis through France and my father being murdered."

“I can’t even imagine. I was scared after the crash,” Danny said. “Certain we’d be caught and Nick would die. After you took care of us, all I could think of was how I needed to get you and Hélène delivered safely.”

“I know you did. I felt it and if I seemed ungrateful, I didn’t mean it. If we have time, I’ll try to make it up to you somehow,” Sophie said.

“Do you have any idea how I feel about you?”

“I have a good idea. Hélène and Nick clued me in.”

“I can’t slow down,” Danny said.

“Then I’ll have to go fast,” Sophie replied, looking at Danny with a big smile.

“Was it hard leaving Hélène back there?”

“Of course. We’ve been through everything together, like sisters. But she knew you liked me and told me so constantly. I think she’s happy that we’re off together. I know for a fact that she’s not afraid to fly.”

Danny laughed. “She’s not jealous? I’d be.”

“Hélène never talks about men. I don’t think she’s ever had a serious boyfriend. She will I guess, when she meets the right guy.”

“And you’ve had tons of boyfriends?” Danny asked.

“And you have a fiancé back home?” Sophie countered. “Sometimes, less is more.”

“Touché,” Danny said, slinking down in his seat. “No. I don’t.”

“I’ve had boyfriends but I tend to scare them away,” Sophie admitted. “I wish I didn’t.”

“You don’t scare me at all. I’m in awe of you. I’ve never felt that way.”

Sophie looked at Danny. He was smiling while looking aimlessly out at the horizon. She knew he was being honest.

The pilot returned and Sophie got out of his seat. As she departed, she said, “Thanks for the flying lesson,” and kissed Danny on the cheek.

“In your unit,” said the pilot, staring straight ahead, “do all the co-pilots get kissed by the passengers?”

“They do,” Danny said, which started both laughing.

There were ambulances already lined up on the tarmac to transport the injured soldiers to the U.S. Army medical facility north of Casablanca. A jeep took Sophie and Danny to the nearby army base, where they stowed their gear in the Bachelor’s Office Quarters. There was one for women, all nurses, and another for the men.

The next morning, Danny visited the U. S. Army Hospital facility to determine his return-to-duty date, thanks to his dislocated shoulder. The doctor told Danny he could return to desk duty at any time, but would be unable to pilot for another four weeks. Danny told the evaluating doctor about the saga in Fériana and added that he had come with Sophie to see Nick off.

“She mean something to you?” the doctor asked.

“Yes. Very much so.”

“How about another two weeks before you report back to Intel?”

That afternoon, Sophie and Danny accompanied Nick to the U.S. Navy Hospital ship for his trip back to the Washington Navy Yard. From there, he would go to Walter Reed Army Hospital in Washington D.C.

Nick demanded to walk up the ramp with his new

crutches. Before boarding, he gave Danny a hug and whispered, “Thanks and good luck. She’s a winner.”

Danny whispered back, “I know, and I know you’re going to be just fine. When I get back stateside, I’ll come to visit first thing. That’s a promise.”

Nick turned to Sophie, as tears welled up in both their eyes. “Thank you for saving my life. I won’t forget you. Say thanks again to Hélène for me.”

“I will,” Sophie said, sniffling.

When Nick reached the top, he waved, turned and disappeared.

“When do you have to go back?” Sophie asked, still looking at the ship.

“Doc said two weeks,” Danny said, “but I’m grounded for a month because of my shoulder.”

“I thought we’d be leaving tomorrow or the day after,” Sophie said, a bit confused. After a moment of thought, she added, “But I’m up for anything.”

“I told the doc about the Fériana saga. He said you and I earned two weeks of R and R. I’d like to see a bit of Morocco. There’s supposed to be some amazing spas and sights in Marrakesh. Will you come?”

“I don’t have any civilian clothes.”

“I do. But for you, we start by shopping here in Casablanca where they have everything you’d ever want.”

“I don’t have money either,” Sophie said, still hesitating.

“Not a problem.”

Sophie smiled and as they walked away, she slid her arm through Danny’s.

“Catching up,” she said. She stopped and took

Danny's hands, pulling both behind her back until they were face to face. Danny could do nothing else but kiss her as she wrapped her arms around his neck.

"Where am I now?" she whispered.

"Way ahead," Danny said.

Sophie laughed.

They walked off hand in hand.

Danny and Sophie went shopping in Casablanca. The second shopkeeper claimed that she had all the latest designs from Paris as of 1940. When she and two assistants came out with handfuls of dresses and laid them out on couches, seat and tables, Sophie started laughing.

"What's so funny?" Danny asked.

"When I was thirteen or fourteen, my friend Marie's mother came back from Paris with all the new fashions. Marie and I and some other mischief makers had the dresses all over her mother's bedroom like this." Sophie spread both hands around and continued, "We put on our own fashion show. We got into so much trouble but my father rescued me from mother's wrath."

Sophie stopped smiling as she thought about her parents. Danny sensed her change in thought and enveloped her in a hug.

"I so would have loved to meet your parents," Danny said, "just to tell them that together they created perfection."

"Thank you," Sophie said. When the smile returned, she started holding up dresses against a mirror.

With a good deal of bargaining, Sophie purchased knockoffs of an Elsa Schiaparelli evening dress and a Madeleine Vionnet Grecian style silk bias cut evening gown.

Danny tried to kiss Sophie outside the third dress shop, but a Moroccan policeman rushed up to scold him. Sophie translated the policeman's rants (public displays of affection were inappropriate in Morocco) and apologized until he went on his way, grumbling. Sophie and Danny laughed together; they were too happy to mind. They headed to the Ancienne Medina to shop for gifts of tobacco, wood ornaments, lanterns, and traditional kaftans.

Exhausted and loaded down with purchases, they found a taxi back to the Army base just as the day drew to a close. Before they separated in the direction of their quarters, Danny took Sophie's hand.

"Would I be crazy to suggest moving out of the BOQ?" Danny asked.

"*What*? Honestly? You want me to stay in a hotel with you?"

Disheartened by her response, Danny didn't answer. Sophie giggled and squeezed his hand.

"I'm teasing you. Yes, let's. We both could have been killed more than once in the past ten days. I'm not depriving myself any more. I don't want to miss another day waiting because ..." Sophie hesitated. "I might have already found what I'm looking for."

Danny smiled and scanned the area. "No Moroccan police." He held Sophie's face in his hands and kissed her.

That night, Sophie and Danny checked into the Anfa Hotel where Roosevelt and Churchill had met in January to plan the war. Danny registered them as Mr. and Mrs. Daniel Booker. The hotel clerk looked at Danny's and Sophie's bare left ring fingers and silently shook his head longer than necessary to get the point across.

As they rode the elevator up, Sophie, a bit upset, said, “Did you see the look on the clerk’s face when he saw we didn’t have wedding rings?”

“I did. Something I’ll fix tomorrow,” Danny said. “Promise.”

Upon entering the suite, both plopped on the bed, exhausted.

“I need a shower so badly,” Danny said.

From the room, Danny made a reservation for dinner in the hotel restaurant. Sophie removed her shoes but lay fully dressed on the bed with her eyes closed. Danny kissed Sophie, then walked into the suite-sized bathroom and turned on the hot water to let the room steam up. The massive, doorless shower had a ten-foot ceiling and hand-painted Moroccan tiles. There was a built-in, tiled bench at a distance from three modern showerheads, including another ‘waterfall’ head on the roof of the shower. Danny turned on all four spigots then stood under them for a delicious moment, marveling at the uber-luxurious surroundings. A heavy, chrome, towel shelf sat on the wall above the bench. On top of the shelf sat a stack of plush Egyptian cotton towels.

As Danny submitted to the rush of water, Sophie walked in quietly behind him.

“This shower is bigger than our bedroom in Fériana,” she said.

Danny spun around but could say nothing, overwhelmed by the sight of her. He slid his hands gently over her bare shoulders, her breasts, and wrapped his arms around her waist, moving her under the falling water. Both felt the warming rush.

“Is it terrible that I’ve undressed you a thousand

times in my mind?" Danny murmured.

Sophie smiled and shook her head and mouthed "No."

He held her face in his hands and touched his lips to every inch of her face. They kissed deeply. She turned, her back to Danny.

"Hold me tight like you did on the mountain."

Danny encircled her in his arms and squeezed as he kissed her neck and let his tongue roam in and around her ear.

Sophie turned back to take in Danny's hard, subtly muscular physique. Using her left palm, she rubbed his upper chest over a smattering of fine light-brown hair while her right hand held softly onto his firmness.

"I'm sorry," Sophie said.

"For what?"

"I seem to have difficulty showing how I feel. When you kept me warm that night, I prayed that we'd be safe in the end to do this. If only once."

Sophie let go of his erection, put both hands on his buttocks and pulled him to herself so that his erection lay flat on her abdomen. She then put her head on his chest and moved slowly up, down, right and left.

"How far ahead am I now?" Sophie purred.

"Light years," Danny said. "Do you have any idea how beautiful you are?"

He tilted one of the shower heads to hit the wall beneath the towel rack. He surprised her by effortlessly lifting her onto the bench, so that his face was level with her breasts. The wet, tiled bench angled downward but she stabilized herself by grabbing the towel rack above her head. Danny caressed each breast softly with his tongue, until her nipples stiffened. Her breathing became short, staccato wisps.

Danny knelt on the shower floor and his hands moved down to her hips. His head urged her thighs apart and his tongue explored the delicate bead he found there. Sophie's breathing became heavy, intermixed with a whispering, raspy, "Oh, Danny." Finally, Sophie let go of the towel rack and grabbed the back of his head with both hands and pulled him harder into her until her body shook to its core.

"I want you inside me now," Sophie purred, still breathing heavily.

Danny grabbed Sophie by the waist again, pulled her off the bench, and pressed her against the shower wall. She wrapped her legs around his abdomen. Danny entered her and rocked her gently against the warm tiles until he released two weeks of dreams. As he softened, he let Sophie slide slowly to the shower floor. Grabbing her face again, he kissed her eyes, nose and mouth softly.

"That was intense," he said.

"You passed me again," Sophie said, still breathing rapidly. "We French have it wrong about American men."

They used soap to wash each other's bodies, laughing for no apparent reason other than the joy of the moment. When the shower started growing cool as the hotel's water heaters emptied, they towel-dried each other, snuck back into the darkened hotel room, and slid under the covers of the bed. Danny, already semi-erect, started caressing Sophie's earlobes with his tongue. The night went on.

Danny and Sophie never made it to their dinner reservation, but awoke at three a.m. and feasted on the box of Moroccan chocolates and dried fruits they had purchased as a gift for Dr. Gaspar.

At nine a.m., Sophie woke again and turned to find Danny on his elbow, looking at her. "How long have you been awake?"

"'Bout a half hour," he said, "I've been staring at you. It's my new favorite hobby."

"Oh, please."

Danny reached over and pushed the hair off Sophie's face. He took a dangling lock of hair and twirled it for a few seconds. He then slid toward Sophie and kissed her on the forehead and then the lips. He slid back but kept staring.

"My father used to twirl my hair like that," Sophie said.

"You must miss him."

"More that you'll ever know."

"I'm sorry you lost him."

After a brief moment, Sophie began dangling her left hand and fingers in front of Danny's face. "What do we do about not having a wedding ring."

Danny laughed. "There's time to fix it. The coach to Marrakech doesn't leave until one p.m."

"Fix it?"

"I'm going to buy you a wedding ring."

"You haven't asked me to marry you yet," Sophie said.

"I might by the end of the week."

"Isn't that the wrong order of things?" Sophie said. "And how do you know I'll say yes? Besides, I'm a terrible cook and a know-it-all. I'd be an insufferable wife. Your family would despise me. Why would anyone want to marry me?"

"I swear I don't care about any of that. I know the

hours you keep and the responsibilities you'll shoulder to practice medicine. If I ask and you don't agree to marry me, I'll turn myself in to the Krauts."

When Mr. and Mrs. Daniel Booker registered at the La Mamounia Hotel, Resort, and Spa in Marrakech that night, Sophie had a faux diamond on her left ring finger with a matching band and Danny sported a thin gold wedding band. She wagged it ostentatiously at check in, eliciting smiles from both desk clerks. Despite the myriad attractions in Marrakech, Sophie and Danny spent most of the first two days and nights in bed or in the private hammam, their private Turkish bath and steam room.

On the third morning, Sophie held up two of the dresses they'd purchased in Casablanca.

"You bought me all these fabulous dresses and I've worn none of them," she lamented with a smile.

"You've worn little of anything," Danny laughed.

"Very funny." She made a face at him. "Today we're going exploring."

They found time to walk the alleys of the Mellah, Marrakech's sixteenth century Jewish quarter. Outside the Slat Al Azama Synagogue, Danny stopped a man who happened to be one of the rabbis. Sophie translated for him, talking the rabbi into a private tour of the synagogue with its exquisite mosaic tilework. After the short tour, and a donation, the rabbi blessed their marriage. On the walk back to the hotel, Sophie laughed that they'd need to atone for their lies to the rabbi.

After three days of a planned six-day stay, Danny and Sophie sat in the hotel restaurant having a sumptuous breakfast of fresh coffee, croissants, and cheese omelets.

"I need to say something which might upset you," Danny said.

All merriment vanished from Sophie's face in an instant.

"What?"

"It's nothing like that. I feel guilty because a thousand miles to the east, the war goes on. Our men are fighting and dying and I could be helping. We're sitting in this magnificent restaurant, dining like Roman royalty, seemingly without a care in the world."

At that moment, a waiter in a tuxedo came to the table and without asking, refilled both their coffee cups.

"Is there anything else I can bring you?" the waiter asked.

Danny looked at Sophie who shook her head.

Danny said, "No, thank you."

The waiter smiled and left.

"See what I mean," Danny said.

"What, you don't have tuxedoed waiters in your mess tent?" Sophie asked.

Danny started to laugh and Sophie followed, then her face became sober.

"Honestly, I've thought the same. Men are getting injured and I could be helping. I swore after learning of my father's murder by the Nazis, that I'd help defeat them."

"You won't regret cutting our holiday short?"

"We'll both regret it more if we stay," Sophie said. "Let's head back to Casablanca and find a plane to the front. Besides, we left Hélène behind and I worry about her. I thought we'd be gone only a few days."

The next day, they took a coach back to Casablanca and stayed at a hotel nearer the U.S. Army Base. Danny went to the air control desk and found a plane leaving in thirty hours to the Thélepte Airfield, now occupied by the Allies who had pushed the Germans north toward Tunis. For their last night in Casablanca, Sophie opted for a French restaurant that offered bouillabaisse Marseille.

"Midwesterners don't eat fish soup, ever," Danny said.

"Your loss then," Sophie replied. "Finally, something we disagree on. You'll have to adapt."

Both laughed. Sophie ordered soup. Danny ordered a steak.

After dinner, Danny took Sophie's hands from across the table. "It's our last night. I need my rings back, if you don't mind."

"I thought they were mine to keep?" Sophie pouted.

"Nope, they're mine," Danny said, holding out an open hand.

"You're keeping your ring on. Not fair," Sophie complained.

Danny slid his ring off, placed it on the table, and held his hand out toward Sophie. Sophie reluctantly slid off her faux-diamond ring and band and placed it on the table in front of her, unwilling to put it in Danny's hand. Danny left the rings sitting between them.

"Do you know Elizabeth Browning, the English poet?" Danny asked.

"I know the name."

"I'm not a poet, but she wrote what I feel, 'I love you not only for what you are, but for what I am with you.'"

“That’s beautiful.”

Danny picked the Sophie’s faux-diamond ring up from the table, came around, and took a knee in front of Sophie. Sophie’s hand went to her mouth.

“I can’t imagine loving you more than I do today, but I know, with the certainty of an army intelligence officer, that I’ll love you more tomorrow. My heart is in your hands. Will you marry me?”

“When?” Sophie asked.

“Tomorrow. There are ten synagogues in Casablanca. Someone will marry us.”

“It’s wartime, is it wise?”

“War and wise don’t belong in the same sentence. I need to know you’re mine forever. You set the terms. Any place you want to go, I’ll go there with you,” Danny said.

“Then, yes,” Sophie said, breaking into happy tears. “Let’s.”

“I was worried you wouldn’t agree.”

“You could have asked me three days ago and I would have answered the same.” Her comment brought a huge smile to Danny. Sophie might not have said yes three days earlier, but she knew the happiness it provided Danny was well worth it.

Danny put the ring back on Sophie’s finger and kissed her hand as the waiter hovered near to the table, befuddled by the strange American ritual he’d just witnessed.

The next morning, Sophie and Danny scoured the synagogues of Casablanca.

The Ettedgui Synagogue, accidently bombed at the beginning of Operation Torch when the U.S. Army landed in Morocco, needed donations. The rabbi spent most of his time trying to raise money to rebuild the damaged temple. Danny offered him three thousand French francs. For that exorbitant sum, Rabbi Menashe agreed to marry them, provide witnesses and a hand-written ketubah, which he would mail to the couple. Danny offered an extra thousand francs if he could ready the ketubah in four hours.

In a musty, rabbi's office, with shattered windows from errant Allied shelling, and two complete strangers as witnesses, Rabbi Menashe married Danny and Sophie. In Sephardic custom, Menashe wrapped the couple in a prayer shawl during the ceremony rather than the European custom of a canopy or 'chuppah.'

When Sophie followed Danny onto the C-47 that night, they each wore wedding bands.

As she settled on the plane, Sophie's thoughts turned to Hélène. She knew that her cousin would find some form of work with the Medical Corps. But the recent victories by the Allies meant the medical facilities could be anywhere within a hundred-mile radius. The only person who knew Hélène by name was Colonel Gaspar. Danny's attempts to reach Gaspar in person from the Army communication's center in Casablanca had proved fruitless. They left messages for Gaspar about their arrival.

"First thing we do," Danny said, sensing her worry, "is find Hélène. I won't report for duty until she's found."

Sophie nodded thanks and hugged Danny's arm. "You think the Army will give you unlimited time until we track her down?" Sophie asked.

"No, unless I don't report," Danny said.

"Great, my husband of one day is court-martialed as a deserter," Sophie said.

The cabin of the C-47 carried only refrigerated food

supplies. The two of them were alone in an unheated cabin. Stacks of wool blankets lay along the inside of the plane. Danny and Sophie each wrapped a blanket around their shoulders and another on their legs.

"I thought the mountain trail to Bou Chebka was the coldest I'd ever be," Sophie said. "I was wrong."

Just as Danny had done days earlier, he had Sophie sit in his lap, placed his new wool flight cap on her head and wrapped his arms around her. This time Sophie didn't utter a word of disagreement.

"You'll be with the medical corps and I'll be with intelligence," Danny said. "We're likely not to see each other very frequently."

"I expect so," Sophie said. "When I was in Belgium after the Bosches invaded, I would work as many as eighteen to twenty hours at a time. I didn't have the energy to think or dream."

"You won't think of me?" Danny asked.

"Probably not," Sophie deadpanned. "But I won't forget the sex in the hot bath in Marrakech or the shower in Casablanca." She tipped her head up and kissed him on the lips and both started to laugh.

"Can we pretend the back of the plane is a hot bath?" Danny asked.

The laughing began again. Without saying anything further, they both drifted off to sleep.

As the plane started its descent into Thélepte, Sophie and Danny were awakened by the co-pilot. Only then did they agree to keep their nuptials secret.

"I have to tell Hélène," Sophie said. "I'll make her take a vow of silence."

"I 'spose," Danny said. "I'll keep the ketubah, you keep the rings."

Verging on being ceremonial, the newlyweds removed their rings at the same time. She looked, with sadness, at the tan mark on his ring finger. Sophie pocketed the rings.

"Ring or not, you're mine," Sophie said.

"And you are mine."

"Are you going to tell your parents?" Sophie asked.

"No. Even if our mail wasn't censored, there's too much to tell them. We'll wait 'til after the war and then we'll do it in person."

"You can't do that. Just walk in one day and say, 'Oh, by the way this is my wife.'"

"You have a better idea?"

"Maybe write that you met somebody you like," Sophie said.

Chapter Twenty-Four

Northern Tunisia

March-April 1943

The C-47 landed at the Thélepte Airfield, thirty minutes from Fériana by Jeep, just as the sun was rising. The pilot told Danny and Sophie that a welcome party waited on the tarmac. The newlyweds spent a moment lost in thought, staring at each other. The reality of the work that awaited them and the enormous stretches of time they would be apart at last sunk in.

They found Hélène on the tarmac, dressed in Army Nurse Corps greens with 2nd lieutenant bars on her shoulder. Another nurse wearing captain's bars was parked in a four-passenger Jeep next to the plane. The cousins ran to each other and embraced. When they separated, Hélène grabbed Sophie by the shoulder and gave her a once over.

"I missed you, but I have to admit you look good. You're tanned and put the pounds you lost back on," Hélène gushed.

"I missed you too. So much to talk about," Sophie said. "Nick said to say good-bye again, and thank you. He's on a hospital boat sailing home."

Danny approached with their suitcases in tow. Hélène gave him a hug.

"Thank you for bringing Sophie back," she said. "She looks fabulously happy."

“Not happier than I am,” Danny said.

“I see you enlisted,” Sophie said.

“Not to deliver babies. But I learned enough from you that they made me a nurse and an officer. I want you to meet someone.”

Hélène introduced Danny and Sophie to Captain Gloria Rezin from Waterloo, Iowa.

“I’ve been assisting in surgery,” Hélène said, “and rooming with Gloria. Go figure, two Jewish nurses.”

Gloria said, “Hélène has been telling me about your adventure all week. You could write a novel about what you’ve been through, but no one would believe it.”

“Do you have any idea where 1st Infantry HQ might be?” Danny asked. “I have to report.”

“Not exactly, but I know that General Fredendall was relieved of duty,” Gloria said, “and replaced by George Patton and Omar Bradley. The hospital units are in Fériana, Thélepte, Kasserine, and Sbeitla. Hélène and I are in Fériana.”

“Where’s Colonel Gaspar?” Sophie asked.

“In Kasserine today, but he moves around,” Hélène said.

“How’s the clinic?”

“What clinic,” Hélène said hollowly. “The Bosches smashed the windows, took everything that wasn’t nailed down, and burned the whole clinic to a crisp.”

“I’m so sorry,” Danny said.

“Also ...” Hélène took a deep breath and met Sophie’s eyes, “They killed Mayor Bahoul and his wife.”

“My God,” Sophie gasped, her eyes filling with tears. Because of us?”

“No,” Hélène said, squeezing her hand. “They

discovered his short-wave radio. They left a path of destruction, smashed the city well, burned down the mosque, and took all the livestock."

"How are the people getting by?" Danny asked.

"The U.S. Army," Gloria said. "They're bringing food and drinking water until the well is repaired. They purchased herds of goats in Algeria and trucked them in for the towns around Fériana and Kasserine."

"My God," Sophie said again. Though she and Danny had chosen to return early, it was still a shock, how quickly the war now rushed to envelop them.

Hélène looked at the large suitcases that Danny had lugged from the plane. "Where'd those come from?" she asked.

"Danny took me shopping," Sophie said, looking guilty. "Everything we bought will fit both of us."

"That's good. All the clothes we left in the clinic were torched."

Sophie dropped the suitcases at Hélène's tent in Feriana.

"Not sure where they'll put you," Hélène said. "I'd like to stay with Gloria. I'm learning and I like her company."

Sophie, surprised, didn't answer immediately. "That's fine. Let's see where they need me. Any chance we could go look at the old clinic? I'm curious."

"It'll break your heart," Hélène said.

The clinic had indeed been scorched inside and out. The walls were blackened, as if they'd been spraypainted with a flamethrower. The root cellar had been pillaged, and the shelving burned to ashes.

"I had to see, I guess," Sophie said.

Hélène said, "I talked to a British officer. He said the Americans aren't as cocky as they were before Kasserine Pass, and they're learning. The overwhelming resources and materiel they bring to the battle will overwhelm the Bosches in the end."

"Have you seen Fatima?" Sophie asked.

"Her husband left her," Hélène said.

"Oh, no."

"It's for the good. She's wised up a bit. She's negotiating with one of apricot farmers. A widower with small children who needs her and is nicer."

"I need to get back to the Kasserine," Sophie said. "I want to meet with Gaspar. They said he'd be back by four."

"You're in the United States Army now. Better start using Army time. Sixteen hundred," Hélène said.

Sophie laughed. "If you start saluting me, I'll punch you."

"Aye, aye, Captain."

Sophie was waiting alone in Colonel Gaspar's command tent when Danny found her.

"Intel is run out of Kasserine but moving north tonight," Danny said.

"I assume the hospital units will follow. Hélène surprised me by saying she wanted to stay with her new buddy, Gloria."

"That bother you?" Danny asked.

"You think it would, but Hélène seemed actually happy. I'll be okay. Fériana had plenty of doctors already and don't need a surgeon. I assume I'll be stationed elsewhere."

"The British Eighth is attacking Gabes on the coast. That's near Djerba. I hope your relatives are okay."

"Me too. I'll tell Hélène. Her family's there."

"I've got to get back to my unit, Mrs. Booker," Danny said.

"You didn't tell me your mother was here," Sophie said, smiling.

"Smartass." Danny kissed Sophie on the lips. "I love you. See you as soon as I can."

Later that evening, Danny wrote a letter to his parents. He couldn't tell them about the plane crash or the escape; it would only be blacked out by the censors. Instead, he told his parents that he was doing well, just homesick like every GI. At the end of the letter, he added:

> *....I met a woman in the medical corps whom I like very much. I won't get to see her too often as we're in different units. She's Jewish!*
>
> *Love,*
>
> *Danny*

Meanwhile, Sophie sat down and returned to waiting for Gaspar and the orders he would bring. She closed her eyes and for the first time since May 1940, all her thoughts brought smiles. Gaspar interrupted her dreams.

"So! The 'Angel of North Africa' is back," Gaspar cried as he entered the tent.

"I'd appreciate it if you didn't call me that," Sophie

said.

“Fine,” Gaspar said with a shrug. “But I can’t stop the others. More than a few have asked about you. I must tell you, your cousin Hélène has been very helpful, speaking French, Arabic and some form of Spanish that she calls Ladino. The French units depend on us for medical care and she’s been invaluable.”

“How can I help?” Sophie asked.

“The Brits control the medical and surgical coordination, but if you’re up to it, the U.S. 48th Field Hospital in Thala, a third echelon facility, has lost two experienced surgeons. One to malaria, the other to appendicitis. They could use the help. A couple of French units have joined us and Hélène said you also speak French and Arabic, as well as German.”

“I do. When do I report?” Sophie asked.

“ASAP. Get your stuff and I’ll have my driver get you there tonight. Like your cousin, I’ll have you sworn in to the United States Army, but as a Captain, the same rank you had in France. The French loaned me a nurses outfit. We’ll send U.S. uniforms for you as soon as we can. CSurg at the 48th is Captain Charlie Harris. He’s not easy to work with, but he’s a good doc and the 48th needs the help. Just report to him. I’ll radio that you’re coming.”

Wearing her French uniform without rank and hefting a large valise, Sophie arrived in Thala and found the 48th Field unit eating in the mess tent. When she entered the tent, the fifty men and women of the 48th turned to gaze at the stranger in a strange uniform.

“Is Captain Harris here?” Sophie asked.

“That’s me. Who the hell are you?”

The man who spoke was in his mid-thirties, already bald, short and carrying thirty pounds of paunch. He seemed out of place. Harris remained seated at the end of a table near Sophie and put a fork full of lamb into his mouth. He made no effort to stand.

"Sophie Sollar, reporting. Did Colonel Gaspar notify you?"

"Nobody's told me shit," Harris grunted. "What kind of uniform is that?"

"French," Sophie said. "Where can I put my stuff?"

"That's French, *Sir*. You're talking to an officer," Harris barked.

Sophie didn't respond. She gritted her teeth and glared at Harris, while most of the tent stopped eating to watch the confrontation.

"You got something to say?" Harris demanded, "like *Sir*?"

"Depends, I guess," Sophie said.

"Depends on what, Miss?"

"Depends on whether I outrank you. Maybe you should be saluting me, Captain, and calling me Ma'am."

Sophie now had everyone's complete attention.

"Nurses, techs, or medics, even if they're fuckin' generals, don't outrank me in the medical tent," Harris said.

"I am a captain in the French Medical Corps and have been sworn into the U.S. Army as a captain," Sophie said smoothly. "My rank dates to 15 May 1940."

"Gimme a break. The Frogs don't have women in their Medical Corps and besides, Frog ranks don't mean shit around here. Tell me when we get to Paris.

Far as I'm concerned you're a private, if that."

"Colonel Gaspar told me two things," Sophie said. "One, your unit is short two surgeons, which I am, and two, you're impossible to work with. Looks like he was spot-on correct."

"You're a surgeon and I'm Napoleon Bonaparte," Harris said, now standing.

"*Vous êtes un connard,*" Sophie snapped.

"What's that supposed to mean?"

"Get some education and learn French. You want me to leave?"

A blue-eyed, first lieutenant in her twenties stood up from her mess plate. "No!" she called. "Please don't leave. We need you."

Harris and Sophie turned to the nurse.

"Are you the surgeon that killed an SS colonel after amputating one of our pilot's legs in the dark? The one they call 'The Angel'?"

"That's me."

"You got my salute, Captain," the nurse said, performing the gesture with emotion. "I heard the story when we were in Tebessa. Couldn't believe it. The 48th could use you. Badly. And there's an empty bunk in my tent."

"Thank you. What's your name?"

"Ruthie Bunnen. Won't you come sit with us? We wanna hear the whole story straight from the horse's mouth."

"Who's the horse?" Sophie asked.

"You are. American slang," Ruthie said. "Better than Seabiscuit."

Abandoning Harris, Sophie joined Ruthie and other

nurses at the table. For Ruthie, it was like Frank Sinatra had just taken a seat next to her. "Also heard you snuck off to Casablanca with a handsome pilot," Ruthie announced to the rest of the table. "Ain't she the cat's meow."

Sophie let Charlie Harris stay in command despite the fact that she technically outranked him. Harris would assign cases as they rolled in, but as soon as a surgeon had completed a case, they automatically took the next case. Harris and Sophie would alternate triage duty to determine the order of cases to be done or if nothing could be done to save a soldier. Though a miserable son-of-a-bitch, Harris was a skilled surgeon who worked as hard as Sophie. It took only two days for them to develop a modicum of mutual respect. Harris, in a rare feat of humbleness, apologized to Sophie for the hubris he demonstrated at their first meeting.

A few days later, another surgeon arrived at the 48th Field Hospital. Lieutenant Bob Tacher had completed medical school, an internship, and one year of surgical residency. Though eager, his surgical acumen was raw. Tacher found his niche as an assistant surgeon to Harris and Sophie while he learned.

Sophie settled swiftly into her new life. She stayed busy, because when she had a moment to herself, she missed Danny with every fiber of her being. She missed the sensation of his body next to hers in bed. Her nightmares of wounds, blood, and severed limbs and her father returned plus the added new worry about Danny.

Five days after arriving at the 48th, Sophie exited the tent for a breath of air. She'd just completed a complicated bowel, spleen and kidney procedure.

Outside the tent, dead soldiers lay in rows of stretchers on the ground, their bodies covered with formal shrouds or sheets.

“Hey, Doc,” a medic yelled. “C’mon over here.”

Sophie approached the medic, who was standing next to one of the corpses. Medic O’Doul was nineteen years-old but he looked fifteen. A cross hung from his neck. He looked like he’d seen a ghost.

“What is it?” Sophie asked.

The medic saluted Sophie, then spoke as if the fear of God possessed him. “This soldier was shot in the chest and pronounced dead. The chaplain gave last rites a few minutes ago, and we moved him here. I’m ‘sposed to gather the belongings and bag’em. But I swear I just saw his hand move. Scared the living bejesus outta me.”

“What’s your name?” Sophie asked.

“Billy, Ma’am, uh Captain, Private Billy O’Doul, from South Boston.”

“Let’s look.” Sophie said, pulling back the sheet. Billy took three steps back not knowing what to expect. He stood squarely behind Sophie and looked away.

The dead soldier was in his early twenties, blond and pale. There was a gory opening on the left side of his chest. Sophie kneeled down to the ground and felt his wrist.

“I’m not sure if there’s a pulse,” she said.

When she placed the man’s arm back to his side, she saw his hand move slightly.

“He did move,” Sophie said.

Billy jumped back another foot. Sophie turned the patient’s neck to see if she could find a pulse in either carotid artery.

"Oh my God," she shouted. "his jugular veins are both distended. They shouldn't be. Billy, get me a large bore needle and a 50-cc syringe. He may be alive and has a cardiac tamponade. Hurry!"

The medic had no idea what Sophie was talking about, but he ran into the surgical tent and returned in seconds with a 50-cc syringe and 14-gauge, large bore, four-inch needle. Without prepping the soldier, Sophie jabbed the needle with the attached syringe under the man's sternum, aiming straight upward toward the heart. Billy O'Doul fell to his knees and with his head down, trying not to faint, and prayed out loud. He then watched Sophie out of the corner of one eye.

As Sophie advanced the needle, she maintained constant negative pressure on the syringe by pulling the plunger back. The needle went deeper and deeper until it reached its end at four inches. Sophie pushed the syringe hard against the skin to press the needle deeper. All of sudden, the fifty-cubic centimeter syringe filled with dark semi-clotted blood. Billy, mouth agape, started crossing himself over and over. Sophie unscrewed the syringe from the needle, squirted the syringe's blood onto the ground, and reattached the empty syringe to the needle. Again she retrieved more dark blood.

The soldier's hands moved first, then his head moved and he took an enormous breath.

"He's not dead. Quick, let's get him into the tent," Sophie yelled, leaving the needle in place.

O'Doul and Sophie picked up the stretcher and quickly moved it into the surgical tent.

"Am I going to die," the soldier whispered.

"No," Sophie said, "not as long as I'm here." Entering the tent, Sophie yelled, "Anesthesia, now. Help."

Sophie and Billy put the soldier directly on an operating table as nurses rushed in. Together with Harris, Sophie sutured a grazed wound to the outside of the left ventricle of the heart which had bled into the pericardium surrounding the heart. The large amount of blood in the pericardium had prevented the heart from pumping efficiently. Billy O'Doul stood to the side during the entire procedure and began to weep as the nurses rolled the patient onto a stretcher to the recovery area.

"He'll be fine," Sophie said, holding onto O'Doul's shoulders. "All because of you."

"Not me. I just saw his hand move," O'Doul cried. "I thought I was seeing things. He was dead and you brought him back to life. I swear you are what they say, 'the Angel of North Africa.'"

"Billy, I'm not an angel. Just a doctor who made the right diagnosis. I've seen this once before in May of 1940 in Belgium. My father who was a surgeon made the same diagnosis."

"Say what you want, I saw you do it. I won't never forget this."

The next day saw a lull in the fighting. Few casualties came to any of the army medical units. As the entire 48th sat in the mess tent for lunch, Danny entered. All eyes turned to him. Sophie smiled, watching Danny trying to find her in the large group. She leaned over to Ruthie. "The pilot from Casablanca came to rescue me."

"No one ever comes to rescue me," Ruthie lamented as Sophie stood.

Sophie walked to a smiling Danny. "Don't kiss me here," she said in a strong whisper.

Together they walked out of the tent and around the corner. They both checked the periphery and, seeing no one, they embraced.

"You did it again," Danny said.

"Did what?" Sophie asked.

"Performed another miracle. It's getting around."

"I did nothing but make the correct diagnosis."

"Right, except they'd pronounced the poor sap dead and gave him last rites."

"That wasn't my doing. I lost two chest wounds last night, back to back. I'm not perfect."

"I missed you so much," Danny said.

"Me too."

"Anywhere we could go and be alone?" Danny asked. "You'd think a real angel would have some pull around here."

"Call me an angel one more time and you'll find out the kind of pull I have," Sophie said, pretending to glower which morphed into a smile. "Hold on a second."

Sophie went back to the mess tent and called Ruthie off to the side. "I need to have a top-secret discussion with Captain Booker," Sophie said. "Any chance I could keep you out of our tent for an hour?"

Ruthie laughed. "Sure. Happy to."

"Thanks."

"Can I listen in?" Ruthie asked impishly.

"Only if you want me to take out your appendix without anesthetic," Sophie replied.

"Go. No one will bother you."

Sophie ran out of the tent.

An hour later, Sophie and Danny left the zipped

tent, flushed and smiling. They returned to the now empty mess tent and sat.

"More to talk about," Danny said. "I've been grounded permanently."

"Why?" Sophie asked.

"The story of our escape made it onto Armed Forces Radio. The Krauts picked up on it and have tried you, me, Hélène, Nick and Omar in abstentia for the murder of an SS Colonel. A reward of a thousand Deutsch marks is offered for any one of us. You, Hélène and Nick are safe. I've no idea what's happened to Omar. I'm at risk if I fly again and get captured, so they've grounded me."

"I'm sorry," Sophie said.

"I argued. They wouldn't listen, but on second thought, I'm not totally sorry," Danny said. "I knew my life was at risk every time I flew. Now, with you, I see life differently."

"And where, exactly, is that life?"

"I don't care. Really. Anywhere. As long as it's by your side."

"Now I want to go back into the tent," Sophie said.

"The tent will have to wait a bit. We've got to win a war first."

Sophie pulled Danny's hand and they went to find Ruthie so Sophie could introduce them.

"Any more flyboys as handsome as you who are looking for an adorable nurse?" Ruthie asked. Ruthie dimpled her chin with her finger and posed, which prompted a laugh from Danny and Sophie.

"I'll ask around," Danny said.

That night, Danny wrote another letter to his parents. He wrote that he was doing well. At the end of the letter, he added:

> *...I'm still seeing the woman from the medical corps. She's beautiful, raised in France, Jewish, and a doctor. She spent a year in high school in Ann Arbor. Her name is Sophie.*
>
> *Love, Danny*

Danny had no intention of telling his parents he had already married Sophie.

Hélène and Gloria arrived by jeep at the 48th Field Hospital on the day after Danny visited and waited for Sophie in the empty mess tent.

"We've so much to catch up on," Sophie said.

"More than you'd ever think," Hélène said. "Our hospital unit, and yours too, I'd suspect, is moving north toward Tunis."

"That's what I heard," Sophie said. "Did you hear that the Bosches are offering a reward for our heads?"

"I did. But Fériana will protect me to the last man," Hélène said.

"They couldn't protect a goat," Sophie said. "Besides, you just said your unit is moving north."

"They will, just not me. I'm staying in Fériana and re-opening the clinic. The village needs me and the army okayed me dropping out. I've learned enough from you and Gloria that I can handle most stuff. The whole town is scrubbing and whitewashing the clinic, while the Army is refurbishing it. I'm hoping you could come once in a while. Gloria will too."

"You'll be there forever, then?" Sophie asked.

"I told the new mayor that I'll stay until the end of the war. Then we'll see," Hélène said.

"Then see about what?" Sophie asked.

"Hélène and I will go to Palestine," Gloria said, interrupting the conversation between the cousins. "And set up a women's clinic somewhere there."

"You two getting along that well?" Sophie asked.

"I've never been happier," Hélène said.

"Nor I," Gloria added.

Sophie nodded, a sudden understanding dawning. "Then I'm happy too. But I heard the Brits aren't letting Jews into Palestine."

"They will after the war, like it or not," Gloria said. "There'll be millions of displaced Jews with nowhere to go."

"We'd like you to join us," Hélène said.

Sophie hesitated.

"There's, uhh. ... I have a lot to consider."

"Are you also considering a guy named Danny?" Hélène asked.

"Yes..." Sophie looked around the mess hall to make sure they were alone. "I'm guessing that if I tell you a secret, Gloria will hear about it anyway."

"Most definitely," Hélène said.

"Fine. Then I'll tell you both, but you can't tell anyone. Promise?" Sophie asked.

Hélène looked at Gloria then back to Sophie. Hélène held up her right hand and Gloria followed. "Promise," both said in unison.

"On the last day in Casablanca, ..." Sophie said,

then hesitated, as she watched Hélène's eyes and mouth open wide in sync,"... we bought two wedding bands, Danny hunted down a rabbi, and we got married."

"*Merde,* what were you thinking? I thought we were sisters. When were you going to tell me?" Hélène asked.

"The whole trip was intense. When we checked into a hotel the second night, the hotel clerk saw that I wasn't wearing a wedding ring. It was a 'if-looks-could-kill' kind of a stare. Danny went and found a phony diamond ring and wedding bands and we wore them for the rest of the trip. Neither one of us wanted me to take them off when it was time to head back," Sophie explained. "So he proposed."

"I hoped this would happen, but not so fast," Hélène said.

"We even have a ketubah, somewhere," Sophie said. "We don't even know if it's legal."

"It's legal by me," Hélène said, then jumped up, ran around the table, and gave Sophie a huge hug and a kiss.

...

By the end of March, the American army had learned some hard lessons from the terrible losses in and around Kasserine Pass. The Germans knew to concentrate their forces in Tunisia just as they had when sweeping through Belgium, the Netherlands and France in 1940. The American defeats early in the African campaign led the Germans to believe that the American armies would never be a threat – a fatal mistake.

General Fredendall, in charge of the southern Tunisian campaign for the Americans, had based his mindset on the trench warfare of the First World War and spread his troops too wide and too thin. After Kasserine, General Dwight Eisenhower dismissed

Fredendall and replaced him with Generals George Patton and Omar Bradley, who understood power concentration and rapid troop movement. Communications between infantry, armor, artillery, and air support became more coordinated, thus removing another shortcoming that characterized the first American battles. Lastly, the British and American armies, fractious with each other at first, learned to work together.

At the end of March, Patton led the U.S. II Corps from Kasserine Pass and pushed the Germans back toward Tunis at the Battle of El Guettar. At the same time, the British 8th Army on the eastern Tunisian coast won the battle of Mareth and Gabes, also forcing the Germans toward Tunis as well. Finally, on April 6th, the U. S. First Army, coming from the west, joined with the British 8th Army coming from the east. With the British Navy controlling the Mediterranean Sea between Tunis and Italy, the German army had nowhere to hide and no way to escape. That said, the German army remained a formidable adversary.

Chapter Twenty-Five

Medjez el Bab, Tunisia
April 20, 1943

It was late afternoon, and 1st Infantry's intelligence tent hummed with activity. Intel had just learned that the 78th Infantry Division had cleared the road from Medjez el Bab to Béja. Four specialists with headphones listened to any and all German messages. Two men sat at the phone transcribing encrypted information from Gibraltar gained from deciphering German messages using the Enigma decrypting machine. Three more men stood over a ten-foot by ten-foot map of northern Tunisia, moving tokens representing the various Allied and German troop formations. Colonel Cap Teller, a bright-eyed, steel-jawed, West Point graduate in his fifties, talked in short sentences with rare, wasted words, unless he was pissed. Teller ran the intelligence section of 1st Infantry. Second to Teller was Danny Booker, now a major.

Danny bounced around the intel tent in a very good mood.

"Why's he so happy?" one of the technicians asked his sergeant.

"He's got a gal at the 48th Field Hospital," the sergeant said. "He snuck out last night. Colonel Teller don't know and I ain't gonna be the one to tell him. Booker's the best staff officer I've ever worked with."

Teller entered the tent and stood beside Danny and the three non-com soldiers working the troop movements.

"Has the 9th British Corps moved?" Teller asked.

It was a moot question. Nobody in 1st Infantry knew exactly how far, or whether, 9th British had moved in the last twenty-two hours.

"We don't know if they've moved northeast to join 8th Army," Danny said. "That was the plan, according to Ike and Alexander. We haven't been able to reach them since 1400 yesterday. It's SNAFU."

"Damn General Crocker, 9th Corps needs someone who can communicate," Teller said.

"Want me to drive over and see what's what? Shouldn't be more than twenty, thirty minutes there and back." Danny asked.

"Damn Crocker," Teller repeated, then added, "No. I need you here, Major."

"We also need their position," Danny said.

Teller hesitated for a long moment, then said, "Against my judgement, okay. Hightail over there and back. Be quick. It's gonna be dark soon."

As the early spring sun sat just atop the mountains to the west, Danny grabbed a road map, ran out of the Intel tent forty yards to his private tent, holstered his .45 pistol, then ran another thirty yards to the motor pool. Three men in three Jeeps sat talking to each other as Danny approached. All three jumped out of their vehicles and stood at attention. Almost in perfect unison, they asked, "Major?" knowing a command would follow.

"Need a ride to the 9th British HQ," Danny said.

The three shrugged, having no idea where to find 9th

British HQ.

"Who's the best driver?"

"I'm senior, Major," said one, who was built like a bantamweight wrestler and brimming with confidence. "Been here with the Big Red One since day one, sir. Corporal Jeff Trop at your service."

"Okay, Corporal, let's go. I know where they were twenty-two hours ago, so we'll start there, at Goubellat. Heading out and then coming right back."

"Aye, aye, sir," Trop said as he started his Jeep. Trop and Danny both carried .45 Colt pistols and an M-1 rifle sat behind their seats on the floorboard.

The seventeen-kilometer trip to Goubellat took twenty-five minutes on the potholed, dirt road as the sun began to set. Entering the village, the telltale signs of a major army encampment lay everywhere. But the village itself looked deserted, with only a few windows showing light behind curtains.

"You speak Arabic?" Danny asked Trop.

"Not a lick, sir."

"Then no use knocking on a door and asking where they went."

Trop shrugged, having no idea what to do next.

"They're supposed to head northeast toward the British 8th, so let's go northeast," Danny said.

Ten minutes of driving on the small dirt road failed to reveal any traces of any army had passed that way.

"Better turn around and head back, Corporal. They didn't come this way," Danny said.

As Trop made a back-and-forth U-turn on the narrow road, gunfire erupted from the bushes. Danny leaped out of the jeep opposite the gunfire, rolled clear of the Jeep, into a shallow ditch, and emptied his .45

blindly into the bushes from which the firing came. Trop, before exiting with Danny, turned back in his seat to retrieve the M-1 from the rear floorboard. He then jumped towards Danny, holding the rifle, but the delay cost him his life.

"I'm hit, Major. Shouldn't have gotten… rifle… sir," Trop gasped.

"You'll be fine!" Danny cried. "Just hang on."

Trop never said another word.

"Trop, give me your handgun," Danny yelled. When Trop didn't answer, he repeated, "I'm out of ammo. Give me your pistol." Danny rolled five feet toward Trop, nudged him, then realized Trop was dead. "Oh, God no."

German yells now came from both sides of the road. Danny had seized Trop's pistol, but with the enemy on both sides, decided against shooting blindly.

"Surrender *oder die*," came a shout from behind him.

Danny turned but could see no one. The consequences of being captured with his own ID thudded in his mind. Rolling next to Trop's lifeless body, he could make a left chest wound even in the dim light. Danny swapped his own dog tag with Trop's. Next, he swapped hats. He then tore his major's oak leaf clusters off his shoulders and hurled them into the bushes. He stripped Trop's corporal chevrons from his shirt, and put them in his pocket. Having done all he could, Danny dropped his pistol, stood up with his arms in the air and yelled, "I surrender. I surrender."

The German squad consisted of eight men. They marched Danny through the bush for an hour before coming upon a German encampment. A few men asked,

"*Sprechen Sie Deutsch*?" Danny knew the phrase and shook his head truthfully no.

Within minutes of entering the encampment, Danny found himself in the back of an unlit two-and-a-half-ton truck. A nervous, young German soldier with an automatic weapon guarded him.

Danny, an intelligence officer, knew that he'd be professionally interrogated at some point but he hadn't enough light or privacy in which to read and memorize Trop's dog tag, engraved with a social security number, name, address of the next of kin, and blood type. He couldn't let the Germans even suspect that he wasn't Jeff Trop.

He tried moving toward the rear end of the truck where a sliver of light came through the canopy. The German guard immediately raised his weapon and said, "Halt."

The truck drove for two hours when Danny smelled saltwater and heard voices along with airplane engines. This meant he was near the Mediterranean Sea and an active airfield. He knew that the German Luftwaffe used at least twenty-five landing strips within twenty miles of Tunis. No plane spent more than fifteen hours at any strip.

The truck stopped, backed up, stopped again at the yell of "*Halt*." The curtain at the back of the truck opened, revealing the rear end of a Junkers-52 airplane, the poor equivalent of the American C-47 transport. Without a word from anyone, the soldier escorted Danny onto the plane, where he joined twenty-three other American, British, Indian, and French prisoners. Guarding the men were seven German soldiers, automatic weapons at the ready.

For the first time since his surrender, Danny had the light and opportunity to study the engravings on

Trop's dog tag. Jeffery J. Trop, serial number '07362639', 'O' for blood type, 'A' for atheist, '41' for the year of his tetanus vaccination. Next of kin was Hazel Trop, 2641 28th Ave W, Seattle Wash. Danny was relieved to see that their blood types matched and that Trop was an atheist. He'd been hoping for anything but an 'H' for the Hebrew faith, although he'd heard that the Germans so far had followed the Geneva Conventions for prisoners of war and did not segregate or treat Jewish prisoners differently.

The plane took off and landed three hours later. During the flight, the guards wouldn't allow any talking and even a whisper from any of the prisoners resulted in one or two weapons being aimed at them.

Danny assumed they were somewhere in Italy. From an airstrip with no markings, trucks took the twenty-four prisoners and seven guards to a POW camp. Danny would soon find out he was in 'Camp 59' in Servigliano, Italy, a small village near the Adriatic coast, one hundred and seventy-five kilometers northeast from Rome.

That night, and for the next three days and nights, different German and Italian interrogators, in groups of two, piled question after question at Danny. For the first five sessions, Danny would repeat Name, Rank, and Serial number after every question and nothing more. By the third day, Danny saw that his interrogators were losing their patience. He also knew these sessions would continue until the interrogators learned something of value. Danny realized Jeff Trop needed to say something, but without a shred of worthwhile military intelligence.

"Okay, I'm tired of the questions. They're dumb. I'm a driver. That's alls I ever did," Danny said.

The German interrogator smiled at the breakthrough, then smiled at his Italian counterpart.

The German continued, “Where was the camp for you and your companion?”

“Middle of Bob,” Danny said, butchering the city Medjez el Bab’s name. “The major, he come up to me and says drive, I be telling ya where we be goin’. That’s alls he said.”

“The officer didn’t tell you where you were going?” the German asked.

“No siree, Bob. I’m just a driver and I don’t know where we was goin’ and I don’t think he knows where we was goin.’ He had a map and was pointing this way and that. At the end, there, we was lost, bad. All of a sudden people was shootin’ at us from both sides of the road. I jumped out quick. Then the major, he tried to jump and got shot. I put my hands up. That’s alls I know.”

The German bought Danny’s deception and realized he would obtain nothing of value and that Jeff Trop was an dumb as a bedpost. The German said something to the Italian next to him, and both walked out of the interrogation room. That ended Danny’s interrogations.

Danny settled among the rest of the non-commissioned POWs, who were mostly Greeks and Slavs who mostly didn’t speak a word of English. At no time did Danny ever mention to anyone that he was not Jeff Trop, a taxi driver from Seattle. Fortunately for Danny, no other prisoner had ever been to Seattle or the Pacific Northwest.

The Italian Army ran the camp, and the only Germans on-site were the interrogators. The only news of the war came from new POWs who could speak English.

Danny knew he could write letters which would be censored by the Germans or Italians and then sent through the Red Cross. Though he wracked his brains, he could think of no way to write his parents or Sophie without giving away his identity. He saw no reason to write to Jeff Trop's family for the same reason. He decided that he needed to wait for the war to end and only then could he make things right. He hoped that his parents and Sophie would not suffer too greatly, but he knew they would. He hoped too that Trop's parents would understand his deception and forgive him if he made it home alive.

Thirty minutes after Danny and Jeff Trop's departure from 1st Infantry Intelligence, Cap Teller started worrying. 9th Corps had communicated with Teller's Intel unit only minutes after Danny had taken off to look for them. The 9th British had headed south first and then northeast to utilize better roads.

In hindsight, Danny should have never left. By the twelve-hour mark, Teller knew something bad had occurred. He had his men call every surgical and medical unit in the vicinity. No one had seen Major Booker or Corporal Trop. The next morning, Teller assumed the worst and listed Danny and Trop as MIA (Missing in Action).

A sergeant in the unit informed Teller that Danny had a girlfriend who was a surgeon in the 48th Field Hospital.

"There's only one broad in the entire surgical corps. The one who took off his copilot's leg?" growled Teller. "She's his girl?"

"That's my understanding, sir. When things were slow around here, the Major would borrow a jeep and run over to the 48th. I think they were close."

Teller's face was grave but unreadable. "You're dismissed sergeant," he said.

Chapter Twenty-Six

Mateur, Tunisia
April 27, 1943

The 48th Field Hospital moved north with First Infantry to a location fifteen kilometers south of Mateur, Tunisia, the site of the next battle. Harris, with the Corps of Engineers, directed the building of the surgical units, while other engineers and medics sped around putting up living quarters.

A corporal came up to Harris, saluted and said, "1st Infantry Intel needs to speak to you. Officer's waiting in your tent."

"Intel. Tell him I'm busy erecting a surgical unit and will get there when I'm damn well done," Harris said. "I've never talked to anyone in Intel. I don't know shit."

"Captain, this was a full-bird-colonel asking. Don't think he's the kind of officer you want to make wait. I told him you were busy. He said he needs to speak with you now."

Harris stormed off to his tent, where he saw a Jeep with a driver waiting outside. The Jeep's motor was running. Harris entered to find Colonel Teller sitting at his desk. Momentarily perturbed by the sight of someone else in his chair, Harris suddenly realized that Teller outranked him by three grades. Hastily, he saluted.

"Captain Harris, sir."

Teller stood. “Captain, we’ve got a problem. You’ve got a female surgeon on your staff?”

“Is she in trouble?” Harris asked.

“No. Her friend, Major Daniel Booker, is MIA,” Teller said. “He went by Jeep to talk to 9th British and never got there. It’s been two days, so it’s not likely he’ll be found. We called every medical unit in Tunisia. He’s either KIA or captured. If he’s not dead, the Krauts will kill him once they find out who he is. He knocked off an SS Colonel with your surgeon friend back in February, and the Krauts want blood.”

“I knew about that. This is terrible,” Harris said. His face was perturbed, as if he were about to say more.

“I’ve got to get back, so I’ll let you tell her. If we hear anything definitive, I’ll let you know,” Teller said.

“You’re not going to tell her?” Harris asked, looking panicked.

“I don’t know her and I’m busy. I didn’t have to come,” Teller said.

“What if she has questions?” Harris asked. “She’s human. Sir.”

“I don’t have any answers. He went off in a Jeep and never came back.”

Harris saluted, and Teller exited the tent and drove off.

“Asshole,” Harris muttered.

Harris went to the surgical tent, where Sophie was operating on a deep laceration to an infantryman’s shoulder. Ruthie Bunnen sat off to the side, reading a magazine. Harris knew that Sophie and Ruthie had become bunkmates and best friends. He went over to Ruthie and asked her step out of the tent. Ruthie followed Harris out.

“We’ve got a problem,” Harris said. “I need your help. I’m not a good people person.”

Ruthie smiled at this truism. “What’s up?”

Twenty minutes later, Sophie had completed dressing her shoulder repair. Ruthie, waiting off to the side, asked Sophie to come back to their tent.

“What’s up?” Sophie asked. “Can’t it wait ‘til after lunch?”

“No,” said Ruthie, avoiding her eyes.

“Did Danny’s presence the other day upset you?” Sophie asked.

“No.”

As Sophie and Ruthie entered their tent, Harris joined them.

“What’s going on?” Sophie asked, sitting on her cot.

“No way to make this easy,” Ruthie said. “Danny’s MIA.”

Sophie’s hand went to her open mouth and her head swiveled back and forth between Ruthie and Harris. “What? No. He’s not flying. He just has a desk job. It has to be a mistake.”

Ruthie shook her head.

“Oh, please God. It’s not a mistake?” Sophie cried.

Harris spoke first. “I’m afraid not. His CO, Colonel Teller, came by an hour ago. Major Booker went out with a Jeep and a driver to talk to the 9th British two days ago. He never got there. They’ve called all the med units and he’s not there either.”

“Please tell me you’re joking. Please!” Sophie begged.

“I can be an asshole, but I’m not that low,” Harris

said. “At this point, he’s MIA. He may have been captured.”

Sophie’s hands went to her mouth as her head started shaking. Her eyes moved rapidly right and left. “That’s a death sentence for Danny. I told you. I told you about it.”

“You did. Anyway, you’re excused from duty until you’re up to it,” Harris said.

“No. This can’t happen,” Sophie cried. Sophie stood, sat down, stood again and walked to the back of the tent facing away from Harris and Ruthie. “It can’t be true. It can’t. Leave me alone. Both of you.”

Harris and Ruthie stood there, unsure what to do.

“I’ll stay with you,” Ruthie said.

“Get out. Go. Now!” Sophie screamed.

Sophie fell on her cot and curled into the fetal position. Harris and Ruthie slowly backed out. As Ruthie turned to secure the tent flaps, deep wails of grief billowed out from inside the tent.

Ruthie returned before dinner as the sun sat atop the peaks of the western hills. The flaps of the tent remained closed.

“Sophie, it’s me Ruthie. Can I come in?” she asked. Receiving no answer, Ruthie repeated the question: “Can I come in?”

Ruthie spread the flaps a bit to peek in and found the tent empty. She found Sophie’s suitcase laying open on her cot with dresses, shoes and scarves from Casablanca and Marrakech strewn around her side of the tent. Ruthie had seen the dresses before, usually after Danny had visited. She ran toward the soldiers on guard duty. The first two men Ruthie questioned had not seen Sophie. The third had.

“Yeah, Ma’am,” the guard said. “The captain said she wanted some breathing space. She didn’t look so good. Face was all puffy like she’d been cryin’ hard.”

“You let her leave?” Ruthie demanded.

“I told her I wasn’t supposed to let anyone leave,” the guard said. “She told me that she was a captain and would do what she wanted and walked thataway.”

Ruthie headed off. On a grassy knoll forty-five yards from the edge of camp, she found Sophie sitting on a rock, staring into the distance at an olive grove in the low rolling hills of northern Tunisia. Off in the far distance, the edges of Lake Ickeul to the north gave a sense of tranquility.

Ruthie tried to approach slowly, but the crinkling of twigs alerted Sophie, who wheeled around.

“I want to be alone,” Sophie hissed.

“Not a good idea out here.”

“I want to be alone,” Sophie repeated, even more fiercely.

“C’mon, Sophie. I’m your best friend here. I know we don’t go back so far, but I’m here for you. Vent, scream, cry, swear, hit me, I don’t care. I know I’d need someone with me.”

Sophie stumbled to her feet and faced Ruthie. The sadness etched on her face took Ruthie’s breath away. The nurse opened her arms and folded her friend into a hug. Sophie screamed “Nooooo,” into Ruthie’s shoulder, then began to sob.

When Sophie’s crying subsided, Ruthie held her left hand. That was when she felt then noticed the engagement ring and wedding band. Sophie saw her looking.

“Danny gave it to me when we got to Casablanca. A

hotel clerk gave us a look when we registered because we weren't wearing wedding rings. The next day, Danny found this fake diamond with matching band and a gold wedding band for himself. We never took them off for the rest of the trip."

"I haven't seen you wear it before," Ruthie said.

"I didn't until now."

"Why?" Ruthie asked.

"On our last night at dinner in Casablanca, Danny suggested I take it off before we returned. I didn't want to. I liked how it felt. It gave me comfort. I hadn't felt that secure since my father died."

Ruthie nodded.

"At the end of dinner, Danny asked for the rings back and it upset me. But I gave them to him. He right away came to my side of the table, got down on a knee, and proposed to me. I said yes."

Ruthie started tearing up. "Oh Sophie. When were you going to get married?"

Sophie hesitated, looked toward the setting sun.

"We were married the next day in Casablanca," she whispered. "We decided not to tell anyone. Our three rings went into my suitcase and Danny kept the marriage certificate. These are our three rings." Sophie held up her left hand. She then went inside her blouse and grabbed a shoelace tied around her neck. On the end was Danny's engagement ring.

Sophie needed a break to collect herself. She, Ruthie and Harris knew it. Fortunately, the 48th Field Hospital had little to do for the next forty-eight hours. Sophie spent most of her time in the tent; Ruthie brought her meals. Each afternoon, Sophie would walk past the same patrol guard at sundown and sit on the rock where Ruthie found her the day she got the news.

On the third day, the US II Corps under Omar Bradley and the British 1st Army under Kenneth Anderson attacked north of Medjez el Bab, burrowing deep into heavily fortified German defensive positions. Both sides suffered huge casualties and the 48th Field Hospital, among others, was flooded with injured soldiers.

Harris went to Sophie's tent and personally delivered the news of the incoming casualties. Without a word, she got off the cot and left the tent. Harris followed her. Sophie stopped suddenly and faced Harris.

"Charlie, we're friends, aren't we?" Sophie said.

"Yes. You may be the only one here who likes me," Harris said.

"I'm in a strange place in my head right now. I've lost my father to the Nazis and that crushed me for the longest time. Now I've lost Danny. I dream I'm a soldier with a machine gun, and I want to kill every Nazi that I see. It's not a good dream. If we get wounded German POWs, I don't think I can treat them. I know it's wrong."

"Hell, Sophie, none of us *want* to treat them. We took an oath as doctors. If you don't do your job, you'll lose who you are. Don't deprive yourself of the only thing you have left."

Sophie nodded curtly. "Thank you, Charlie." Sophie followed Harris toward the surgical tent and did exactly what she had taken an oath and been trained to do.

Like Belgium in May 1940, the number of injured soon overwhelmed the Allied medical staff. Sophie and Harris, along with Bob Tacher and two additional surgeons brought in the week before, worked eighteen-to-twenty-hour days and nights for the next week.

At two a.m. on April 30th, Harris nudged Sophie and Ruthie awake.

“Incoming,” Harris said. “The French XIXth were overwhelmed and they’re shipping overflow injuries to us. They’ll be here in twenty.”

Sophie and Ruthie knew the drill and were dressed and ready to work minutes later as ambulances started to arrive. They stood by as two French medics brought in the first patient, a moaning soldier with wounds to his abdomen and thigh.

The leading French medic, his back to Sophie, asked, “Où allons-nous” in French.

“Ici,” Sophie responded, pointing to an operating table. The medic turned around and his face and Sophie’s face lit up immediately.

“Sergeant Kilie,”

“Doctor Sollar.”

Kilie and the other French medic placed the patient on the OR table. Once settled, Kilie leaned into the ear of the patient and said, “Don’t worry. You’ve got the best surgeon in the world taking care of you. She’s my friend, she’s French, she’s an angel, and you’re going to be fine.”

“I’m sorry we can’t spend time talking about the last three years. I’ve got work to do,” Sophie said in French.

“I understand and I have to get back too,” Kilie said. “I’d hoped I would run into you. Everyone knows about the ‘Angel of North Africa.’ No one believed we were friends.”

With his medic partner watching, Sophie planted a kiss on each of Kilie’s cheeks. She turned to his partner and said, “It’s all true. Henry and I go way back and are best of friends.” Sophie turned to the injured patient as Kilie and his partner ran back to their ambulance.

On May 2nd, General Omar Bradley stopped by the 48th Field Hospital. Everyone from doctors to supply personnel gathered to listen to their leader. Sophie and Ruthie stood together.

“I want to thank Captain Harris and the entire 48th Field Hospital,” Bradley said. “The number of men this unit has saved in the past week humbles me. I know how hard you’ve worked day and night. As an aside, some of the units wanted to know if, when they’re deployed, the 48th will be close. Something about ‘angels’ here.”

Ruthie nudged Sophie forward with her elbow. Sophie stepped back, looked at her friend, and whispered, “Don’t you dare.”

Bradley continued, “It may be quiet for a time, but it won’t be long before we’re back at it. I know the 48th can handle anything we throw at ‘em. Anyway, thank you again.”

En masse, the 48th saluted their general and he saluted back.

Everyone in the 48th knew what the ‘angel’ comment meant. When Bradley departed, most came by to congratulate Sophie.

“We’re all angels,” she said.

…

By May 1st, the Allies had achieved all of their immediate goals and the fighting leveled off. The Allies, which included the US II Corps, the British First Army, the French XIX Corps and the British 8th Army, redeployed positions and re-armed.

On May 5th, the Allies, in force on all fronts, attacked.

On May 7th, the British 8th Army under General Bernard Montgomery entered Tunis and the US II Corp under Omar Bradley, who had replaced George Patton, entered Bizerte.

...

The 48th Field Hospital worked day and night taking care of casualties, only getting some rest on May 8th.

Six days later, on May 11, 1943, all Axis resistance ended with the surrender of just under a quarter million German and Italian troops.

On May 12th, 48th Field Hospital began packing up equipment when they received a visit from Colonel Teller, Danny's boss. Escorted by Harris, Teller came looking for Sophie.

"Permission to enter," Harris said, standing outside Sophie's tent.

"C'mon in," Ruthie yelled.

Harris and Teller entered. Sophie and Ruthie acknowledged their entrance with nods, but continued to pack. No one in the 48th had been saluting anyone in the chaos of the last few weeks. Teller's jaw stiffened and he stood stock still. Harris quickly understood what Teller's posture meant. He turned, saluted, and said louder than normal, "Colonel, Sir, may I present Captain Sollar, a cracker-jack surgeon loaned to us by the French, and First Lieutenant Bunnen, a skilled and able surgical nurse."

Sophie and Ruthie quickly realized the faux pas, stood to attention, saluted, and said together, "Colonel."

Appeased, Teller responded, "I'd like a word with the Captain."

Sophie asked, "Is this about Major Booker, sir?"

"Yes."

"If you don't mind, I'd like Lieutenant Bunnen by my side."

"As you wish," Teller said. He turned to Harris and said, "You're excused, Captain."

Harris saluted and exited the tent.

Sophie sat on her cot and Ruthie stood by her side. Sophie reached up and took Ruthie's hand.

"The Krauts gave Major Booker's dog tag to the Red Cross a week ago. We have no other information."

"Nothing about where his body might be?" Sophie asked.

"No, Captain. I'm sorry. Just a dog tag," Teller said, head down.

"I see," Sophie said faintly. Ruthie squeezed her hand.

"However," Teller went on, "we've learned that the driver assigned to the Major, a corporal by the name of Jeffery Trop, was taken prisoner and is now in a POW camp in Servigliano, Italy. Of course, we have no way of communicating with Corporal Trop at this time. Unless the corporal escapes, we're not likely to learn the details of Major Booker's death until after the war. It's also possible that the corporal will be moved north to another POW camp closer to Germany."

A dim light went on behind Sophie's eyes.

"Might I write to Corporal Trop?" Sophie asked.

"You can try, through the Red Cross. The US and the Krauts will censor everything except how lonely or homesick you or they may be," Teller said. "Some camps allow mail, many don't. I can't promise anything you send will get through."

Teller stood for a while. Sophie and Ruth could think of nothing more to ask.

"For what it's worth," he added, "Major Booker was the best staff officer I've had the privilege to work with. The rest of my staff would agree. He was smart, intuitive, hardworking, and a friend. We are sorry for his loss. We knew you two were ... good friends."

"For what it's worth, Colonel," Ruthie interrupted, "Sophie and Danny were husband and wife."

Teller's head popped back. "That's not on the Major's record."

"No, it wasn't," Sophie said. "Nor mine. We were married on March 3rd in Casablanca. Danny kept the marriage contract."

"His belongings have been shipped to his parents in Detroit, if I remember correctly," Teller said.

"Yes. Danny's from Detroit."

"At this point, there's nothing I can do to change your status. You'll have to take it up with the Army. I have no idea what you need to do or who you talk to."

"Thank you for coming," Sophie said. Sophie stood, and together she and Ruthie saluted Teller, who saluted back, turned and exited.

Just like she had the night Sophie learned Danny was MIA, she cried on and off until morning. "He's gone, Ruthie. He's gone."

Ruthie, as she had every night that Sophie couldn't stop wailing, got off her cot to comfort and hug her bunkmate. "You and me, we'll make it through this. I'm here for you."

Later that day, Sophie sat in Harris' tent to listen to

the orders for 48th Field Hospital.

"Don't know when or where," Harris said, "but they're amassing troops and supplies in Tunis, Tripoli and Algiers for something. Must be an invasion. I'm guessing southern France, Italy, maybe Sicily, Greece or even Normandy. Doesn't make any difference to us. We follow where the Army goes."

"I'm in," Sophie said. "I don't care how long it takes."

"Glad to hear it," Harris said. "You doing okay otherwise?"

"Still angry. I'd like to take a week off and head south to Fériana to see my cousin."

"Go and come back ready to work," Harris said.

Sophie hitched a ride on a C-47 and flew into Thélepte at the old airfield. Broken planes, American and German, filled the edges of the runway. External signs of the armies that had traipsed back and forth through southern Tunisia for over three months, whether German or Allied, remained everywhere. The Tunisian villagers' emotional scars would last for a generation. Sophie donned a head scarf and hitched a ride for the thirty-minute trip to Fériana.

Nearing the clinic, Sophie saw a line of chairs outside the front door filled with seated women waiting to be seen. When they saw Sophie, they began to scream "Safiyah, Safiyah!" and ululate. Sophie smiled and stayed outside to greet those she knew.

With the noise, Hélène and Gloria ran out the door of the clinic.

Hélène, spotting Sophie, shouted, "You're here," and greeted her cousin with a tremendous hug, pulling Sophie off the ground. Gloria stood in the doorway, grinning.

"You're staying," Hélène insisted, once they separated.

"Only a week," Sophie said. "The Army is preparing for an invasion. Where and when, we don't know."

"Oh, we hoped you'd stay," Gloria said. "We need you."

"I'll help this week, but I'm still needed on the front lines." Looking to Gloria, Sophie asked, "You're here for good now?"

"Yes," Gloria said, her eyes darting to Hélène. "It's my home now."

"Let's get inside," Hélène said. "Are you okay?"

"Not really. I've sad news to tell you."

Sophie followed Hélène and Gloria into the freshly painted clinic. Everything had been replaced courtesy of the U. S. Army: beds, tables, instruments, shelving, plumbing, and electric fixtures. Two women, both pregnant, sat on exam tables, waiting for either Hélène or Gloria.

"Nice," Sophie said, looking around. "Let's sit."

"What's the news?" Hélène said as she grabbed Gloria's hand.

"Danny ... was killed in action."

Hélène's hand flew to her mouth and her eyes filled with tears. "Oh no. That's terrible," she said. "When, how?"

"We don't know the particulars. I saw him on April 19th and he spent the night. He left camp in a Jeep on the afternoon of April 20th and never returned. The Red Cross delivered his dog tag a month later. The jeep driver who was with him is a POW in Italy. That's all we know."

"How are you doing?" Gloria asked.

"How you'd expect - shitty. I didn't believe it at first because he'd been grounded after the threats against all of us for killing that SS Colonel. Then the battles came, and I didn't have the luxury of mourning. Some days, we're up to our elbows in injured men. Lucky to get two or three hours of sleep at any time. I didn't have time to be depressed."

"Been there, done that, after Kasserine Pass," Gloria said.

"I've lost six pounds," Sophie said. "I'm tired all the time, I've missed two periods, and I sleep with one eye open, waiting to be called or thinking of Danny."

"We won't wake you for the week. That's a promise," Hélène said.

Anyway," Sophie continued, "I'm just so angry at the Bosches. First they took my father. Then they took Danny and all our plans for the future. I'll stay in the Army until the war is over, and help however I can. After that, I don't know."

"You can always join us, you know," Hélène said. "Here or in Palestine."

"I have nowhere else to go, so yes, I was hoping I might still join you," Sophie said.

Hélène stood and gave her cousin another hug. Then she and Gloria went to treat the two women patiently waiting to be seen.

Hélène and Gloria had moved to a two-bedroom apartment next door to the old mayor's home while the clinic underwent renovation, but then they stayed. The joy of having medical care for women overrode the gossip about the odd relationship between Hélène and Gloria. The townspeople said nothing.

Sophie tried sleeping alone in the new clinic bedroom that night. As soon as the light went off, visions of Danny dying, war injuries, SS Colonel Gunther, and her father swirled in her head. She needed Ruthie, or Hélène, or someone, anyone, just to be there for her. Sophie picked up her pillow and sheets, exited the clinic, and walked around the corner to Hélène and Gloria's apartment. She pounded on the door until Hélène answered.

"I can't sleep alone," Sophie said. Her eyes were haunted.

Hélène understood, said nothing, and opened the door. "Come in."

Hélène brought an army cot into the bedroom she shared with Gloria, and laid the cot on the floor next to her side of the bed.

Gloria, now sitting up, said, "We're here for you."

Sophie nodded and mouthed, "Thank you."

Sophie made it through that night and stayed the week next to her cousin and Gloria. When the week was over, Sophie returned to the 48th Field Hospital, anxious to help prepare for the invasion of Europe.

Her first morning back, Sophie vomited after breakfast.

Chapter Twenty-Seven

Tunis, Tunisia
June 1943

In the middle of June, the 48th Field Hospital moved to Tunis to continue preparations for an invasion. General Gaspar, the Chief Medical Officer for 1st Infantry, came by to conduct inspections. Gaspar had been elevated to Lieutenant General and he brought promotions with gold oak leaf pins for both Harris and Sophie, elevating them to major. Sophie demanded that Harris be promoted first, even by a minute. Although technically the higher-ranking captain, Sophie wanted no part of being the CSurg and running the unit. Harris thanked her for the consideration. Harris, who continued to be disliked by most of the staff on a personal basis, ran a very successful unit with high morale. Moreover, he was courteous to Sophie and she was touched by it.

After pinning on their promotions, Gaspar took Sophie aside and told her how sorry he felt after learning of Danny's death.

"I talked to Teller over in Intel and he told me you two were married. That right?" Gaspar asked.

"Yes," Sophie said. "Danny had the marriage contract done by a rabbi in Casablanca. We were never sure whether it would be valid, but we didn't care."

"I might not have let you two go if I thought you'd marry the guy," Gaspar said.

“If you hadn’t, we’d have used the Imam in Fériana and done it that way,” Sophie said.

That got a laugh from Gaspar. “You been in touch with his family?”

“No. They didn’t know we were married. They might figure it out when they get Danny’s locker. Maybe after the war, I’ll write to them. It’s a lot to think about.”

“Yeah,” Gaspar said. “Anyway, sorry for your loss. Harris has told me a few times that you’re the real deal. People are still calling you the ‘Angel of North Africa.’”

“I wish they wouldn’t. I’m just human, I make mistakes and I don’t save everyone. I don’t need the pressure of being a miracle worker.”

“To a wounded soldier, it helps to think an angel is looking after them,” Gaspar said gently. “You’re a powerful presence. No need to deny them that.”

Sophie remained silent, knowing that Gaspar was right.

“Another thing,” Gaspar went on. “The French XIXth helped quite a bit in the last push to Tunis. I met with the head of their medical team, a General Leveque. He said he knows you.”

Sophie’s face broke out into sunshine.

“I know Maurice. He was a good friend of my father from the First War. My father and I worked with him when the Germans invaded Belgium catching the French medical units unprepared. He commandeered us.”

“I told him about your father. He was deeply saddened.

“They were good friends,” Sophie said.

“That said, he wants you back.”

“What did you tell him?”

“Absolutely not. You’re ours. But I might trade you for the Louvre, the Eiffel tower, and a case of Chateau Lafitte Rothschild Bordeaux every year.”

Sophie smiled. “You wouldn’t.”

“No. You’re too valuable to let go. Anyway, Leveque laughed at the offer and said to say hello.”

“If you see him again, please say hello from me.”

“I’ll do that.”

“There’s also a sergeant under Leveque named Kilie who told me about your surgical feats on a moving train. He also said to say hello again.”

“I saw him briefly when the French XIXth got swamped,” Sophie said.

“Just so you know, Major, there’s a lot of people cheering for you.”

Sophie nodded.

Gaspar left to visit other hospital units and make promotions.

Sophie’s rare and intermittent vomiting lasted for only a few days after returning from Fériana. She assumed she had eaten something on her visit. Although the nausea dissipated, she felt fatigued much of the time. Ruthie, playing the friendly psychiatrist, thought the lull in the fighting had finally given Sophie the chance to be depressed.

Ruthie knew she needed to take Sophie’s mind off Danny’s death. At night, before bed, Ruthie would talk of their plans after the war. “I want seven kids, a big house, and two dogs, somewhere warm, maybe San Diego. I just have to find a guy who agrees.”

Every night, she changed cities, house size, number of children and animals.

Sophie would laugh at the suggestions each time and it diverted her attention from her sadness. Ruthie then demanded that Sophie say what she might do at war's end.

Sophie told Ruthie that she'd most likely go to Palestine with Hélène and Gloria, or she might return to France and restart her practice in Metz. Some nights, Sophie toyed with the idea that she might move to the United States, but not to Detroit or Ann Arbor. Those places, close to Danny's family, would not allow closure.

Ruthie became more and more sisterly to Sophie, doing everything she could to cheer up her bunkmate. Ruthie continued to encourage Sophie to keep thinking about her future, but not to make any decisions until after the war. The diversions helped.

Sicily had been selected for invasion the previous January by Roosevelt and Churchill at the Casablanca Conference. Only a few knew.

The invasion of Sicily would be called Operation Husky. The combined forces of the Allies would be led, as in Tunisia, by the British General Harold Alexander. George Patton would lead the U.S. 7th Army and Bernard Montgomery would lead the British 8th Army.

The invasion of Sicily began on July 10, 1943. The British landed at the southernmost part of Sicily while the United States landed to the southwest. The Americans secured their beachhead by that evening. By the third day, the American-controlled beachhead went fifteen miles into Sicily. On July 13th, the capture of the Biscari airfield cleared the way for medical hospital units to land.

The temperature in Tunis on July 14th measured one-hundred-ten degrees Fahrenheit at two p.m. Every member of the 48th worked and sweated, packing the essentials for the flight to Sicily scheduled the next day.

That afternoon, Ruthie entered her shared tent to find Sophie asleep.

“Wake up,” Ruthie murmured, nudging her friend. “We’ve got a staff meeting before mess.”

Sophie shook her head and sat up. Sweat stains covered her tee shirt.

“We’ve been sweating like pigs all day and it’s not getting cooler. Better take a shower before the meeting,” Ruthie said.

“I’m beat,” Sophie said.

“You need to shower; it’ll make you feel better. I’m going over to the PX to buy some toothpaste. I’ll meet you in the shower.”

Sophie trudged off to the communal showers. The water temperature in the elevated water tanks, baked in the hot sun, measured ninety degrees.

Sophie, eyes closed, relaxed under the spray. She planned to stay under the relaxing waterfall as long as she could, never mind how hot it was. As she stood transfixed by the water, her thoughts went to the shower in Casablanca with Danny. A faint smile crossed her face.

When Sophie opened her eyes, she saw Ruthie, returned from the PX. Ruthie, head atilt in curiosity, was staring at Sophie.

“What are you looking at?” Sophie asked.

“Your body,” Ruthie said.

"This isn't some sexual thing, is it?"

"No dummy. When was your last period?"

"March. But what's it to you?" Sophie turned away and started scrubbing her arms. "My periods disappear with stress. When I fled France in 1940, I went six months without a period. Trust me. I'm stressed and happy that I don't have to deal with periods."

"I've been in the shower with you, what, five to six times a week for three months? You've lost weight but your breasts are bigger than they were six weeks ago. And your abdomen looks rounder."

"Not possible," Sophie said, continuing to scrub herself.

"Jesus, Sophie, you're a doctor. I think you're pregnant. You gotta be checked," Ruthie insisted gently. "You can't go into a war zone pregnant. No way. I won't let you."

"There are no pregnancy tests available in any of the units," Sophie said harshly. "If we send my urine out it would take weeks. We used protection every time. I'm not pregnant, and I'm going to Sicily."

"No, you're not," Ruthie said. "The last flight doesn't leave until sixteen hundred tomorrow. There's a gynecologist in the 37th who's seen two of our nurses. We're going to see him tomorrow morning."

Sophie, frustrated, didn't answer. She moved under the shower head. There was only the sound of rushing water pounding her head as she considered the possibilities. After a moment, she stepped out of the waterfall

"If it'll placate you," Sophie said, "then fine, I'll go. Let's not talk about it anymore tonight and don't tell a soul what you're thinking."

Surprisingly, Sophie slept through the night. The

next morning, Ruthie had to rustle her out of bed. Together, they went to the motor pool to borrow a Jeep and Ruthie drove across Tunis to the 37th Field Hospital group. During the ride, Sophie had little to say and seemed to be in a trance-like state, staring glassy-eyed at the hustle-bustle of the early morning Tunis traffic.

Not surprisingly, chaos ruled at the 37th Field Hospital too, as everyone was also packing equipment to be shipped off to Sicily.

Ruthie led the way and Sophie, curiously quiet, followed. After a few queries, they located Major Marv Sisken, a gynecologist from San Diego.

"What's up, Major?" Sisken asked, looking at Sophie.

"This is Sophie Sollar," Ruthie said, "a surgeon in the 48th. I think she's pregnant. She won't believe me."

Sisken turned to Ruthie. "You're doing the talking for the Major, Lieutenant?"

"Yes, we're best friends and bunkmates," Ruthie said. "We're supposed to ship out to Sicily later today. I had to drag her here."

"My breasts are larger and I haven't had had a period since March," Sophie said.

"Have you been sexually active?" Sisken said.

"Yes, in April," Sophie said, blushing, and held up her wedding band. "I – I'm married…or was. We used protection every time."

"And where is your husband now?"

Sophie took a deep breath.

"Major Booker was in 1st Infantry intelligence. He was captured and killed by the Nazis on April 20th," Sophie said.

"I'm sorry for your loss," Sisken said. "But all the exam tables and speculums are packed."

"We're not leaving until you examine her," Ruthie said.

Sisken sighed heavily. "Why did I have a feeling you'd say that. Fine. There are still some tents up with cots. Follow me."

As they walked, Sisken asked Sophie questions. "Have you had morning sickness?"

"A few weeks ago, I was nauseous and vomited a few times. Not since then."

"Are you fatigued?"

"We're a surgical unit. We're always fatigued."

"Any mood changes?"

"I just lost my husband. Yes."

They approached a tent.

"You want to stay out here and guard the door, Lieutenant?" Sisken asked Ruthie. "You both know this whole thing is off the record. Got it?"

"Sure," Ruthie said.

Ten minutes later, Sisken walked out of the tent. "She's dressing."

"What do you think?" Ruthie asked.

"Honest opinion?" Sisken asked.

"What else?"

"Ninety-nine percent chance she's pregnant. I'm thinking eleven, twelve weeks."

"Oh, shit," Ruthie said.

"She's the one everybody calls the 'Angel?'" Sisken asked.

"Yes."

"Big loss for the 48th."

"Yes," Ruthie said. "Terribly, awful, big."

Sisken nodded agreement and walked away as Sophie exited the tent, looked at Ruthie, exhaled, and said, "Thank you. We've got to get back to the base and tell Harris."

The trip back across Tunis took longer than expected. By the time Sophie and Ruthie got back to camp, the trucks had already departed for the airfield. Panicked, Ruthie grabbed her suitcase and together they rushed off to find a taxi to the airfield.

In the taxi, Ruthie found Sophie again lost in thought. "You okay?"

"Yeah. I'm good," Sophie said. "Thank you again for having me checked."

"You'd have done it for me."

"I would have. You'll tell Harris?" Sophie asked, "and get it all straight. Don't tell him I'm sorry. I'm not. I thought maybe I'd go anyway but if it gets crazy busy, I'd be putting the baby in jeopardy. I can't do that to Danny."

"Danny?"

"It's his child, so to me, it's him whether it's a boy or girl. I can't go."

"Good choice," Ruthie said.

"I knew you were right. I dreamt only of him last night, Fériana, the escape, Casablanca, Marrakech, the nights in our tent. I told him about the baby. He asked me to take care of it."

Ruthie sniffled and wiped a tear with her sleeve. She needed to say nothing more.

When they arrived, all but one of the C-47s had departed. Major Harris and all the doctors and nurses were already airborne. Sophie and Hélène reported to the air controller, a master sergeant in the AAF, holding a large sheath of bound papers.

"You two were AWOL," the controller said. "Major Harris was pissed. Big time."

"Is that the last C-47 for the 48th?" Sophie asked.

"Yep, 'W37' on the side." The controller held up the sheath of papers. "You two are the only ones on the manifest. I've had to move your names from three previous flights. If you don't make this one, you'll have to swim to Sicily. This C-47 is filled with equipment. There are a few seats in the cabin behind the cockpit."

"Thanks, Sarge," Ruthie said.

Neither Ruthie nor Sophie told the sergeant that Sophie had no intention of getting on the plane. Only Ruthie carried a suitcase as they both rushed to the C-47, 'W37' marked on the fuselage. As they neared the plane, an AAF corporal stood in the open side door waving them on. When Sophie and Ruthie made it to the door, the right propeller turned over in a cloud of fumes, smoke and noise. Sophie and Ruthie had to scream directly into each other's ears to be heard.

"You'll tell Harris everything when you get to Sicily?" Sophie yelled over the prop noise.

"Yes. We'll miss you. I'll miss you," Ruthie yelled back. "If it's a girl, don't do anything stupid like name her Ruth."

"If it's a boy, I'll name it Ruth anyway."

Sophie hugged Ruth and both started to cry.

"You're the best friend ever," Sophie yelled. "Take

care of yourself. Tell everyone good luck from me. We'll find each other after the war."

"Will do. You have my home address," Ruthie yelled. "Where are you going to go now?"

"I'll stay for a few days with a family I know in Tunis. Then to Fériana, to be with my cousin and work in the clinic. Hopefully I can get my head straight." Sophie yelled.

The right propeller turned over, making the noise level louder than ever.

"Is the controller watching us?" Sophie screamed.

Ruthie, hoarse from yelling, looked back to where the controller had been standing. Not seeing him, she shook her head no and gave Sophie a thumbs up.

Sophie ran toward an airfield exit, away from the controller. Once clear of the plane, Sophie turned back to Ruthie and watched the corporal grab her hand and pull her up and through the door.

Returning to the empty base, she put on one of her favorite outfits from Casablanca, the Elsa Schiaparelli evening dress. She took her suitcase, and walked out in search of a taxi that could take her to the Benoliel's house.

A Focke-Wulfe 190 German fighter plane shot down the USAAF C-47 plane numbered 'W37' twelve miles short of Sicily. All lives were lost. The United States Army listed Major Sophie Sollar and Lieutenant Ruthie Bunnen as aboard the plane.

Sophie had no way of knowing the plight of USAAF 'W37.'

Late that night, a copy of the plane's manifest in hand, Charlie Harris laid his head on his desk and cried. He had lost not only First Lieutenant Ruth Bunnen, but his best and only true friend in the 48th, Major Sophie Sollar. At last, Harris pulled himself together and called General Gaspar to tell him of the crash. He would need at least two surgeons to replace Sophie. The 48th Field Hospital held a ceremony for Sophie and Ruthie two days later. Colonel Cap Teller, Danny's CO, came to pay his respects.

Chapter Twenty-Eight

May 1943
Detroit, Michigan

Marty and Linda Booker had known of Danny's MIA status since the 25th of April. Though not overly religious, they started attending services every Friday night at Temple Israel, a reform synagogue which had opened only days before the Japanese bombed Pearl Harbor. Services were held at the Detroit Institute of Art until a permanent sanctuary could be built. After every service, the Bookers sought out Rabbi Leon Fram for solace.

On Saturday, May 22nd, Phillip Booker, Danny's sixteen-year-old brother, answered a knock on their front door at 4 p.m. At the door stood two U. S. Army officers in dress uniforms: one a colonel, the other a captain. The Colonel held a telegram in his hand.

Phillip yelled, "Mom, Dad, come here! It's about Danny, I think."

Marty and Linda rushed out of the den.

The colonel spoke. "Permission to enter."

Marty opened the door and the officers entered.

"You are the parents of Major Daniel Booker of the United States Army Air Force?"

Linda had already grabbed Marty's arm and started to cry.

"Yes, we are," Marty said.

The Colonel read from a telegram. "The Secretary of War has entrusted me to express his deep regret that your son, Daniel, was killed in action in Tunisia on April 20th of this year while on patrol. The Secretary extends his deepest sympathies to you and your family in your loss. The letter is signed by J. A. Ulio, Adjutant General, United States Army."

Linda Booker collapsed in Marty's arms and both slid to the floor. Per her wishes, Danny's room would remain untouched indefinitely.

Two months later, the U.S. Postal Service delivered Danny's footlocker with all his possessions to the Bookers' front door. Neither Marty nor Linda had the fortitude to open it. Marty and Phillip put the footlocker in Danny's bedroom. Three weeks later, Phillip asked if he could open the locker, and both parents gave him permission, although Linda was reluctant.

Phillip discovered dress and fatigue uniforms, toiletries, a Detroit Tiger baseball cap, a baseball glove and ball, flying magazines and a framed photograph of his family. Unexpected was a French-English dictionary and a primer on basic French. Even more curious was a one-page, folded letter or document in an envelope, hand-written entirely on plain, unlined paper in an unusual form of cursive Hebrew. Phillip showed the document to his parents. Marty and Phillip could pronounce Hebrew writing in printed block script called 'Assyrian' but had no idea how to read or interpret what the document meant.

"What do we do with this?" Linda asked. "I wish I hadn't let Phillip open the trunk."

"I suppose we'll bring it to the rabbi and see if he can decipher it," Marty said.

"Good idea," Phillip said.

"No. Not now," Linda said. "It won't bring my son back. I can't take any more news. It will only make us sadder. Leave it be."

Marty agreed. Phillip, usually curious, didn't want to upset his mother further. So he refolded the paper and replaced it in the original envelope.

"I'll put it on Danny's bookshelf," Phillip said, as he headed off.

The document would be forgotten and remain untouched for two years.

...

Sophie's arrival surprised the Benoliels, but they were only too happy to see her. They had been fortunate to escape the Nazi roundup of Jews in Tunis.

Sophie spent an entire evening telling the family her saga of Djerba, Fériana, the war, Danny and Nick's crash, the escape, Morocco, her marriage and Danny's death. With the children present, she omitted the part about the SS colonel and her pregnancy. Sophie fibbed that she had seen enough war and resigned her commission. She would head to Fériana to be with her cousin and work the clinic they had established.

Later that evening, with Laila, now seventeen, but absent the younger children, Sophie filled in the gaps about Colonel Gunther in detail. Again, she omitted her pregnancy.

"I've been through a lot and still have nightmares," Sophie said. "I don't want to scare anyone if I start crying."

"What can we do?" Jeanne asked.

"Might I sleep in Laila's room on the extra bed? I do better when I'm not alone."

Avram and Jeanne looked at Laila.

Laila didn't say a word, she only stood and came over to Sophie and gave her a hug.

Sophie stayed for two days and three nights. She made it a point to go out alone to lunch with Laila and give her sisterly advice. In the three years since Laila announced she would be a surgeon at dinner, her goals had changed. She now considered nursing a better fit. Sophie supported this choice, much to her parent's delight.

Eight hours on a bus in the middle of summer, wearing a head scarf in 105-degree heat, left a sweaty, tired Sophie in the middle of Fériana. The bus stop was near the open-air market in the center of town. It was close to dinner time, and the vendors were packing up their goods. Within minutes of disembarking, the women at the market had surrounded Sophie, chanting, "Safiyah, Safiyah," ululating in joy, over and over. One woman took her suitcase, two others grabbed Sophie's hands, and all together they proceeded to the clinic surrounding Sophie like worker bees surrounding their queen.

"What are you doing here?" cried Hélène with a mixture of bafflement and delight. She and Gloria thought Sophie was already in Sicily with the Army.

Once inside, Sophie removed her scarf and outer garments and sat heavily at the table. Gloria brought her a large pitcher of lemonade, half of which Sophie quickly drank down.

"We thought you were going with the army?" Gloria asked.

"I'm out," Sophie said.

"Did something bad happen?" Hélène asked. "You told us that you were committed to the end."

"I guess it depends on what you call bad. It was a surprise, that's for sure," Sophie said.

“You’re killing me. What is it?” Hélène asked.

“I’m three months pregnant. The army regulations won’t let me go to Sicily, so where better than here?”

“Oh Sophie,” Hélène said, instantly understanding.

“At least it’s kosher,” Gloria said. “You were married and have your rings on.”

“Funny you should say that,” Sophie said. “I don’t have any official documentation of being married. The wedding rings don’t mean a thing and Danny kept the ketubah in his locker. The army didn’t know we were married, so the whole lot of his stuff along with the ketubah were sent to his parents.”

Sophie went into her blouse and extracted Danny’s wedding band, still on a shoestring.

“This is all I have of him. I never take it off,” Sophie said.

“I know for a fact that the footlocker won’t get there for months,” Gloria said.

“Still,” Hélène said, “you’ll have to write his parents.”

“Danny’s parents didn’t know we were married. He only told them he was seeing me. That’s it. How do you think it will go if I send them a letter saying, Oh, by the way, Danny and I were married and I’m expecting your grandchild?”

“Could go either way, I suppose,” Gloria said.

“What do you mean?” Sophie asked.

“They could believe you or not. No way to tell,” Gloria said.

“Nothing like surprising a grieving family,” Sophie said, “with the news that their son was trapped by some floozy who got herself pregnant. Please send money to this address."

"What'll you do?" Hélène asked.

"I'll send a letter asking for the ketubah or a picture of it at least and tell them no more. What's the worst that could happen?"

"They could burn the ketubah if they haven't already tossed it," Hélène said. "That's the worst."

"But I have to do something."

That night Sophie penned a letter to the Bookers and mailed it from Fériana. She had no idea when or if the letter would make it to Detroit. She sent an identical letter a week later but gave it to a patient who was heading to Tunis and would post it there. Only the first letter mailed from Fériana would arrive.

July 20, 1943

Dear Mr. and Mrs. Booker,

My name is Sophie Sollar and I was Danny's girlfriend. He told me that he mentioned me in his letters. I am so sorry for his loss. May his memory be a blessing to all who knew him.

I know that Danny's footlocker has been sent to you in Detroit. In the footlocker, Danny had kept a document of mine written entirely in hand-written Hebrew that I need badly. If you have this document, I hope you could mail it or a copy or photograph of it to my friends in Tunis: Avram Benoliel, 43 La Fayette Aller, Tunis, Tunisia. I'm living in a small village with my cousin and the postal service is spotty here at best.

Sincerely,

Sophie Sollar

Hélène and Gloria prepared the extra bedroom in their apartment for Sophie. Sophie stayed there for two months before attempting more independence via a move back into the clinic bedroom. She lasted two nights alone, then moved back to Hélène and Gloria's apartment indefinitely.

Chapter Twenty-Nine

Detroit, Michigan
September, 1943

On a warm, humid, September night, Marty Booker entered through the garage door at dinner time. He greeted Linda with a kiss and a "What's for dinner?"

"We got a letter today from a woman named Sophie something who claims to have been Danny's girlfriend," Linda said.

"Danny did say he was seeing someone named Sophie," Marty replied cautiously.

"Yes, but we never knew more than that."

"How many Sophies could there be writing to us? What did she have to say?"

"How sorry she was about Danny and that she needs that funny-looking document from Danny's footlocker. She wants it, or a copy of it, mailed to her in Tunisia."

"Should we send it?" Marty asked.

"I suppose. You think we should find out what it is first?" Linda asked.

"I talked to the rabbi. He said he'd look at it but probably can't translate it unless it's from the Old Testament. He gave me the name of a friend who might be able to do it."

“Maybe just send it, then. I don’t want to know because it’s not going to bring Danny back. I can’t think of any reason that Danny would have had a Hebrew document. It must be hers.”

“Let’s send a copy. The letter said that would be okay,” Marty said. “But I think we should wait. I can’t imagine how difficult it’s going to be to get a private letter mailed to Tunisia during the war. This isn’t going through the U.S. Army post. It might get lost.”

“Maybe we’ll wait for the war to end before we mail it. I put her letter next to the document on Danny’s shelf.”

“I agree,” Marty said, kissing his wife on the forehead.

Neither parent told Phillip about the request.

Chapter Thirty

Servigliano, Italy
September 1943

The day Danny arrived at Servigliano, he decided, given an opportunity, he would try to escape. He also knew that no one spoke English in rural Italy. He set about learning as much Italian as possible from the guards.

Danny's three years in intelligence gave him some perks, unknown to most soldiers. He collaborated often with British Intelligence and considered some of their officers among his closest friends. He shared dinner one night with the officers in Harold Alexander's intelligence section and learned of a ploy the British were using to aid Allied prisoners of war if they were able to escape.

Packages and mail, delivered through the Red Cross, arrived weekly for the POWs. The game Monopoly was often included in those packages. Danny had discovered that the British Intelligence Agency, MI-6, sometimes doctored the Monopoly game tokens to contain wads of silk that showed the locations of nearby safe houses. A small magnetic compass would also be imbedded at the bottom of one of the tokens, as well as currency of the local country, hidden in the piles of Monopoly money. The 'rigged sets' would have a red dot placed in a corner of the board which appeared to be a printing error.

Aware of this British ploy, Danny grabbed a Monopoly set every time one appeared looking for the red dot. Absent the dot, he gave away the first two sets he'd taken. During the last week in August, he obtained one of the doctored sets. He pocketed the compass, a few thousand Italian lire, and a silk wad that showed safe houses within fifty miles of Servigliano. Danny waited, hoping an opportunity to escape would occur. He didn't wait long.

In early September 1943, the POWs at Servigliano heard that the Italians had surrendered. Still, the camp Commandant refused to set any prisoners free.

...

In 1943, the Allies and the Russians took the war to the Third Reich. The Germans suffered a massive defeat at the Battle of Stalingrad in February 1943. Afterward, the Russians began pushing the Germans westward. The invasion of Sicily, or Operation Husky, began on July 10, 1943. A month later, the Allies had driven the Axis forces, ground, naval and air, from the island. For the first time since 1941, the Allies had complete control of the Mediterranean Sea and free reign for their merchant ships.

The Italians had had enough of the war and the fall of Sicily lead to the toppling of Benito Mussolini's government on July 25th. The Allies invaded the Italian mainland on September 3rd, 1943, and that same day, the Italians signed an armistice taking them out of the war.

Germany, alone and angered by the Italian truce, responded by attacking Italian troops in Italy, France and the Balkans. Germany set up a puppet government in Rome and by September 12th, they had occupied all of Italy still under their control.

From the day of the armistice signing on September

3rd to mid-September, many of the Italian guards at the various POW camps simply opened the gates, allowing the prisoners to flee. It would take the Germans two weeks to regain control of all the POW camps. The Commandant of the Servigliano POW camp, Colonel Bacci, however, was a hard-core fascist who decided to keep the prisoners until the Germans arrived.

On September 14th, word that the Germans would arrive in Servigliano spread around the camp. Some prisoners made a dash for the gates, but were stopped by the few remaining guards, who fired warning shots. The Senior British Officer, in the camp, Captain J. H. Derek Miller, threatened Bacci with an all-out riot if the guards didn't open the gates. Captain Miller signed a form which gave him responsibility for any POWs who might be killed by local fascists or Germans. Bacci agreed and ordered the gates opened. The prison emptied.

...

Danny and a small group of Americans loaded as much food as possible into their pockets and rushed openings in the camp fences. When the guards fired shots over their heads, the Americans skulked back to the center of camp. Everyone believed that if the Germans took the camp, they'd all be shipped north. The best time to escape was now.

Moments later, men started yelling, "The gates are open! The gates are open!"

Danny and his cohorts fled. He'd told his friends that if they stayed together in a large group, they would all be caught by the local Fascists or German patrols and be killed or returned to another camp. With Danny's advice, his friends fled in singles and pairs. Everyone headed south toward Allied lines. Danny stood at the gate. It dawned on him that if the masses headed south, the Germans would catch most of them.

He turned and headed north, alone, hoping only that he wouldn't be caught.

Danny travelled only at night, staying hidden during the day. His plan was to stay hidden until the Allied armies arrived or he'd be found by a friendly resistance group. From within ravines and or behind tree trunks, he saw trucks loaded with German soldiers on their way south.

By the third day, Danny's plan to stay hidden fell apart – he had run out of food. Sooner or later, he'd need some luck and hoped to find a family who wouldn't turn him in to the Germans or Fascists. The crude silk map from the Monopoly game suggested that a safe farmhouse existed outside a small village named Corridonia, twenty miles north of the prison. He found what he thought was the farm, and watched all day from a tree limb.

The farmer lived there with his wife and four children, two boys and two girls. Danny guessed the children's ages ranged from four to twelve. Danny watched the man kiss his wife for no apparent reason. She pushed him away and they started to laugh. Later, the farmer and his wife played soccer with all of the children. For no specific reason other than a tiny spot on a map and the man's loving behavior, Danny hoped the family would have no ties to the Fascists. He knew his decision depended on luck and nothing else. At dinner time, Danny approached and knocked on the door of the farmhouse. He hoped his primitive Italian would suffice. If the farmer appeared unfriendly, he was prepared to run.

The farmer's wife answered the door. She gasped and held her hand over her mouth at the sight of the bedraggled, unshaven fugitive. Danny, equally frightened, backed away from the door, ready to flee. Her husband rushed to the door but was not armed.

The farmer was a dark, swarthy man with a pleasant smile. He stood about five foot five, seven inches shorter than Danny. His wife was slightly taller than him, with a lighter complexion and wispy brown hair.

"*Sono Americano. Ho fame. Per favore,*" Danny said.

The farmer repeated, "*Americano*?"

"*Si.*"

The farmer strode past Danny into the courtyard, looked around for others, friends or foes. Surmising that Danny had no accomplices, he turned and pushed Danny into the farmhouse. Inside, Danny saw all four children at the table. They stopped eating, their eyes wide. Each swiveled their heads between Danny and their parents trying to figure out what to do.

The farmer spoke very fast, his hands waving right and left. The two older children got up from the table and closed the curtains to every window. While the children scurried around, the farmer brought a stool to the table and sat Danny down.

"Mangia," the farmer's wife said, placing a bowl of homemade spaghetti in front of Danny. She sat across from him and folded her arms.

Before Danny took a bite, he pointed to himself and tried his meager Italian. "*Grazie. Mi chiamo Danny Booker.*"

"*Mi chiamo Carlo Scavuli.*"

"*Mi chiamo Beatrice Scavuli.*"

The children each gave their names, giggling shyly.

Famished, Danny dug into the spaghetti which was covered with a delicious homemade marinara sauce with small pieces of meat. Danny could have easily eaten six helpings, but he refused by waving his hands.

Beatrice disregarded the hand signals and put a large second scoop on his plate.

When Carlo left the house for a moment, Danny stood and put all the Italian lire on the counter in front of Beatrice.

"*Grazie*," Danny said.

Beatrice, surprised, looked at the wad of cash, smiled, and put it in her apron pocket. She said, "*Grazie*," back to Danny.

After dinner, Danny tried to help clear, but Carlo pushed him back to his seat. As Beatrice cleaned, Carlo brought out an old, dog-eared world atlas.

"*Dove*?" Carlo asked.

The older children stood aside as Danny opened the atlas and found the United States.

"Here," Danny said, then corrected himself. "*Qui*."

He pointed to Detroit, saying, "Detroit."

"Ah, Detroit," Carlo said. "*Automobili*."

Danny smiled and said, "*Si*. Automobiles." He then pretended to drive a car recklessly, which delighted the children.

Danny then asked Carlo the same question he'd been asked: "*Dove*?"

Carlo turned the pages to the Province of Macerata and pointed to Corridonia.

Danny read the map, butchering the pronunciation of Corridonia to Car-eye-doo-nia.

The entire family laughed and Danny shrugged.

Danny searched the map until he found a city nearby Corridonia on the Adriatic Sea. He pointed at Ancona. Carlo nodded agreement. Danny walked his fingers over the map, asking how long it would take to walk to Ancona.

"*Due giorni,*" Carlo said slowly.

Danny didn't understand 'due giorni.'

Carlo pulled a calendar off the wall and pointed to *Lunedi,* the Italian word for Monday.

"*Uno giorno,*" he said, then pointed to *Lunedi* and *Martedi,* the word for Tuesday, together. "*Due Giorni.*"

Danny nodded to show he understood 'two days.'

Carlo said slowly, "*Due giorni. Andiamo a Ancona.*" Carlo pointed to Ancona on the map, pretended to drive a car, and then pointed to Danny and then to himself. He repeated, "*Due giorni.*"

"*Grazie,*" Danny said, shaking Carlo's hand. "*Grazie, grazie.*"

Beatrice tugged at Danny's clothes. He wore a ratty wool coat given to him at Servigliano, but his shirt and pants came from Uncle Sam. Beatrice pointed to the U.S. Army issued olive green shirt and pants and said, "*Americano. Non buono.*"

"*Si,*" Danny agreed.

Beatrice waved for Danny to give her his pants and shirt. She kept waving until he understood. With the children rolling on the floor with laughter, Danny, making funny faces, stripped down to his underwear. Pretending to sniff the pants, Beatrice made a face of exaggerated disgust. A fresh wave of laughter rocked the children. That night, Carlo brought Danny a wool blanket and a straw pillow, then waved for him to follow into the root cellar. Danny laughed to himself as he realized he was to hide in a cellar again, just as he had in Fériana. In the kitchen above, Beatrice first washed Danny's clothes, dyed them black, then hung them before the hearth to dry.

The next day, Danny worked as a farmhand alongside Carlo, Beatrice and the two older children, harvesting cantaloupes and putting them into the back of an old, broken-down Austro-Fiat AFL truck with bald tires. Danny was given a pair of old shoes bigger than anything Carlo might have worn, their provenance a mystery, plus a frayed flat cap.

The next morning, Carlo again opened the cellar door at five a.m.

"*Andiamo,*" Carlo said with a wave of his hand.

Danny climbed out of the cellar, where Beatrice greeted him with a cup of brutally strong coffee, a small loaf of bread and some cheese. Danny hugged Beatrice and said, "*Grazie.*"

Carlo repeated, "*Andiamo.*"

With the truck full of melons, Danny sat in the passenger seat beside Carlo. The old truck coughed, spewed, stalled, and shook, but made it to Ancona.

As they neared, Carlo grew tense, watching everyone in the street. Danny understood his concern but had no idea what to look for other than armed German soldiers, whom they passed in modest numbers. As they drove near the seaport, Danny saw a Star of David on the side of a small building on a street named Via Astagno. The doors and windows on the building were boarded up.

"*Qui,*" Danny said and pointed to the Levantine Synagogue of Ancona. "*Qui.*"

Carlo pulled the truck to the side of the road and stopped. He gave Danny a curious look and asked, "*Ebreo*?"

Danny nodded and said, "Ahh. *Si.* Hebrew, *Ebreo.*"

Danny used two hands to shake Carlo's right hand and added, "*Grazie, grazie.*" He was about to jump out of the car when Carlo pulled him back. Without a word, Carlo handed him the entire wad of Italian lire he'd had given to Beatrice on the first night in their house.

Danny nodded and said, "*Grazie.*" He closed the truck door and walked toward the synagogue. If he ever got out of Italy alive, Danny hoped he'd return one day to thank Carlo and Beatrice.

Danny knew he could not stay with the Scavullis any longer. He also knew that Italian synagogues had been shuttered and many Italian Jews rounded up by the Nazis. Given his limited knowledge of speaking Italian, he hoped that he might find someone, perhaps a caretaker for the synagogue, who might be helpful.

He walked around each side, only to find all the doors boarded except one small side door, secured by an old padlock. Danny found a bench twenty yards farther down Via Astagno and sat, hoping that someone would enter the small door to the synagogue.

At two p.m. an elderly woman, perhaps seventy, bent over, gray hair bound in a tight scarf, approached the synagogue and turned toward the side of the padlocked door. Danny stood and walked quickly to the same side of the temple to find the padlock missing. He opened the door, entered, and closed the door.

On the main floor of the synagogue, he found the woman dusting the candelabras adorning the temple. She heard Danny's footsteps and turned, giving him a look of curiosity. Danny took off his double flat cap and the woman shook her head vigorously, tapping her head with her hand. Danny replaced his hat, forgetting for a moment that Jewish men of religion always have their heads covered.

She smiled.

Danny said, "*Sono Americano. Sono Ebreo.*"

The woman gave Danny a look of concern.

Danny repeated, "*Sono Americano. Sono Ebreo.*"

The woman finally understood and waved for Danny to follow her. She led him into an office filled with books in Italian, Spanish and Hebrew. She pulled out a chair and had Danny sit, then closed the door behind her as she left. Twenty minutes later, a man in his late sixties with a white beard, wearing a black suit topped with a fedora, came in. He removed the fedora to reveal a kippah underneath.

Danny stood and said, "*Sono Americano. Sono Ebreo.*"

The man smiled and said in perfect King's English, "Welcome to Ancona. I'm Rabbi Giovani Brando. I was an assistant rabbi at the Spanish Synagogue in Manchester, England, before coming home to Ancona. How can I help you?"

"I escaped from Servigliano a week ago."

"Along with hundreds of others, so I hear. Congratulations on making it this far. I won't ask you how."

"I wouldn't tell you," Danny said.

"So, how do we get you south of the Nazis, eh?" Brando asked.

"Yes. If possible."

"Whoever helped you to get here has you looking the part of an Italian farmer but one word from your mouth and it's over. Capish?"

Danny nodded. "Yes."

"First," Brando said, "you can't stay in the synagogue. With the Nazis, we don't even come here for services."

"Where then?"

"With me."

"Let me guess, to your root cellar?"

"Yes. I'll need to talk to someone in the Resistance and see if they have any ideas."

"Good. I have no ideas, other than I hate boats," Danny said.

Danny stayed in Brando's cellar and ate like a king for the next two days. On the third day, an hour before dawn, Brando and Danny exited Brando's house.

"Where are we going?" Danny asked.

"When you told me you hated boats, it gave me an idea," Brando said. They walked to the Ancona docks. Danny boarded a fishing boat owned by Brando's wife's third cousin, a man named Marco Rossi.

Marco, who wasn't Jewish, had fished the Adriatic his whole life, as had his father and grandfather. Being a practical man, Marco sold his catch exclusively to Mussolini Fascists and Nazis. Marco used the profits to support the La Resistenza, an umbrella term for the loose coalition of resistance groups in Italy. His double life guaranteed Marco safety from reprisals after the war's end.

Marco's boat was a thirty-five-foot diesel trawler called *'La Bella Luna.'* It had its normal crew of three men, plus Danny. They soon set sail south towards Bari, Italy, at the top of the heel of the Italian boot which was already under Allied control. For the next two days, Danny lay in the hold of the trawler, puking. On the morning of the third day, a British destroyer patrolling the southern Adriatic boarded the La Bella Luna. The HMS Wheatland's two tenders approached the fishing boat loaded with armed Marines. Marco gladly transferred his worthless deckhand to the larger ship. On the destroyer, Danny continued to be plagued with sea sickness. On October 1, 1943, the HMS Wheatland finished its Adriatic patrol and dropped Danny at Bari, Italy, before heading to its home port in Malta.

Danny had lost seven pounds during his seven days at sea. He spent the first day at a British army hospital unit outside Bari, getting IVs. The next day, feeling stronger, he started to look for 1st Infantry. The Brits would not issue Danny an official ID, telling him that he would need to obtain papers from the U.S. Army.

Danny learned that 1st Infantry remained outside Messina, Sicily, and the unit would be transferred to England in November. From Bari, Danny found a plane heading to Reggio Calabria across the narrow strait separating Italy from Sicily.

Once in Reggio, Danny found a ride to the ferry crossing at Villa San Giovanni and arrived at the docks in Messina at sundown. With some luck, he found a Jeep heading toward the 1st Infantry encampment and arrived at ten p.m.

Danny underwent the most difficult part of his day at the sentry gate to 1st Infantry. Out of uniform and without ID, he had only letters written by the captain of the HMS Wheatland and the doctors at the British Army hospital. The sentries thought Danny should be placed into the 1st Infantry's brig until his identity could be established. Danny pleaded with the senior sentry, a sergeant, to call Colonel Teller in intelligence. Icily, the sergeant complied.

Phone at his ear, the sergeant listened for a minute, then rounded on Danny.

The sentry and his partner drew their service revolvers and pointed them at Danny.

"You're under arrest. Major Booker died in Tunisia.

So you must be a spy," the sentry snarled.

"May I have the phone for a second," Danny pleaded.

The sentries exchanged looks. The sentry in charge handed Danny the phone, but kept the gun trained on him.

"Is this Colonel Teller?"

"No. Teller's not here. This is Major Kim Margolis. Who the hell are you? It's not Daniel Booker."

"It *is* me, Danny Booker. I'm not dead."

"I don't believe you. Teller received your dog tags from the Red Cross."

"I don't know you, but Colonel Teller's nickname is Cap, though his full name is really Alphonse. He's from Santa Fe, New Mexico, his wife's name is Adeline, his dog's name is Queen and he played double-A baseball for a Cubs' farm team in Boise, Idaho. He quit when he got accepted to the Academy. You want more."

Margolis said, "Holy crap. I'll be there in five minutes."

Danny spent the next three hours in front of Margolis and two other intelligence officers as he recounted his full story. The interview lasted until three-thirty a.m.

"Unbelievable," Margolis said.

"I've got three things I need to do," Danny said.

"How can I help?"

"Not sure. One, I need to let my parents know I'm alive. Two, I need to contact Corporal Trop's family in Seattle to let them know about their son. Three, I need to find the 48th Field Hospital and talk to one of their doctors."

“The 48th is already in England,” Margolis said. “You can try to send a telegram to your parents but it would be a thousand times easier when we get to England. No idea what to do about the family who thinks their son is a POW. I’d start with Teller, who’ll be here at sixteen hundred this afternoon.”

“I’m good with that,” Danny said. “I’m going to need clothing, new ID, and a solid night of sleep. The ground is still rocking from seven days on the Adriatic sea. God, how I hate boats.”

Danny slept until two p.m. the next day, caught leftovers from lunch at the mess hall, then received some army-issued clothing. Afterward, he ran to the Intelligence tent, hoping that Colonel Teller had arrived.

Teller saw Danny immediately. “I wouldn’t have believed it if anyone else had told me. But Margolis convinced me it was you.”

“It’s me, sir,” Danny said.

“Let’s take a walk,” Teller said. “There are things you need to know.”

Danny followed Teller out of the tent. The ‘things you need to know’ Teller mentioned had stirred a feeling of foreboding in him.

The 48th Field Hospital is in England,” Teller said.

“Margolis told me, sir.”

“Major Sollar is not with them.”

“You know Sophie? Where is she?”

“I met Major Sollar and her bunkmate in Tunis to deliver your dog tag. Her CSurg, a Major Harris, said she was the best surgeon he’d ever worked with and even after hearing you were MIA, she continued to work just as hard. She was personally commended by

General Bradley who visited the 48th."

"That's Sophie."

"I also learned from Major Sollar that the two of you had married in secret."

"Oh, you found out. We thought it best to keep it secret."

"I'll get to the point," Teller said, as he stopped to face Danny. "Major Sollar and her friend Lieutenant Bunnen died in a plane crash on the way to Sicily on July 15th. I attended the memorial service. I'm so sorry for your loss."

Danny wavered and Teller stepped closer. Danny waved him off and bent over for a moment. He finally stood, glassy eyed, and took a huge breath. Teller put his hand on Danny's shoulder but said nothing.

"Knowing I'd see Sophie again was what kept me going. I ... I ... I don't know how to process this," Danny said.

"It's your call, Major, but if you need to take time off to see your family, whatever, I'd understand."

Danny turned away, not wanting Teller to see him cry.

"That said, we genuinely could use your experience for the invasion of France. You think you could come back after you've straightened things out?"

Danny wiped his eyes with his fists then turned around. "There's too much to do here to go home. Sophie and I felt the same way. She knew she was needed and went back to work after she thought I was dead. I just need some time to write my folks. Give me a few days."

"I hoped you'd say that. It's an honor to serve with you, Major," Teller said.

Danny wrote his parents to say that he was alive and promised a detailed letter describing his ordeal would be forthcoming. He then had the War Department notify Jeff Trop's parents that Jeff had died trying to escape a Nazi POW camp. Lying to the Trops bothered Danny; he vowed to make things right after the war.

He spent the next two days writing his parents the promised letter. He knew the censors would cross out much of what he'd written. He didn't include any names of the people who'd helped him, nor the places he'd passed through. Nor did he mention Sophie, their marriage, or her death. After he finished writing the nine-page letter, he painstakingly copied it, this time including all the names and places omitted in the first letter. He added an additional four pages describing his love for Dr. Sophie Sollar, their marriage, and her untimely death. He mailed the abbreviated letter to his parents, and stashed the longer version in his suitcase, to be mailed stateside at the end of the war.

The next morning, he woke early and had coffee and a donut. In Sophie's memory, he would work harder than he ever thought possible. It was time to win the war.

Chapter Thirty-One

Fériana, Tunisia

November 8th, 1943

Hélène and Gloria decided the fetus needed a name. Sophie disagreed, saying she didn't want to get attached to a name and then not use it. Secretly, she already had one but didn't want to share that tidbit of information.

Hélène suggested finding a temporary name, but one that would never, ever, under any circumstance, be considered. Gloria's idea of 'Pork Chop' had Sophie in stitches and would be the baby's moniker until D-Day, D for Delivery.

The pregnancy, by best estimates, had reached thirty-eight weeks. With Gloria watching, Hélène had Sophie lay on a table to be examined.

"The cervix hasn't dilated," Hélène said, "but I'm guessing you're thirty-eight weeks, give or take. Pork Chop could come at any time. The baby's head is still up. I'd hate to see it descend in the breech position."

"How 'bout I stand on my head for the day. Pork Chop might get the hint," Sophie said.

"You're not serious, are you?" Gloria asked.

Hélène and Sophie started laughing. "If you haven't figured Sophie out yet, you're a slow learner," Hélène said. "She's told that to pregnant women in breech position for the past three years. They think she's serious, and I have to spend twenty minutes pleading with them not to try."

Gloria gave Sophie a look and then all three started to laugh. Four months in Fériana with Hélène and Gloria had changed Sophie. She smiled constantly, didn't let little things bother her, slept better and, most surprisingly, turned into a practical joker. Simply said, Sophie laughed often, wore a smile and looked forward to being a mother.

Not tempting fate, Sophie remained in the guest bedroom in Hélène's apartment.

"If Pork Chop is still upside down by next week, I'll try to rotate it," Hélène said. "That's not fun."

That week, the new mayor of Fériana presented Sophie with a hand-crafted bassinette made by local artisans out of limbs from an apricot tree. Sophie removed the second twin bed in the unused clinic's bedroom and placed the new bassinette next to the remaining twin bed. Hélène and Gloria remained privately concerned that Sophie's nightmares would return if she stayed alone in the clinic with only the baby.

Sophie continued to see patients until the following week. Her contractions became more frequent after a false labor, and the breech position hadn't changed. Despite her best efforts, Hélène could not rotate Pork Chop out of breech.

On November 19th, just after dinner, Sophie's water broke and she went into active labor. Six hours later, Pork Chop's rump crowned. It was a dangerous moment: breech deliveries could get stuck in the birth canal, cutting off the baby's oxygen supply. With Gloria sitting at the head of the bed encouraging and comforting Sophie, Hélène screamed at an exhausted Sophie to push with each contraction. Sophie, in turn, would yell back, "We should have left you on the goddamn mountain!" The retort confused Gloria but Hélène and Sophie would laugh.

Hélène delivered Pork Chop, a beautiful, healthy, screaming girl, ten minutes later. Gloria took the baby to clean her as Hélène massaged Sophie's deflated abdomen to deliver the placenta. When Gloria laid the naked baby on Sophie's bare chest, all three women wept tears of joy.

"Thank you," Sophie said through her tears. "I only wish Danny were here to see his daughter."

Hélène and Gloria, holding hands, agreed.

"I can't call her Pork Chop anymore," Hélène said. "She's too precious."

"I've had a name from the day I found out I was pregnant," Sophie said. "Ruth Sollar Booker."

Sophie placed Danny's wedding band, still on her shoestring necklace, into the baby's palm, knowing that the baby would reflexly grab it. Baby Ruth didn't disappoint and firmly grabbed the ring.

Despite Hélène and Gloria insisting that Sophie and little Ruthie should stay in the apartment's second bedroom, Sophie moved into the clinic's bedroom. Her nightmares, already rare, disappeared on the day of Ruthie's birth. If Sophie did awaken, she had only to look over at her sleeping daughter for comfort. "I feel like Danny's with me at night," Sophie explained to Hélène. "I feel safe."

Two weeks later, Sophie returned to seeing patients. Two women in the village volunteered as wet nurses, allowing Sophie to work full time. Sophie kept Ruthie in the bassinette until her first birthday, then she brought back the original second twin bed and snuggled it against hers. Little Ruthie Booker was the apple of all

Fériana's eye.

Chapter Thirty-Two

Beaminster, England
Spring 1944

On June 6th, 1944, Operation Overlord began on D-Day, putting United States, British, and Canadian forces onto the Normandy Beaches.

Using Enigma deciphers, French resistance messages, and a complete knowledge of Allied strengths, Major Danny Booker put paratroopers in key positions behind German lines. Two weeks later, the Allies had secured the beachhead and controlled fifteen miles into the Normandy countryside.

The 1st Infantry's intelligence section and the 48th Field Hospital moved from England to Normandy.

Despite struggling with depression, Danny spent much of his free time driving over to the 48th Field Hospital to comfort injured soldiers.

Fall came. In October, Teller promoted Danny to Lieutenant Colonel and threw a celebration marking Danny's one-year return from captivity. Danny quietly realized that it also marked the one-year anniversary of his learning about Sophie's death.

That month, Teller and Danny made a three-day trip to London to meet with American and British Intelligence units regarding resistance fighting groups in France, Belgium, Netherlands, Norway, and

Denmark.

On the second night, Danny found himself in a British pub next to an English cryptanalyst named Captain Susan Tapper. She hailed from Bletchley Park, the center of Allied code-breaking during the war. Danny and Susan had met that same afternoon during the intelligence meetings. As they downed pints of ale, Danny learned that Susan had lost her husband, a pilot in the RAF, during the early days of the Battle of Britain in August 1940. Sometime during the evening, Susan put her hand on top of Danny's. Danny began to cry. The story of his love for Sophie poured out of him. Susan turned out to be a wonderful listener.

"You are in no way ready for a relationship," Susan said. "Go back to France, help us win a war, and then try me again."

Danny thanked Susan and told her he'd reconnect when his head was on straight.

"I'd like that," Susan said.

...

By early spring of 1945, the Allied armies from the west and the Russian armies from the east had entered German territory. The German army in the north of Italy had already surrendered. Desperate for troops, old men and young boys were conscripted into the German army as the death knell of the Third Reich approached.

Hitler committed suicide in a bunker with his girlfriend, Eva Braun, on the night of April 30th. On May 5th, the German army surrendered unconditionally and on May 8th, 1945, or V-E Day, the German government signed an official armistice.

Three months later, August 14th, 1945, the Japanese surrendered unconditionally after two atomic bombs leveled the cities of Hiroshima and Nagasaki.

World War II had come to an end.

Chapter Thirty-Three

August 1945

Fériana, Tunisia

Sophie, Hélène, Gloria and little Ruthie sat at the dinner table in Hélène's apartment.

"I can't believe you've not heard a word from Danny's family about the ketubah," Gloria asked while cutting up pieces of cheese to put on Ruthie's high chair.

"Tank you, Auntie GoGo," Ruthie said.

"I've also written to Ruth Bunnen's address in Illinois," Sophie said. "I would have guessed she wouldn't have stayed for the duration. Haven't heard a word but then our mail service is God awful."

Gloria added, "Where's the Pony Express when you need them."

"What's that?" Hélène asked.

"Horseback mail delivery in the U.S. from St. Louis to California in the 1860s. It failed miserably after two years."

"Now that the war is over," Hélène suggested delicately, "maybe you need to go to the U.S., meet his family, and get that ketubah."

"I can't go there without them knowing that I had Danny's daughter," Sophie said. "I need visas for both of us. That means Ruthie and I would have to travel to Tunis and go to the embassy. I have no proof that

Danny and I were married or that Ruthie is his child."

"Your army service should help," Gloria said.

"I'm not sure I can prove that either, here in Tunisia. I think I'd have to go to Washington. I'll wait until October when I know the Benoliels are back from Marseille. Perhaps something will arrive in the meantime."

Lieutenant Colonel Danny Booker had served for over four years. Fort Benning, Georgia, AAF flight school at the Army Air Forces Pilot School in Coffee County, Georgia, the USS Leedstown at sea, Morocco, Algeria, Tunisia, the POW camp in Italy, Sicily, England, France and finally Germany.

It was in Bremen, Germany, that Danny received his orders to report to Fort Riley, in Manhattan, Kansas, by Tuesday, August 29th, 1945, to be honorably discharged from the United States Army.

Danny telegrammed his parents that he'd be home in Detroit no later than the middle of September. He asked his father to wire three thousand U.S. dollars to him in Bremen, Germany and would explain why when he returned.

Danny exited an Army Air Force C-47 in Rome on a flight from Bremen. He spent the next five days scouring Rome for a used truck. With a bit of good fortune, he found a 1938 Fiat 626 NM truck which had been used sparingly by the Italian army. He wrangled the price down to a thousand U.S. dollars and spent another two hundred dollars for new tires.

Danny next scoured the big hotels of Rome for names of interpreters who might have a week free and an automobile.

Danny found Lorenzo Defidio, an out-of-work tour guide for the Thomas Cook Travel company.

The next day, Danny and his truck headed to Corridonia, Italy, followed by Lorenzo in his 1939 Fiat 500, affectionately known to Italians as the 'Topolino.'

The Scavulis knew that Danny would arrive with a translator, but they were speechless when the new truck arrived in their yard. With tears in their eyes, everyone embraced.

Danny and Lorenzo stayed for two nights. Beatrice's homemade pasta with the rich, meat sauce was just as good as Danny remembered and the morning coffee she offered could awaken the dead.

Danny, Lorenzo, and all the Scavullis helped pick melons and placed them in the bed of the new truck.

On his last night and now with Lorenzo's help, Danny could explain his air crash, escape over the Atlas mountains, the secret marriage to Sophie, his capture, and escape. Finally he reached the tragedy of learning of Sophie's death.

By the end of the saga, Beatrice was crying so hard, she asked to be excused. When she finally returned she said she'd pray that Danny would find someone to replace Sophie.

Danny responded that he'd met someone in London before D-Day but wasn't ready to make a commitment at the time. He thought that after he'd gone home to see his family, he might head back to London before returning to work.

As everyone stood by the Lorenzo's 500 before the drive back to Rome, Danny repeated the first words he had said to Beatrice and Carlo at their door in 1943, "*Sono Americano. Ho fame. Per favore,*" to which Carlo responded, "*Sono Italiano. Prego.*" Danny nodded and started to cry as he hugged his two saviors.

Danny and Lorenzo headed to Ancona next. Unfortunately, Rabbi Giovani Brando had returned to Manchester, England, in October, 1943, soon after placing Danny on *'La Bella Luna.'* The synagogue remained boarded up. Danny then headed to the docks only to find Marco Rossi at sea.

The time had come for Danny to head back home and put his life in order without Sophie.

Arriving in the United States at the US Naval base in Norfolk, Virginia, on August 22nd, 1945, Danny called his parents long-distance. Before coming home, he told them, he needed to go to Denver to see his injured co-pilot, Nick Pascavage. Then he would go to Seattle to provide closure to the Trop family, who had lost a son. From Seattle, he'd come home to stay. Safe from the censors, Danny mailed the long letter he had written that explained, in detail his four-year army service and marriage to Sophie.

Danny had crashed his Grasshopper after being shot down by the Germans and Sophie had also lost her life in a plane accident. Although not particularly superstitious, Danny had heard people say that things happen in threes. He decided that getting on an airplane was a luxury and he now had all the time in the world. He would take the train to Fort Riley, Kansas, to be discharged, then to Denver, to Seattle, and then home to Detroit.

Danny arrived in Denver, Colorado, a week later. He found Nick at home and doing well. Nick had mastered the use of a prosthetic leg and worked full-time at the family hardware store. He'd met a nurse during rehab at the Denver Veteran's Hospital and the wedding date was set for the following July. Danny promised to come.

Nick had talked often of Sophie, or Safiyah, and the miracle of his surgery and survival. The news of her death shook Nick and his family. They had all hoped to meet the 'Angel of North Africa' someday. Nick could see that Danny was uncomfortable talking about Sophie. Enough so that Nick moved the conversation to another topic.

At the Denver train station, Nick pulled Danny aside.

"Thanks to you and Sophie," Nick said, "I'm alive and doing okay. I've put my lost leg behind me and I'm thankful for every day."

"I'm happy for you," Danny said.

"I can see you're not okay. You need to get on with your life. Find someone who'll make you happy again."

"Funny you should say that. I met a woman, a widow named Susan, in London, who decoded German messages. Her husband, an RAF pilot, was killed early in the war. I wasn't ready then but I think I'll go back to Britain before restarting my law practice."

"That's the spirit," Nick said. "The real Danny's in there somewhere."

Nick and his family tearfully waved Danny off at the train station.

Danny arrived in Seattle, Washington on September 4th. He stayed downtown at the Roosevelt Hotel. He called the Trop's home that night and told his mother, Hazel, that he'd been with Jeff when he died. He was in town and needed to tell the family the complete story of their son's heroism. Having learned Trop's address by heart during captivity, he went the next morning to the Trop home on Magnolia Bluff. There he met Jeff's parents, an older sister and an uncle, a veteran from World War I.

Danny explained in detail what had happened on April 20th, 1943, in Tunisia and why he switched identities. Danny would never forget the sacrifice Trop made, he said. He apologized for the pain he might have caused them during the period they were led to believe that their son had survived and was a prisoner of war. Danny spent the entire day with the Trop family and gave them, and himself, the closure needed.

Danny returned to the Roosevelt Hotel that night. His plan was to leave on the morning train heading east to Detroit. He would rejoin his father's law practice and try to restart his life after finding out if Susan Tapper was still available. If so, he'd return to England first.

Phillip Booker, Danny's brother, who'd recently graduated high school, would be attending the University of California, Berkeley, after Labor Day with hopes of becoming a mathematician. Phillip attended a Wednesday afternoon program at Temple Israel about Zionist hopes for an independent Jewish state in Palestine. Phillip had read that the lecturer, a Mr. Ze'ev Cohen, had lived in Palestine on a Kibbutz for ten years.

After the lecture, Phillip brought the mysterious Hebrew document from Danny's shelf with him to see if the lecturer could explain its meaning. After everyone had cleared out of the temple, Phillip approached Mr. Cohen with the document.

Phillip told Cohen that, at the time, his mother didn't want to renew the suffering of Danny's death, so the document had gone untranslated, then forgotten.

Cohen looked at the document and laughed. "This is a ketubah written in Solitreo, a cursive form of

Hebrew used by Sephardic Jews in the Ottoman empire for writing Ladino."

"Huh? Solitreo? Ladino? Ketubah?" Phillip said, totally confused.

"Spanish or Sephardic Jews don't speak Yiddish, they speak Ladino, a form of Spanish."

"And ketubah?" Phillip asked, having no idea of the word's meaning.

"A ketubah is a marriage certificate," Cohen said. "Your brother was married. Usually ketubahs are very ornate and beautiful documents in color. This ketubah must have been written in a hurry without any flourishes."

"That makes sense. Our family had no idea Danny was married until we received a long letter from him a week ago."

Cohen went on, "It says here that Daniel Booker was married to Safiyah Shaloub Sollar on March 3rd, 1943, at the Ettedgui Synagogue in Casablanca, Morocco, by Rabbi Moises Menashe and witnessed by two men."

"We received a letter from a Sophie Sollar asking for this," Phillip said. 'My parents didn't think we could send anything to Tunisia while the war was going on, so we didn't."

"Safiyah is the Arabic equivalent of Sophie. Sophie Sollar is your sister-in-law. She may need proof that she is married," Cohen said.

"Was," said Phillip. "She died in a plane crash later that year."

"That's a shame," Ze'ev said.

Phillip thanked Cohen and headed home. Once there, he found Danny's detailed letter, brought it down to the kitchen, poured a glass of orange juice, and leafed through the pages until he got to the part about Sophie's death.

Talking to the kitchen wall, he read aloud, "Sophie and her bunkmate, First Lieutenant Ruthie Bunnen, a surgical nurse, died in a plane crash on July 15th 1943, flying with the 48th Field Hospital from Tunis to the Bacari airfield in Sicily."

Phillip then looked at Sophie's letter, dated July 20, 1943, asking for the ketubah and realized immediately that the dates were impossible. Sophie had died in a plane crash five days earlier.....unless she hadn't.

Phillip mumbled to himself, "How's that possible?" He then answered his own question: Sophie wrote the wrong date on the letter, Danny had the wrong date for the plane crash, someone else wrote the letter and used Sophie's name, or Sophie was alive.

Phillip turned to the Kelvinator refrigerator to find Danny's itinerary posted on the door with a magnet. He took the itinerary, hopped on his bicycle and rode to a Western Union office twelve blocks away on Seven Mile Road near Wyoming Avenue. From there, for fifty cents, Phillip sent a telegram to Danny Booker at the Roosevelt Hotel in Seattle.

5 September 1945

To: Mr. Daniel Booker

c/o Roosevelt Hotel 1531 7th Avenue, Seattle, Wash

Sophie Sollar sent a letter to mom and dad wanting the ketubah. The letter is dated July 20,' 1943. What do you think it means? Your letter says she died in a plane crash on July 15, 1943.

Phillip

When Marty and Linda Booker returned home that evening, Phillip explained what he had discovered.

“It must be a mistake,” Linda said.

“Or someone’s used her name and is pulling a fast one and wants money,” Marty said.

“Danny said she was a surgeon. Surgeons aren’t supposed to make mistakes,” Phillip said. “Anyway, I sent Danny a telegram. If it’s ...”

The phone rang and the room fell quiet. Marty answered the phone.

“Will you accept a collect call from Daniel Booker,” the operator asked.

“Yes,” Marty said, then announced. “It’s Danny. Phillip, you talk to him.” Marty handed the phone to Phillip.

“Dad, is that you?” Danny asked.

“No, it’s Phillip. Listen. We got a letter in 1943 written by someone who signed it Sophie Sollar. She wanted the Hebrew document you had in your footlocker, which we just found out is a ketubah. She wanted it sent to a family named Benoliel in Tunis. The letter is dated July 20, 1943. That’s all we know.”

“That’s impossible. Sophie died in a plane crash on July 15th. You’re sure about the date on the letter?” Danny asked.

“Absolutely,” Phillip said. “What do you think?”

Phillip waited for Danny’s response but heard nothing. “Danny, are you still there?”

“I’m cancelling my train trip. I’ll fly home,” Danny said. He disconnected the call.

Danny landed at the Willow Run airport the next

evening after taking flights from Seattle to Minneapolis to Chicago to Detroit. Marty, Linda and Phillip met him at the gate.

After the obligatory hugs and kisses, Phillip handed Danny the letter from Sophie to the Bookers asking for the Hebrew document. The family sat on a bench as Danny read and reread the note.

"It's her handwriting," Danny said. "I'd stake my life on that. But could she have written the wrong date?"

"You know this family, Benoliel?" Linda asked.

"They're a family in Tunis who took her in when she fled France and before she went to Djerba, the island where she was born."

"What do we do?" Linda asked. "Can you call someone? Call this family she knew?"

"We can't call Africa," Danny said. "Maybe send a telegram. God knows how long a letter might take. The Benoliel family might have moved. Sophie's cousin, Hélène, might have moved as well. Let's get home and think on it."

On the car ride home, Marty suggested that the U.S. Embassy in Tunisia might be able to track down the Benoliels. Phillip thought that Danny should write the Benoliels and wait.

Linda settled the conundrum. "I'm your mother. I know you. Your wife might be alive. You need to go to Tunisia now. You won't be able to sleep until you find out."

"You think so, Mom?" Danny asked.

"Absolutely. And I'm going with you. If she's there, I've got a daughter-in-law. If she's not, you'll need someone by your side."

"It won't be an easy trip. You up to it?" Danny

asked.

"Are you kidding? This will be the trip of a lifetime with a son I haven't seen in four years."

Four days later, Danny and Linda arrived late at night in Tunis via New York and Paris. On the flight to Tunis, Danny had suggested that Linda wear a scarf covering her head whenever they went out in public. Linda had no intention of wearing a scarf in summer. She caved at the airport when she saw no women without their heads covered. They stayed at a hotel near the airport, and early the next morning went to the address on the letter to see the Benoliels.

Linda spent the entire taxi ride calming Danny.

Much to their dismay, the Benoliel house was locked. A peek in the window suggested no one had been living there for a while. They went next door to see if a neighbor knew the Benoliels' whereabouts. The neighbors spoke enough English to tell Danny and Linda that the Benoliels spent summers in Paris and Marseille and would be back in late October.

Danny wrote a note to the Benoliels, explaining his dilemma and giving an address in Detroit. He slipped the letter through a slot in the front door.

To his mother, he floated his next best idea. "We'll go to Fériana. If her cousin Hélène is still there, she can explain what happened. If Hélène isn't there I have no idea what to do."

After failing to find a car rental agency, Danny bought a used 1938 Citroën Traction Avant for $900 U.S. dollars. He made a deal with the salesman that he'd sell the car back to him for $800 two weeks later.

The next morning at five a.m., Danny and Linda set off for Fériana, three hundred kilometers away. They stopped for gas in Kairouan and ate a late breakfast at the Continental Hotel. They drove through Kasserine and Thélepte before reaching the outskirts of Fériana at three p.m.

"I don't know where exactly their clinic is," Danny confessed, staring at the village ahead. "All of the time I was here, I was locked in a secret room in the cellar. I crashed south of the village."

Danny drove around the south side of Fériana for fifteen minutes before seeing a clinic with a red crescent painted on the side, which denoted medical facilities in Muslim countries. Parking outside the clinic, he saw a long line of women waiting in chairs for appointments.

"This has to be it. I can barely breathe," Danny said.

"Business looks good," Linda said.

Danny laughed, easing the tension. "God, Mom, you're so Jewish."

Danny and Linda got out of the car and they approached the clinic entrance.

Linda stopped Danny. "Wait. You said this clinic is for women and I don't see any men around. You can't go in. Someone might be undressed."

"You're right," Danny said, his lip trembling. "I'll go wait in the car."

Before his mother could say anything else, Danny strode quickly to the vehicle and sat in the front seat with the door open. His eyes were closed and he took deep breaths as he tapped nervously on the Citroën's steering wheel.

Linda approached the clinic as a young girl around two-years old came running from around the side of the clinic and past Linda. The toddler, with black, curly, unruly hair and large brown eyes, pushed hard on the front door and stumbled in. Linda followed the little girl into the clinic. She found two women sitting next to exam tables. Another woman, very pregnant, had her legs in stirrups while a female practitioner conducted a pelvic exam.

A woman, Caucasian, tall and thin with dark hair, approached Linda.

"*Ni qadar ni aawnek*?" Gloria asked.

Linda shrugged. "Do you speak English?"

Gloria said, "Of course. How may I help you?"

"I'm looking for a woman named Sophie Sollar."

The request surprised Gloria. She stared at Linda trying to guess why an unknown, middle-aged, apparently healthy, Caucasian, female tourist in southern Tunisia would ask for Sophie.

Just then, little Ruthie grabbed Gloria's skirt and insisted, "'*Ana jayie.*"

Gloria turned to Ruthie, bent over, and moved the unruly, mop of hair off the toddler's face. "In a moment, Sweetie, I'm talking to this nice lady." Gloria stood and turned back to Linda. "Sorry. She's a bit spoiled. So, why would you be looking for Dr. Sollar?"

"I'm Danny Booker's mother."

Gloria's hand went to her mouth. "Hélène, Hélène, this is Danny's mom."

Hélène, having finished the pelvic exam, stood at the sink washing her hands and turned quickly. "Give me a second."

"I'm Gloria, Hélène's partner. Hélène is Sophie's cousin."

Hélène ran over. "You're Danny's mom?"

"Yes, and you're the Hélène from the trip over the mountains?" Linda asked.

"Yes. I never thought I'd meet you. Gloria and I are sorry for your loss. Danny meant so much to us."

"Loss? What loss? What are you talking about?"

Hélène and Gloria looked at each other, confused. They turned back to Linda, uncertain what to say.

Linda, also confused, swiveled her head between Hélène and Gloria.

"Danny died in the war," Gloria said.

"That's crazy. My son's alive. Danny's alive," Linda said.

"Danny was killed by the Nazis outside of Medjez al Bab in 1943," Hélène said. "The Red Cross delivered his dog tags."

"I'm his mother. He's not dead."

"Where is he?" Hélène asked.

"He's sitting in a car outside the door."

Hélène bolted for the door. Danny had already exited the car and approached the clinic front. Hélène saw Danny and jumped into his arms.

"Oh, Danny. Oh, Danny," Hélène kept repeating as she kissed him with tears pouring down her cheeks. Danny finally let Hélène down.

"We all thought you were dead. Oh, my. I think I need to sit down," Hélène said. "This is too much."

Danny helped Hélène move to a vacant chair from the waiting row outside the clinic. Ruthie came out the door and stood between Danny and Hélène.

The impatient two-year old pulled on Hélène's sleeve, "'*Ana jayie.*"

"You can eat later," Hélène said to the girl who

frowned and crossed her arms.

Linda and Gloria followed Ruthie out the door and stood next to Danny.

"Is this your daughter?" Linda asked Gloria.

"You don't know, do you?" Gloria asked. She looked to Danny. "You don't either?"

Linda and Danny shrugged, having no idea what Gloria was talking about.

"We came here to see what happened to Sophie," Danny said. "The Army told me she died in a plane crash on her way to Sicily."

Hélène stood to face a smiling Gloria and said, "I'm feeling better now. Can you believe this?"

"Not in a million years."

Hélène turned back to Danny. "There's a person in the village who knows the whole story in detail about Sophie."

"Who's that? Someone from the 48th?" Danny asked.

Hélène evaded the question and said, "Pick up the baby. Her name is Ruthie. You and your mother follow me."

Hélène pulled a scarf from her pocket, covered her head and headed away at fast pace. Danny picked up Ruthie, who didn't seem to mind, and off Danny and Linda walked, trying to keep pace with Hélène.

As they walked, Danny yelled ahead at Hélène, "Who are we seeing?"

He got no response.

Danny asked again which caused Hélène to walk even faster.

Three turns on unmarked streets and a hundred

yards later, they arrived at an large open-air market that sold fruits, vegetables, meats, and odds and ends.

Hélène scanned the market and spotted Sophie from the back, her arms loaded with sacks of fruits and vegetables and her head covered. Hélène turned to Danny and said, “Hold onto your daughter and don’t move.” Hélène turned and ran into the market.

“What?” said Linda sharply. “Whose daughter?”

Danny, confused, looked at Ruthie, then back to his mother.

Hélène approached Sophie, turned her around, and held her shoulders firmly, blocking Sophie and Danny’s view of each other. Sophie’s arms were laden with bags of produce.

“Why are you here?” Sophie asked. “You have patients.”

“Give me the bags,” Hélène said. “I’d hate to see a week’s wages rolling around the market.”

“I’m not going to drop the bags,” Sophie said. “Let me go.”

“Not until you give me the bags,” Hélène demanded.

“Why are you doing this?” Sophie asked, irritated.

“Because, when I let you go, all hell is going to break loose. Give me the bags.”

“No. Let go of me, you’re acting crazy.”

“Not as crazy as you’ll be.” Hélène let go of Sophie’s shoulders and stepped aside to allow Sophie to see Danny, smiling, walking, then running toward her with Ruthie in his arms and Linda following.

Sophie’s mouth dropped open. She was seeing a ghost. She let go of the bags, which fell to the ground just as Hélène predicted. Out rolled onions, apricots, apples, and a melon.

"Sophie. Sophie!" Danny yelled.

Sophie pulled her head scarf back as she ran over rolling apples and apricots toward Danny and Ruthie.

Danny handed Ruthie to Linda just as Sophie jumped into his arms.

"Please, God, let you be real," Sophie sobbed.

"It's me. I thought you had died," said Danny, as he twirled Sophie around.

"We thought you were dead too," Sophie gasped, as they smothered each other in kisses.

Linda, now fully understanding the reality of the situation, looked at the baby in her arms. "Oh my God. You're my granddaughter. You're my granddaughter." She squeezed Ruthie tight.

Ruthie, having no idea why she was being smothered by a stranger's love, started crying and reaching her hands out for Hélène. Hélène stood to the side, beaming. Hearing the baby's cries, Hélène gently lifted Ruthie onto her hip and hugged Danny's mother.

Sophie, back on the ground, reached under her abaya and pulled out Danny's wedding band, still tied on a shoestring.

"I never took it off," Sophie said.

Danny untied the string and replaced the wedding band in its proper place.

Together, all started to bawl and laugh at the same time.

Chapter Thirty-Four

Tunis, Tunisia
September, 1945

Because Sophie and Ruthie had only Tunisian passports, they needed visas to travel to the United States. Linda Booker had brought a photocopy of the ketubah, but it didn't help. The American Embassy in Tunis had no one to read Hebrew. Even if the ketubah could be read, the embassy officer said it was not sufficient proof that Sophie had married Danny and that Ruthie was his child.

Danny remembered that General Omar Bradley had been asked to run the Veteran's Administration immediately after World War II. Taking no chances, Danny telegraphed Bradley at both the VA and the War Department asking help in getting Major Sophie Sollar of the U.S, Army Medical Corps, the 'Angel of North Africa,' and their daughter into the United States.

Frustrated but hopeful, the Bookers left the Embassy and returned to their hotel. Danny went back to the Embassy every day, awaiting a response from Bradley.

Anxious but with nothing to do, Linda demanded that they tour Tunis. Sophie went to the hotel's front desk and asked for a list of English-speaking guides. Number four on the list was Omar Sadar.

Lunch that afternoon with Omar took three hours, time needed to explain the two and one-half years since

Danny, Sophie, and Hélène had parted ways with Omar in Bou Chebka.

Omar explained that he went into hiding in Algiers given the death warrant offered by the Nazis. He didn't return to Tunis until the Nazis had been defeated.

Linda Booker admitted that each story warranted a novel.

Omar gave the group an amazing two-full-day tour around Tunis. Even better, Omar's sister, who had a two-year-old daughter, babysat Ruthie on both days. Omar wouldn't accept payment for the tours. In kind, Danny promised he would arrange a visa for Omar to visit the United States.

Four days later, the American Ambassador to Tunisia received a telegram from General Omar Bradley. Bradley, a national hero, wrote that anyone who delayed or denied visas for 'The Angel of North Africa,' Major Sophie Sollar of the 48th Field Hospital of U.S. Army Medical Corps and her daughter would receive his wrath. The next day, Danny, Sophie, Ruthie and Linda boarded Air France for Paris, and then home.

As Danny had needed to square the events around Jeff Trop's death, Sophie needed to meet and talk to Ruthie Bunnen's family in Glencoe, Illinois, and introduce little Ruthie to them.

After getting settled in Detroit, Danny, Sophie and Ruthie drove to Glencoe, just north of Chicago. Ruthie's family, like the 48th Field Hospital and the U.S. Army, believed that Sophie had died in the same plane crash. A death prevented because Ruthie Bunnen knew that Sophie was pregnant.

Danny and Sophie had a marriage celebration at Temple Israel that November. Rabbi Fram gave his blessings to the couple and little Ruthie. He told the audience of three hundred that the ketubah from Rabbi Moises Menashe of Casablanca was one-hundred percent valid, as was their marriage. Guests included Nick Pascavage and his fiancée, Lieutenant General Cap Teller, Major Charlie Harris, Hélène Al-Hadef, Gloria Rezin, Omar Sadar, Ruth Bunnen's parents and numerous members of 1st Infantry's intelligence section and the now defunct 48th Field Hospital unit.

The highlight of the event was Omar greeting Hélène for the first time. He snuck up behind Hélène and hoisted her over his shoulder as he had in Fériana before putting her in the trunk of the SS Colonel's auto. Omar put Hélène down immediately and they hugged.

Two months later, Sophie announced that she was pregnant again. Charles 'Charlie' Booker was born the following June.

Epilogue

Starting in 1950, Danny and Sophie went to the annual reunion of the 1st Infantry Division –'The Big Red One.' the oldest continuously serving division in the U.S. Army. They would attend every year.

In 1953, Danny and Sophie moved into a new house in Detroit on West Outer Drive near Vassar. Danny's law practice flourished and Sophie found meaning in working for the Veteran's Administration Hospital in Detroit. Every month or so, she'd run into a patient who served in the North African campaign, many of whom reminded her of her moniker as the 'Angel of North Africa.'

Sophie never revisited Metz, France, but she did correspond with Louise LaFleur. Her reason – too many sad memories. She knew exactly where the Nazis had murdered her father and had no desire to reawaken that terrible event.

...

Sophie had so many days of the year that evoked memories, good and bad. She knew them all.

Birthdays, anniversaries, and the day in Fériana that Danny, holding Ruthie, walked into the market. On those days, Sophie found it impossible not to smile.

The day her father was murdered, the day her mother died, and the day she thought Danny had died weighed heavily on her. The worst, curiously, was July 15th every year, the day Ruthie Bunnen died in a plane crash that by all rights should have killed Sophie.

Ruthie, besides being an amazing friend, saved Sophie's life by demanding she be checked for a pregnancy.

This July 15th, 1953, a Wednesday, and the ten year anniversary of Ruthie's death, was worse than most. To make matters worse, this was first year that both children were away from home. Ruthie had left two weeks earlier for Camp Tamakwa, in Algonquin Park, Ontario, Canada, and Charlie was away with Marty and Linda at their cabin on Lake St. Clair.

As Sophie sat in the kitchen, alone, nursing a cup of coffee, she started tearing, thinking of her friend and how much Ruthie had meant to her. Danny entered the kitchen in a business suit to find Sophie wiping her eyes with the sleeve of her pajama top.

"What's up?" he asked, then answered his own question. "Oh, it's the 15th," as he took a seat next to Sophie.

Sophie nodded that the day meant something. "I would have been on that plane. She stopped me. Ruthie only ended up on the last flight out because of me."

"Tell you what," Danny said. "My trial finished three days early, so I've little to do in the office other than paper work. It's your day off and the kids are gone. Let's do something together."

"You'd do that?"

"In a New York second. I can't have you moping."

"What do you have in mind?" Sophie asked.

Danny took a sip from Sophie's coffee cup then a smile went from ear to ear. "A Marrakech morning. You remember those?"

Sophie smiled, wiped the remaining tears, took Danny's hand and walked him upstairs to their bedroom.

That night, lying in Danny's arms, Sophie, dreamt only of showers and baths in Morocco.

ABOUT THE AUTHOR

James Gottesman M.D. is a Urological Oncologist who has been writing most of his adult life. He has authored more than 100 scientific papers, medical book chapters, research grants, operative consent forms, and computer programs written in BASIC and HTML. His first book, *The Road Back Isn't Straight* was published in 2013. *The Search of Grace,* his second novel, was published in 2014, *Can't Forget*, his third in 2016, *Stab Wound* in 2019, *An Enemy to Love* in 2021, *In Flew Enza* in 2022, and now *The Angel of North Africa*.

Dr. Gottesman graduated from UC Berkeley and UC San Francisco Medical Center and did his Urology training at UCLA. He was Clinical Professor of Urology at the University of Washington in Seattle. He lives on Mercer Island, Washington, with his wife, Gloria, three sons, nine grandchildren, and dog, Biscuit.

www.ingramcontent.com/pod-product-compliance
Lightning Source LLC
LaVergne TN
LVHW010639110826
845149LV00014B/2888

* 9 7 8 0 9 9 1 1 5 5 7 6 7 *